The
Suite
Spot

ALSO BY TRISH DOLLER

FOR ADULTS

Float Plan

FOR TEENS

Something Like Normal

Where the Stars Still Shine

The Devil You Know

In a Perfect World

Start Here

The Suite Spot

TRISH DOLLER

ST. MARTIN'S
GRIFFIN
NEW YORK

First published in the United States by St. Martin's Griffin, an imprint of St. Martin's Publishing Group

THE SUITE SPOT. Copyright © 2022 by Trish Doller. All rights reserved. Printed in the United States of America. For information, address St. Martin's Publishing Group, 120 Broadway, New York, NY 10271.

www.stmartins.com

Designed by Omar Chapa

Library of Congress Cataloging-in-Publication Data

Names: Doller, Trish, author.
Title: The suite spot / Trish Doller.
Description: First edition. | New York : St. Martin's Griffin, 2022.
Identifiers: LCCN 2021044034 | ISBN 9781250809476
    (trade paperback) | ISBN 9781250847423 (hardcover) |
    ISBN 9781250809483 (ebook)
Subjects: LCGFT: Novels.
Classification: LCC PS3604.O4357 S85 2022 | DDC 813/.6—dc23
LC record available at https://lccn.loc.gov/2021044034

Our books may be purchased in bulk for promotional, educational, or business use. Please contact your local bookseller or the Macmillan Corporate and Premium Sales Department at 1-800-221-7945, extension 5442, or by email at MacmillanSpecialMarkets@macmillan.com.

First Edition: 2022

10 9 8 7 6 5 4 3 2 1

Bountiful, extra curvy, overweight, fat, plus-size . . . no matter which word you claim, you are beautiful. This one's for you.

Be advised, some of the thematic content within contains sexual assault and mentions of child death and suicide.

April

CHAPTER 1

Backpfeifengesicht
German
"a face badly in need of a fist"

Maisie hops from one foot to the other, her oversized backpack flopping up and down as we wait on the front porch for Brian to pick her up. For the past two days, she's been chattering nonstop about spending the night with Daddy. How they're going to eat cheeseburger Happy Meals, color pictures of mermaids, and stay up all night watching Disney princess movies. She'll probably conk out by eight thirty, but I love her optimism.

Her backpack contains an orange-and-white-striped tank top, pink polka-dot shorts, eight pairs of underwear, sock monkey–themed pajamas, a purple toothbrush, a box of crayons, a brand-new mermaid coloring book, her beloved plush giraffe named Fred, and—inexplicably—a snorkel tube. I gently suggested she leave the snorkel tube at home, but she insisted she might need it.

Maisie chants in sync with her hops, *"Hap-py Me-uhl! Hap-py Me-uhl!"*

All I can do is hope Brian won't let her down.

I don't have a romantic story of the night Brian and I met. Not even a meet-cute. We met at a bar when we were both a little drunk and sunburned after a day on Los Olas Beach. He called me "blondie" and bought me a margarita, and I was flattered. The only other guy who'd looked my way that night had said, "Pretty face. Nice tits. Too bad the rest is . . ." He didn't finish the sentence. He curled up his nose like my body was too disgusting to consider. Brian thought I was hot, so I slept with him.

"Maybe we should go in the house and get a cold drink while we wait," I suggest, realizing Brian is fifteen minutes late.

Mom gives me a pointed look through the screen door. She doesn't say anything, but words are unnecessary when her expression is barbed with meaning. Like I need to be reminded that Brian is unreliable. Tightness gathers in my chest thinking about it, and I take a deep breath to make sure my lungs work.

Inside, Maisie flatly refuses to remove her backpack as I lift her onto a barstool at the breakfast counter. I pour her a glass of guava juice while Mom offers her a couple of peanut butter cracker sandwiches.

"Daddy will be here soon," Maisie declares, fervent with unwarranted faith in a man who spends most of his free time playing *Overwatch*. To be fair, she's only known him for three years, so he hasn't had as many opportunities to disappoint her. And it's not Maisie's fault I accidentally procreated with the most irresponsible man in Fort Lauderdale.

When Brian pulls into the driveway in his tricked-out blue Hyundai, I catch Maisie from falling as she launches herself off the barstool to greet him on the porch. I need to check myself, because I've been known to do the same. Brian may have peaked in high school, but that hasn't stopped him from being adorable.

"Daddy, I told Mama you would be here soon." Maisie throws her arms around his thighs and squeezes. "And now you are!"

"Here I am." He ruffles her hair as he offers me a dimpled grin.

"Did you remember to bring a car seat?" I ask, torn between giving in to that grin and yelling at him for being late. The tightness in my chest expands and it feels like I have a school of live fish swimming circles beneath my sternum. "Or do you need to borrow mine again?"

"Um . . ." His shoulders sag.

I hit the button on my key fob with a sigh, unlocking my car. "What time do you plan on bringing her home?"

"I have a delivery shift in the afternoon, so maybe after breakfast?" Brian hefts Maisie's car seat, transferring it.

"That's fine."

"You could join us," he says. "Meet us at Lester's on your way home from work."

Hanging out at Lester's Diner used to be our thing. We'd sit for hours, nursing bottomless cups of black coffee because we were broke. Even after Maisie was born, she'd sleep in her carrier in the booth beside me while Brian and I shared an order of loaded fries. Four years later, I'm still living with my mom. Brian and I haven't moved in together, much less gotten married. My

life goals shifted into low gear when I got pregnant. And Brian
has never stopped being broke, because he spends all his money
on video games and modifications for his stupid car. Objectively,
he's useless, but also *super* hard for me to resist. My resolve wob-
bles. It's that damn grin.

"Mama, please?" Maisie begs, and I crack open like a Cad-
bury Creme Egg.

"Okay, baby. I'll see you in the morning." I lean down to
give her one more hug. As I rise, Brian kisses my cheek and I
lightly push him away. "Get out of here, and don't drive too fast
with your daughter in the car."

Brian also spends a lot of money on traffic violations.

When they're gone, I stop at the mailbox. Cable bill. Water
bill. Coupon flyer. There's also a postcard from Anna. After my
sister lost her fiancé, Ben, to suicide, she took his sailboat and
went to sea alone. I thought it was selfish and irresponsible, especially when she hardly knew anything about sailing. But as
I hold a photo of the Caribbean island where Anna has been
staying the past few months, I'm jealous that she walked out
of her life and into a better, happier one. I don't want her to be
unhappy, but we got along better when we were both miserable.

I turn over the postcard.

Living the dream!

I love my sister, but . . . I hate her a tiny bit.

As I come in the front door, Mom steps out of her bedroom.
She's never been Brian's biggest fan, so she frequently disappears
when he's around. She shakes a warning finger at me. "Don't let
him back into your life again, Rachel."

"We have a kid together," I say, heading to my room for
a nap before work, ready to draw the blackout curtains on my

world for a few hours. Ready for the anxiety fish to rest. "Like it or not, Brian is part of my life."

"All I'm saying is, he's never going to change."

Mom has told me so many times that I can do better, but no matter how often I listen to Lizzo on repeat, there's a quiet voice in the back of my head that wonders if Brian Schroeder is the best I'm ever going to get.

•   •   •

The hotel where I work is a Miami Beach luxury high-rise, but it also features private oceanfront bungalows that cost more per night than my mother's monthly mortgage payment—and are nearly as big as our house. Celebrities and politicians are frequent guests, and we're especially popular with foreign soccer stars and their families. Our VIP guests can call the concierge desk and get almost anything their hearts desire.

I'm not officially a concierge—at least not yet—but I'm the night reception manager, which means it's my responsibility to meet the overnight concierge needs of our VIP guests. Most requests aren't much different from those of regular guests: more towels, a pair of tweezers, an additional fluffy robe. But sometimes they get a little more creative. Like the parents who asked for thirty extra pillows so their kids could build a fort. Or the time I had to send one of our valets to the nearest all-night sex shop for an assortment of toys, including a leather riding crop. One regular guest wants a glass of raw milk with her 5:00 A.M. post-yoga breakfast, so we arrange a local dairy delivery every morning at four thirty—practically fresh from the cow—for the duration of her stay. And once, when I was nearly finished with my shift, the Beckham family required a security sweep for paparazzi in the seagrass around their bungalow before they stepped out onto the beach for the day.

Maisie is the biggest joy of my life, but working at Aquamarine runs an awfully close second. I love the atmosphere, the energy, and the pride in knowing our guests could have chosen any hotel in Miami Beach, but they chose ours because we'll make sure their stay is as close to perfect as you can get.

It's nearly ten when I clock in and log on to the digital concierge portal. Ms. Whitaker is staying with us tonight and the dairy has already been scheduled to deliver her raw milk. There are only a handful of requests for wake-up calls and early airport limousines, but anything can happen between 10:00 P.M. and 7:00 A.M.

Cecily peeks her head into the office. She's been the evening concierge for the past ten years and I secretly covet her job. I don't mind having to fetch sex toys for a visiting dominatrix, but Cecily was once tasked with buying a Maserati for a Saudi Arabian prince.

"Thought you should know that Blackwell is here," she says. "He checked in earlier tonight."

Peter Rhys-Blackwell is . . . well, no one is exactly sure what he does for a living. His Wikipedia entry calls him an entrepreneur, a promoter, and a real estate developer, but mostly he's known for being seen with celebrities and splashing out cash like he prints it himself. He's in his late sixties. Recently divorced from wife number four. He can be exceptionally generous and thoughtful, but according to the staff whisper network, he can also be racist, misogynistic, and homophobic. And I can attest to the fact that he has difficulty keeping his hands to himself.

His behavior is tolerated because most of us can't afford to do otherwise. Standing up to someone like Blackwell takes a safety net many of my coworkers don't have.

"Appreciate the heads-up," I say, offering a silent prayer that Blackwell is already asleep in his bungalow and stays that way for the rest of the night. Not likely, given that Miami Beach never sleeps, but one can hope.

I spend the first hour of my shift making late-night dinner reservations, booking car services, and ordering an extra-large anchovy pizza for a couple of drunk Australian rugby players camped out in the lobby. Right before my dinner break, I deliver a bottle of Tylenol to a guest with a pained back. After scarfing down a Publix Cuban sandwich and a Diet Coke, I return to the desk as the front doors swing open. Blackwell strides into the lobby wearing white Gucci driving loafers, a giant gold watch, and a pink Hawaiian shirt covered in parrots and palm leaves paired with white shorts. His cologne reaches me first.

I step out from behind the reception desk and give him a welcoming smile. The employee handbook requires it, but after this many years, it's automatic. "Good evening, Mr. Rhys-Blackwell. Enjoying your stay at Aquamarine?"

"Always a pleasure to see you, Rachel."

I'm surprised he knows my name until I remember I'm wearing a name tag. "You too, sir."

"How's your little one?" he asks, dipping a hand into the pocket of his shorts and pulling out a money clip. "A daughter, right?"

"Yes." That he legitimately remembers I have a daughter softens me, and when my smile widens, it's authentic. Talking about Maisie has that effect on me. Every single time. "She's nearly four."

"I remember when my youngest was that age." He peels a bill off the stack of cash in his hand, and I pretend not to notice. First, because it's unbecoming behavior for an Aquamarine employee. Second, because it still boggles my mind that someone could have that much cash casually sitting in their pocket. Blackwell has hundreds, while I'm lucky if I have a quarter for the Aldi shopping cart. He says, "She was hell on wheels."

"I've been fortunate so far." I tap my knuckles lightly on the desk. "Maisie is an awesome kid."

"With a mother like you, how could she be anything else?" Blackwell leans in, pressing the money into my palm with one hand as the other comes to rest between my hip and my ass. "Have a bottle of Macallan and a cigar—nothing cheap—sent to my bungalow, will you, sweetheart?"

"Certainly, sir." I take a step back before his touch can become a grope. "Right away."

Blackwell makes a low, satisfied hum in his throat that kind of creeps me out, and winks. "Such a good girl."

He saunters in the direction of the doors leading outside to the bungalows. As Peter Rhys-Blackwell encounters go, this one wasn't too icky. I glance down to find a one-hundred-dollar bill in my hand. There's no rule that says I can't accept tips, but I don't feel completely comfortable keeping this much money. Except, Maisie's birthday is coming up, and she's been begging for a bike with training wheels. I tuck the cash into the pocket of my uniform skirt. I'll decide later.

Ordinarily I'd notify the bar manager of Blackwell's request and he'd have someone from his staff deliver, but it's Friday night, and the bar is crowded. Instead I double-check the portal to see which brand of cigar Blackwell prefers and then add it to his room charge, along with the bottle of twenty-five-year-old whiskey, and prepare the room service tray myself.

The air is pleasantly cool as I wheel a wooden bar cart along the bungalow path, and the sound of the waves washing against the dark, empty shore is soothing. There's too much ambient light to see more than a few stars, but there's a kind of peace that comes with knowing they're up there all the same, moving steadily across the night sky. That if you get lost, the stars will guide you home.

I knock on the bungalow door. "It's Rachel with your room service."

The door opens and Blackwell stands in front of me with his Hawaiian shirt hanging open, his hairy belly peeking through the space between. Not something I've ever wanted to see, but at least he's still wearing his shorts. The housekeepers claim he sits around in his underwear while they clean his room. Blackwell steps aside and gestures me forward. "I didn't expect you to be my delivery girl. Come in! Come in!"

I roll the cart into the suite.

"Pour me a glass, would you?" Blackwell asks, picking up the cigar. He takes a sniff. Seemingly satisfied, he rejects the cigar cutter I provided and pulls a small metal knife from his pocket. He opens the blade and slides the end of the cigar through a hole in the handle, then closes the blade, slicing off the tip. People I know don't smoke fancy cigars much less have their own cutters, so the whole process is kind of fascinating. He glances up to see me watching him. "Have you ever smoked a cigar?"

"I haven't." I turn my attention to the Macallan bottle as he holds a match to the cigar, his cheeks puffing in and out until the tobacco catches the flame.

Blackwell holds the smoldering cigar out. "Wanna try?"

I crinkle my nose. "No, thank you. How do you take your whiskey?"

"Got any of those little stones?"

"Yes."

"Perfect."

I open the ice bucket and use a pair of tongs to place a few of the chilled whiskey stones in a glass, followed by a generous pour. I'm surprised to find the liquor smells like campfire and cinnamon. I thought it would smell like . . . I don't know . . . gasoline or something equally flammable. Rich people always seem to love the most disgusting-sounding things, like truffles, caviar, and soup made of dried bird saliva.

"Do you live around here, Rachel?" Blackwell asks as I offer him the glass.

"Fort Lauderdale."

"I have a friend who lives up that way," he says. "You familiar with Seven Isles at all?"

Seven Isles is a neighborhood of multimillion-dollar homes with swimming pools and waterfront views. I bite back a laugh at the idea that I would know someone who lives in that neighborhood, but I can't stop myself from smiling. "I've passed through on my way to the beach. I mean, it's kind of low-rent."

Blackwell chuckles, rattling the stones in the glass as he points at me. "You're sharp. I like you."

"Thank you," I say, relieved that he's being charming and friendly. "Well, I should get back to work. Is there anything else you need, Mr. Rhys-Blackwell?"

He takes a big slug of whiskey and places the glass on the bar cart. "You could stay."

I laugh. "What?"

"Have a drink with me."

"I'm afraid I can't, sir," I say, adding a touch of regret that I don't really mean. "It's against the rules."

He gives me a conspiratorial grin. "Break the rules."

"I really ca—" His lips mash against mine and his hands grab great handfuls of my ass. It happens so quickly, it hardly seems real. Until his tongue pushes into my mouth and he rubs himself against my pelvis. I shove him away and he staggers back a couple of steps.

I attempt to leave, but he comes at me again, pressing the flat of his hand against the door, beside my head. Trapping me in his room. This time his grin isn't conspiratorial or charming. It's predatory, and I'm scared of what he might do.

"Isn't it your job to give the customer whatever he wants?" Blackwell asks. "You're such a sexy girl, Rachel. Let's have a little fun."

"Let me leave." I try to muster as much authority as possible, but my voice quavers. My heart is thumping violently behind my rib cage. "Please."

Blackwell leans in, as if he might kiss me again, then laughs softly. He releases the door and holds up both hands, like he's innocent. No harm, no foul.

I yank open the door.

"You should be grateful." He leans against the frame as I step out onto the bungalow path. I want to run, but I don't want any of our other guests to think something's wrong. "Most guys don't want to fuck a fat girl."

My better angels tell me to ignore Blackwell. To get away from his door as quickly as possible. Let it go. But I pause, straighten my shoulders, and turn to look him square in the eye. "Well, now you're entirely free to go fuck yourself."

CHAPTER 2

Bérézina
French
"a sense of panic associated with a huge defeat"

For the next twenty-eight and a half minutes, I replay the scene in my head, pausing to wonder if I gave Blackwell the wrong impression, if I somehow led him to believe I was interested. Maybe I smiled too brightly. Maybe I was unintentionally flirty when I chatted with him about Maisie. I rewind to when he gave me the one-hundred-dollar bill. There are rumors that concierges worldwide discreetly break the law to supply drugs and other illicit entertainment to guests. Was that his way of trying to pay me for sex? Did he see the money as some sort of contract? I fast-forward to when I told him to go fuck himself. Could I have read the whole situation wrong? Maybe he was only joking. Was I too harsh toward the man who grabbed my ass and kissed me without permission?

A minute later, when Jack Fulton—general manager of the

hotel—calls the desk, my insides are a snarled knot of anger, fear, and unease.

"I got a call from Charlie Tennesley," he says, referring to the CEO of the hotel group that owns Aquamarine, along with a third of the other hotels on Miami Beach. "He says he had a disturbing conversation with Peter Rhys-Blackwell, who claims you made a sexual advance at him, and that when he turned you down, you physically and verbally assaulted him."

My knee-jerk reaction is to laugh. This must be some sort of joke. But Jack doesn't laugh with me. He responds with utter silence.

"That's not true," I protest. "Blackwell ordered a bottle of whiskey and a cigar to his room. I delivered it, and when I got there, he kissed me and insinuated that the concierge policy includes me having sex with him."

Jack clears his throat. "According to Mr. Rhys-Blackwell, when you didn't get your way, you shoved him and used profanity—"

"I pushed him away while *he* was groping *me*."

"And another guest overheard you tell Mr. Rhys-Blackwell to—and I quote—go fuck himself."

"Out of context it sounds bad, but—"

"Unfortunately, it's his word against yours, Rachel."

"So, Tennesley is going to believe the man who pays thirteen hundred dollars a night instead of the employee who makes thirteen dollars an hour," I say, and again I'm met with a chasm of silence. "Of course he is."

"Blackwell has been a loyal customer for years."

"And I've been a loyal employee for years," I point out. "He's a creep, Jack. Almost every employee has an abuse story about him. The housekeepers dread going to his room because they never know if he'll be wearing clothes."

"No one has ever filed a formal complaint against him," Jack says. "If he's treated the staff poorly, why hasn't anyone ever said anything?"

"Because they need their jobs."

Jack sighs heavily. "Look, Rachel, we're having this conversation because Tennesley himself called me in the middle of the night, demanding that I fire you. Blackwell will settle for an apology. Is it possible you misunderstood his intentions? You need to remember that he's from a different, less politically correct era. And not every situation is a Me Too moment. Apologize and this will all go away."

My eyes go wide, stunned that Jack would defend Blackwell, despite centuries of evidence that men will believe other men before they'll believe women.

"Peter Rhys-Blackwell put his hands on my body and kissed me without my consent," I say. "He suggested having sex with him was included in our company policy and when I tried to leave his bungalow, he barred the door. Consider this a formal complaint. I will not apologize."

Jack is quiet for a long moment and in his silence, I hear my career imploding. Rage flares inside me and I want to scream in my defense, but the impulse is almost immediately swamped by a wave of hopelessness. A career I spent nearly ten years building, gone in an instant because the Blackwells of the world always get their way.

"Collect your belongings," Jack says finally. "Security will escort you out."

• • •

"Sorry I have to do this," Charlton says as he walks me through the employee entrance into the parking lot. We started the night shift at Aquamarine together—Charlton as a security guard and me as a desk clerk. We were promoted around the same time too, and it's been an ongoing joke between us that one day we'll run the hotel. Now he's carrying my box of personal effects as he escorts me to my car. It feels like a bad dream without the anticipation of waking up. "And I'm sorry this happened to you."

"Thank you." I blink rapidly to keep the tears at bay. Not yet. Peter Rhys-Blackwell took my job, but he doesn't get my dignity. "I'll be okay."

I don't know if that's true. I have built-in childcare. I have a roof over my head that won't be immediately threatened by this sudden loss of income. I've got savings to keep me afloat for a couple of months. But getting fired has blasted a hole not only in my dreams but in my heart. I love this hotel, even as I walk away from it for the last time.

I open the back-seat car door, and a sippy cup of rancid juice rolls out, hitting the ground with a plastic crack. The carpet is freckled with Cheerios and I hope Charlton doesn't notice the musty funk coming from the damp beach towel crammed under the seat from our last trip to the beach. He doesn't mention the mess or the smell. He slides the box onto the seat.

I reach in and take out a white envelope. Inside is the one-hundred-dollar bill that Blackwell slipped me another lifetime ago. "Will you do me a favor?"

"If it's not going to get me arrested," Charlton says. "But even then, I might consider it."

Laughing makes me feel a little better. I hand him the envelope. "Will you deliver this to Blackwell's room before you leave? Tell him it's from me."

I doubt Peter Rhys-Blackwell will be shamed by getting his money back, but keeping it doesn't feel like a consolation prize for losing my job. It makes me feel tainted.

"I can do that." Charlton pulls me in for a quick hug. "Don't let this get you down. The Rachel Beck I know is going only one direction, and that way is to the top. Be good to yourself." He bends over and picks up the sippy cup, holding it out and away like it's filled with toxic sludge. He grins. "And clean your damn car."

I take the long way home, driving up A1A instead of taking the interstate. I feel calmer than I should. Like I might be okay. But as I cross the Haulover Inlet Bridge—leaving Miami Beach behind—anxiety hits me like a sucker punch. All my limbs are trembling as I pull off the road and into a parking lot. My heart rate spikes. I can't get enough air. And the fish in my chest— God, it feels like my heart is moving around inside my body. And it's about to explode. I throw open the car door and stagger down to the beach, kicking off my heels as I take big, gasping breaths. I collapse on the sand and lie back, spreading my arms wide like a starfish. I focus on the rhythm of the waves and the slice of white moon hanging above me.

I stay there an exceptionally long time.

Until my pulse returns to normal, and my breathing slows. Until the moon gets blurry, and tears trickle down into my ears.

"What am I going to do?" I say aloud, but there's no answer.

The first rays of sun have gathered along the horizon and the moon is gone when I finally stop crying and stand. I feel hollowed out as I brush the sand off my skirt and get back in the car.

•   •   •

I try to sneak into the house, wanting nothing more than to get in bed and stay there . . . maybe forever. But Mom is brewing a pot of coffee and her brows pull together when she sees me. "Where's Maisie?"

"Oh shit. I forgot." I rummage through my purse until I find my phone and then quickly text Brian. Can't meet for breakfast. Please bring Maisie home instead.

"Rachel . . ." Mom begins. Her worry radar is finely tuned and always scanning, so she can tell something is seriously wrong. It doesn't help that my eyes are puffy from crying and there's sand sticking to my feet. I probably look like I'm doing a walk of shame.

"Mom, this night feels like it's lasted a week," I say as Brian texts back. No problem. "It sucked. And I really, really don't want to talk about it."

She makes an indignant noise I ignore as I walk into the bathroom, where I shed my clothes, shower off the sand, and change into my pajamas. Eventually I'll have to tell her what happened. Together we earn enough to pay the mortgage, cover our bills, and keep the refrigerator stocked. I pay a little extra on my student loans whenever I can and put the rest into savings. We don't splurge on vacations, but we also never go to bed hungry. We should be okay until I find another job. No need to worry her unnecessarily. For now, I only want to turn off the endless Blackwell reel in my head.

I'm tipping into sleep when the door cracks open, spilling light into the room. Maisie comes in and climbs up on the bed with me. "Mama, are you sick?"

"No, baby, only sleepy." I stroke her soft hair. My sister and I had white-blond hair when we were little girls—Anna still does—but Maisie inherited Brian's dark brown hair and brown eyes. "Did you have fun with Daddy?"

"I got a cheeseburger Happy Meal with apples and milk," she says, and I'm relieved that Brian didn't let her have soda. "But we went through the drive-through because Eden came over."

"Did she stay all night?"

Maisie nods.

I rocket out of bed and through the living room. From the window, I can see his car still idling in the driveway, his attention fixed on his phone. I'm wearing my pajamas and my feet are bare as I dash outside.

"What the hell is wrong with you?" I shout, slapping my palm on the closed car window, making him jump. The window whirs as it slides down and Brian grins at me as if I'm not making a spectacle of myself in front of the entire neighborhood. But Blackwell took the last fuck I had to give. "You were supposed to spend the night with Maisie, not your girlfriend of the week."

"It was kind of a last-minute thing—"

"You know what?" I shake my head and shrug. "It doesn't matter. I'm done."

"Babe—"

"I lost my job tonight, Brian." I cut him off before he tries to woo me with endearments and dimples. "And I realized, after four years of waiting for you to commit to me and Maisie . . . I give up. Losing you couldn't possibly hurt worse than getting fired. At least I loved my job."

His smile falters. "Wait. You got fired?"

"That's not the point," I say. "How long do you think it will take before Maisie figures out she can't count on you? If you're going to break her heart, I'd rather you do it now, while she's too little to remember."

He looks confused. "What are you saying?"

"If you can't be fully present for your daughter, then you might as well not be around at all."

Brian snickers a little, rolling his eyes. He thinks we're doing the same dance we've done for the past four years. We blow up. He dates someone else for a few minutes. He makes a half-hearted attempt to be a decent boyfriend and father. And like a fool, I've always fallen for it. Not anymore. This dance is over.

"Call me when you calm down," he says, his window gliding up.

I turn and walk back into the house, and when his tires squeal out of the driveway, I don't turn to look. Eggs are soft-boiling on the stove and Mom is laying out a German breakfast of cold cuts, cheeses, and warm Berliner *Schrippen* rolls.

"Maisie," I say, "did you and Daddy go to Lester's for breakfast?"

"No."

I pull in a deep breath and let it out slowly, taking a small plate from the cupboard. I slice one of the rolls and make Maisie a half sandwich with salami and Havarti, along with a little dish of blueberry yogurt. She's been eating Oma's German breakfast since she was a baby, so cold meats and cheese in the morning normally don't faze her. I settle her at the coffee table with Fred and a fairy coloring book I've been saving for this kind of occasion.

"Mama?" she says.

"Yes, baby?"

"Are you mad at Daddy?"

"A little bit."

"Me too," she says. "He didn't color with me, and he doesn't ever tell me bedtime stories."

My broken heart fractures even more. I refuse to speak ill of Brian in front of her, so I lean down and kiss the top of her head. "Maybe later we can go to the park near the beach and look for gopher tortoises."

"Okay," she says, her tongue poking out as she uses a purple crayon—her current favorite color—to fill in a fairy's wings. "Mama?"

"Yes, Maisie?"

"Ich liebe dich."

I push away the tear that tracks down my cheek and kiss the top of her head again. "I love you too."

Back at the breakfast counter, Mom hands me a plate. "Are you going to tell me what's wrong?"

"I, um—I was fired last night."

"What? Why?" She keeps her voice low, but I double-check to make sure Maisie isn't listening. She's completely absorbed in her artwork. I share the whole story with Mom as I fill my plate, then hold my breath as I wait for her reaction. She's at least a decade younger than Blackwell, but she left her home country to follow a man, so she might not share my opinion. I'm half-afraid she'll tell me I was overreacting and should apologize.

"That is so unfair." There's an edge of anger in her voice, and she wags her egg spoon at me. "You should sue that *verdammtes* hotel."

"I don't want to sue the hotel, Mom. I want to forget this ever happened."

"What will you do?"

I spread a bit of red currant jelly on my roll. "Find another job, I guess."

"Are you worried other hotels won't hire you because you were fired from Aquamarine?"

"Well, I wasn't, but I am now." I hadn't considered that I might have ended up on some no-hire list. I drop the roll. "I need to go lie down."

"You need to eat."

"Mama, when are we going to the park?" Maisie pipes up from across the room.

I sigh. "As soon as I'm finished with breakfast."

"Okay," she says. "Eat faster."

•   •   •

Maisie climbs the playground structure at Hugh Taylor Birch State Park while I sit on a bench and scroll through employment websites on my phone. There are always plenty of housekeeping positions available. I don't think I'm too special to clean hotel rooms—that was my first job out of high school—but it feels like something to fall back on. A last resort kind of thing. I apply for a couple of reception manager jobs at chain hotels, even though a decade of experience and a degree in hospitality management make me feel overqualified. I don't know what else to do—like when Dad left, and Mom had to take a second job so we wouldn't lose our house. She kept going because she didn't really have a choice. I have slightly more financial stability than Mom did, but I can't afford to wallow in my misfortune any more than she could.

My phone rings with a call from Cecily. We usually only see each other when she's going off shift and I'm coming on, so we're not close, but I guess I'd call her a friend.

"I heard what happened," she says. "Jack said you were pursuing other opportunities, but Charlton told me the truth. I'm sorry."

"Thanks."

"How are you feeling?"

"Scattered," I say. "One minute I get so angry, I want to punch something, and the next I want to cry. The minute after that, it doesn't seem real. I keep pinching myself, hoping it's a nightmare."

"You haven't had time to process," Cecily says. "But one of the reasons I called is because I have a lead for you. One of my college sorority sisters used to be married to a guy who is starting up a brew hotel—kind of a hybrid microbrewery and boutique hotel—and he's looking for someone to manage it."

"That sounds great, actually. I love specialty hotels."

My secret someday dream is to own my own hotel, something like the little art deco boutique hotels on Collins in Miami Beach, with just a few cozy rooms and a small restaurant with patio seating.

"The catch is that it's in Ohio," Cecily says.

"Oh." I'm a little disappointed. "Maybe not."

"I thought the distance might make it a long shot," she says. "But I'm going to text you his information anyway. If your situation changes, you'll have it."

"Thanks again."

"I wish . . . I'm sorry . . . I'm not . . ." She trails off, leaving me to fill in the blanks. I understand what she can't bring herself to say. If Cecily had been sexually harassed out of a job, I don't know if I would have spoken up on her behalf. Would her standing in solidarity with me have made a difference? Or would we both be unemployed? My face flushes with shame, but the instinct toward self-preservation is strong. Especially when you're living paycheck to paycheck.

"It's okay," I say. "I appreciate you calling to check on me."

"Hang in there."

"I will." I let out a small, mirthless laugh, thinking about four years of waiting around for Brian. "I've gotten pretty good at that."

CHAPTER 3

Desenrascanço
Portuguese
"the act of disentangling oneself from a difficult situation by using all available means to solve the problem"

"So, most of our bookings are for a single night," Ed says, leading me behind the reception desk during my orientation for the night reception manager position at the Sunway Hotel in Fort Lauderdale.

I was only unemployed for two days before I landed this job. Technically, it's the same job I had at Aquamarine, but the atmosphere is wildly different. The tiny Sunway lobby is decorated with dusty fake palm trees and chairs that look like they haven't been updated since 1988. There's a janky ATM in the vestibule, and the reception desk looks like a wall, making me wonder if the desk clerks frequently find themselves in need of a protective barricade. The general manager is wearing jeans and sneakers with his company-issued golf shirt, which is oddly informal to someone who wore a skirt and heels every night. And is currently—apparently unnecessarily—wearing a skirt and heels for her first day on the job.

"Our guests are basically just looking for a place to crash before their early-morning boarding calls on the cruise ships at Port Everglades or flights out of FLL," Ed continues. "They roll in late and check out early. Night desk is busier here than a lot of other hotels."

"That's fine," I say. "I like busy."

"Once in a while you'll get a homeless person hanging out in the lobby, especially in January and February, when the temperature dips," he says. "They usually leave when you ask, but if they get belligerent, call the cops. Oh, and if anyone calls the front desk to complain about fighting, take down the room number where the fight is happening and call the cops. Don't engage."

Working at this hotel when the weather turns cold enough for homeless people to loiter is not the future I imagined for myself. Maybe I shouldn't have jumped at the first job offer I got, but I don't know how to sit around and do nothing. I nod and fake a smile. "Got it."

Ed walks me through the check-in and checkout processes, introduces me to daytime staffers I may never see again, and takes me on a tour of the property. The hotel is made up of three four-story buildings with a pool in the middle. There's a charcoal grill and a few picnic tables, one of which is occupied by a couple of housekeepers taking a smoke break. One of them gives Ed the finger under the table, but he's too busy talking to notice.

Our next stop is a hotel room. The floors are gray tile—a

smart choice because carpets in hotel rooms are disgusting—and the beds are covered with industry-standard white duvets, but even updated fixtures in the bathroom can't completely disguise the shabbiness. Most of these guests probably don't care, but the rooms and bungalows at Aquamarine were immaculate in comparison.

After two hours of orientation and training, Ed sends me home. As I hurry to my car, I try to look for the silver lining of this job. My daily commute has dropped by twenty minutes each way and I no longer need to use the interstate, but I can't seem to muster much excitement about saving gas money.

This is not a lifetime commitment, I remind myself. *Maybe something else will come along.*

A call from Anna pops up on my dashboard screen as I'm heading toward the day-care center to pick up Maisie.

"Mom told me what happened," Anna says. "Are you okay?"

"Mostly," I say. "I took a job at the Sunway Hotel on Marina Mile."

"Oh God. That place is terrible."

I laugh. "I know, right? If Satan designed a level of Hell specifically for me, it would be working at the Sunway for all eternity."

"Did you try to find something better first?"

The question makes me bristle, even though I don't think Anna means to be insulting. I don't always know how to talk to my sister. Sometimes it feels like she leads a charmed life. I mean . . . no. That's not fair. She lost her fiancé to suicide. Losing my job doesn't even approach that kind of tragedy. But Ben was wildly in love with her, and after his death—when she foolishly went to sea in a boat she really didn't know how to sail—she ended up meeting Keane. In the time I've spent trying to make one man love me, Anna's had two. I try not to resent her for that, but sometimes I can't help myself. I swallow my annoyance.

"I did," I say. "But my choices were either a shitty job in a nicer hotel, or the same job in a shittier hotel. I made a lateral move. Sort of."

"That makes sense," she says. "And it will look better on your résumé."

Not wanting her to think I'm completely pathetic, I tell her about the hotel in Ohio.

"Oh my God, Rachel, that sounds perfect for you," Anna says. "Why aren't you pursuing it?"

"Ohio is so far away, and Mom is here."

"Are you planning to live with her forever?"

I bristle again, but this time I have legitimate cause. "Of course not, but I don't want to take Maisie away from her."

Anna sighs. "Did you ever think that maybe Mom deserves to put herself first for a change? I mean, she hustled to make ends meet when we were kids, and now she spends every night babysitting Maisie. Maybe she'd like to meet someone special or go out for drinks with friends."

This is how we always end up arguing. She pushes my buttons and I push hers. "Maybe Mom is happy with the way things are."

"Are you?"

The question throws me. Mostly because I'm not sure of the answer. I've always thought happiness was something on the horizon: that I'd get there eventually.

"You always say I was selfish for walking out of my life," Anna continues. "Maybe I was. But I was so comfortable with my pain that if I had stayed in Florida, I'd probably still be miserable. Not everyone finds magic outside their comfort zone, but maybe you should learn more about that job before you reject the idea outright."

"I, um—" Normally it's my job to dish out the unsolicited advice. But she's not wrong. "I'll think about it."

"Mom could come visit you up there," she says. "Flying to Ohio is a lot cheaper than flying to wherever Keane and I happen to be on any given day."

"Where are you?"

"We're anchored in Little Bay in Montserrat," she says. "We'll be here for about a week, then head to Antigua."

Anna sailed from Florida all the way to Trinidad—sometimes alone, sometimes with Keane—and they've been meandering their way back up the Caribbean chain for the past year. He takes delivery jobs to keep them afloat financially. Anna has talked about coming home so Mom and I can meet Keane, but they've also been preparing for a transatlantic crossing to Ireland, where his family lives.

"Do you ever get homesick?"

"Sometimes, but Keane is my—"

"I have to go." I interrupt her with a lie, afraid she's going to say that Keane is her home. I don't want to hear that. Not now. I don't want to end this phone call feeling jealous. "I'm picking up Maisie from day care."

"Give her a big hug for me."

"I will."

"Ich liebe dich," Anna says. We never say those words in English. It's like we come right up to the brink of love with each other, but never go all the way over. *"Call the guy in Ohio."*

"Fine." I laugh. Sisterhood is complicated. "I will."

• • •

Maisie is tucked in for a nap when I step out into the backyard and pull up Cecily's text message on my phone. Mason Brown. 419-555-1769.

I settle into the hammock swing hanging from a thick live oak in the middle of the yard. It's a messy old tree that drops a blanket of leaves so dense, there's no grass beneath the circle of its canopy. When Dad was around, he'd set up a tent under the tree so Anna and I could camp. Invariably, I'd be frightened by the night sounds and end up in my bed, leaving Anna alone to face the imaginary dangers of the backyard. Maybe she's always been braver than I am.

I take a deep breath for courage. Release it. And make the call.

"Whatever you're selling, I'm not interested," a gruff male voice says before I've even had a chance to say hello. "And take my number off—"

"Wait," I say, trying to get my verbal foot in the door. "I got your information from Cecily Mercer. She said you're looking for a hotel manager."

"Oh. Yeah. I am." His tone is slightly less abrasive, but still wary. Like I might be trying to scam him into buying an extended warranty for his car.

"My name is Rachel Beck. I'm interested in the job."

"I'll text you my email address. Send me your résumé."

"Right now?"

"You can wait until the Fourth of July if you want, but I can't guarantee the job will still be available."

"Um . . . okay." I hang up without saying goodbye, though I highly doubt Mason Brown cares. What a bizarre conversation. Is he having a bad day or is he always kind of a jerk? As I head inside the house, I'm tempted to ask Cecily if Mason's personality is the reason that he's someone's ex-husband, but she wouldn't have given me his number if she thought it was a waste of my time. Now I'm as curious about this prickly hotel owner as I am about the job. I send my résumé before I completely lose my nerve.

Five minutes later, my phone rings.

"The job is yours if you want it," Mason says without preamble.

I laugh. He can't be serious. "Just like that? You don't want to call my references or ask me about my experience?"

"Are you lying?"

"No, of course not."

"Then I'm not sure what you expect me to ask," he says. "Your qualifications look great."

"Thanks, but . . . could you maybe tell me about the hotel?" I say. "The only thing Cecily mentioned is that it's in Ohio."

"It's called the Limestone Inn and Public House, and—"

"That's a lot of name," I say.

"Well, not every hotel can be called Aquamarine," Mason says dryly, and heat flares in my cheeks as I realize I've interrupted a potential employer to question his choice of names. For the hotel. That he owns. During an interview, albeit an unorthodox one.

"Good point. Sorry."

"Anyway, the brewery is incorporated into the ruins of an old winery, with ten individual cabin plots among the surrounding trees," he says. "It's a pretty small operation, so the manager position basically includes running the reservation desk, arranging transportation, scheduling staff, and overseeing housekeeping. Salary is forty grand, along with benefits and furnished housing, if you need it."

"This all sounds . . . pretty perfect," I say. "So please forgive my asking: Why haven't you filled the position already?"

"Because the hotel is on an island in Lake Erie called Kelleys," Mason says. "And for three, sometimes four months out of the year we can get socked in by ice. We'll get small planes, but no ferries. Most everything shuts down. I don't know what your life is like in Fort Lauderdale, but even when the island is at its busiest in the summer, there's no fancy supermarket or movie theater, and if you want sushi, you'd better have a boat."

"Oh."

"Yeah," he says. "Which is why I haven't filled the position."

On nights I don't have to work, I'm usually curled up on the couch with a book or watching a movie with Maisie, so I'm hardly the wildest twenty-eight-year-old on the planet. I don't even remember the last time I went out to a club with friends. But I like going to the beach, and occasionally I get a craving for shawarma. Kelleys Island might be too isolated—even for a homebody like me.

"Did you offer me the job because you're looking for someone with my qualifications?" I ask. "Or will any warm body do?"

Mason gives a short, humorless laugh. "Fair question. But frankly, you're overqualified. I'd be a fool if I didn't at least try to hire you."

"Well, you've managed to make this job sound as unattractive as possible," I say, and this time he surprises me with genuine laughter. "Can I take some time to think about it?"

"The ferry starts running next week, so I'll need an answer fairly soon."

As I disconnect the call, I don't know how to feel about this opportunity. The hotel sounds incredible. The weather sounds potentially terrible. And Mason Brown . . . well, he's one big question mark of a human being.

I pour myself a glass of wine, plop down on the couch with my laptop, and pull up the hotel website. The page is under construction. Weird, but it's possible their bookings are done over the phone, especially if the island is small. Or maybe the hotel was closed for the winter. If I were running the place, I'd at least upload a few high-quality photos and some contact information.

Next, I google Kelleys Island.

It's a heavily forested, incredibly green island, with a tiny downtown and a few fun-looking restaurants and bars. Visitors can rent bikes and golf carts to tour the island, and paddle kayaks along the shore. There's even a beach. It's not so hard to imagine myself there, checking guests into their cabins, or maybe sending one of my employees to the ferry dock in a golf cart to transport guests to the hotel.

But when I add *winter* to the search, the trees are skeletal and brown, and there's snow everywhere. I find a photo of a man showing off his ice-fishing catch, the bloody fish lined up in a row on the frozen lake. I was born in South Florida, so I've never seen real snow. When temperatures drop, I may have to wear jeans or pull on a sweatshirt—occasionally socks if my toes get cold—but I've never worn gloves or a winter scarf. I don't even own a proper coat. The thing is, even surrounded by ice and covered in snow, Kelleys Island is starkly beautiful. And I find myself tempted in a way I could have never imagined.

I do a Google search for Mason Brown. There are dozens of results, including a Scottish soccer player, a high school baseball coach, and an Ivy League professor of anthropology. I'm about to include the word *brewery* in the search when Maisie comes out of the bedroom wearing a Notorious RBG T-shirt and a pink tutu that she wasn't wearing before her nap.

"Hi, Mama. Whatcha doin'?"

"Hey there, sweet girl." I close the laptop and set it aside as she climbs up beside me. "I was waiting for you to wake up."

"Do you have to go to work?"

"No, I get to stay home with you tonight."

Her face lights up and she claps. "Can we watch *Star Wars*?"

"How do you know about *Star Wars*?"

"Daddy let me watch it on the baby 'puter," she says. It kills me in the best way that she still thinks tablets are baby computers, so I never correct her. And I let the questionable parenting on Brian's part slide. It doesn't matter anymore.

"I like the princess and the robots, but the guy with the black thing on his face is scary," Maisie says, adding quickly, "but I didn't have any bad dreams."

"We can watch until Oma gets home from work," I say, switching on the TV. "But if you get scared, we'll stop to talk about it, okay?"

As we snuggle on the couch, watching the *Star Wars* opening crawl, I let myself imagine what working at a brew hotel on an island in Lake Erie might be like. Without pictures on the website, I don't know what the individual cabins look like, but in my head, they're minimalist with nature-hued textiles—like Aquamarine, only woodsier. My dream of owning a hotel has always been one that takes place in a hazy future. After Maisie starts school, so I don't have to work nights. After paying off my student loans. After moving out of my mom's house. After—

Maisie squawks as I stand up. "Where are you going, Mama?"

"I have to make a quick call," I say, stepping into the bedroom. "I'll be right back." I close the door and dial Mason Brown. It rings several times, and I'm about to hang up when he answers.

"It's Rachel Beck," I say. "I have more questions."

"Okay."

"I have a three-year-old daughter, so if I were to accept the job, I'd need a place for both of us," I tell him. "Would that be an issue?"

He inhales and I wait for the frustrated exhale, signaling that I've asked for too much. Having kids can be a deal breaker, and not only in business.

"No," he says, finally. "That would be fine."

"Are you sure?"

"Positive."

"What about finding a babysitter or some sort of day-care situation?"

"Shouldn't be a problem."

"Okay, before I say yes, there's something you need to know." I cross my fingers and hope for the best. "I was fired from Aquamarine because one of our VIP guests wanted me to have sex with him. When I turned him down, he told the CEO of the hotel chain that I was the aggressor. I don't have any way to prove that I'm telling the truth, but . . ."

"I believe you."

"You do?"

"Generally speaking, men are assholes," Mason says. "So, odds are in your favor that you're telling the truth. The offer stands."

"When do you want me to start?" The words spill out of my mouth and I'm stunned. I'm not the impulsive Beck sister. I'm the planner. The pros-and-cons-list-maker. But when I place my hand on my chest, the only sensation I feel is excitement building.

Am I really doing this?

"Could you be here next week?" he asks.

I'm really doing this.

Even though he can't see me, I smile. "Definitely."

CHAPTER 4

Sisu
Finnish
"a stoic resilience, determination, and hardiness"

"Absolutely not. Rachel, you can't be serious," Mom says, taking last night's leftover broccoli-and-rice casserole from the oven. When I came out of the bedroom after my call with Mason, she was getting home from work. After I realized I'd forgotten to start dinner, I told her why. "*Was ist* wrong *mit* the job you have?"

She's been living in the United States since before I was born but never completely lost her accent. She speaks fluent English, so when German starts creeping into the conversation, I know she's freaking out.

"Surely you can see that the Sunway is a huge step backward," I say.

"*Na ja,* but there must be a nicer place where you can work. There are so many luxury hotels in South Florida." Mom scoops some casserole onto Maisie's plate, then hands me the serving spoon.

"At least a third are owned by Charlie Tennesley's hotel group," I explain. "And I'm probably banned from the rest. Blackwell knows everyone."

"You don't know that."

"No. You're right."

"See," Mom says. "Now you can stop with this *quatsch* about moving to Ohio."

As she tries to listen while Maisie explains the plot of *Star Wars,* I steal a glance at my mother. She's only fifty-seven and still rocks the pale-blond look, even though it comes from a salon these days. She also has luminous skin. Hardly any wrinkles. Anna will probably look exactly like her when she's middle-aged. I take after Dad, which is not a bad thing—he's handsome for a deadbeat—but Mom and Anna are another level of beautiful.

"Do you ever think about dating?"

"Where did that come from?" Mom asks.

"Dad's been gone for . . ." It's been so long, I need to do the math. "Nineteen *years,* and you've never talked about any other men. Have you dated anyone since he left?"

"Oma, do you have a boyfriend?" Maisie asks.

Mom rolls her eyes. "Who has time for boyfriends?"

"You would if I took the job in Ohio," I say. "You could downsize to a condo and not have to worry about repairs or yard work. You could go for drinks after work with your friends. You could sign up for a Tinder account."

"*Halt die Schnauze,*" she says, pinching her fingers together like a closing mouth. She rolls her eyes again, but she's fighting a smile. "Tinder account."

"Why not? I'm sure a lot of old geezers would swipe right on you."

She laughs. "I don't need a man. I have my girls."

"Mom, I'm taking the job."

"I think you're making a mistake."

"You thought Anna was making a mistake when she went sailing," I point out. "But look how that turned out."

"You're not Anna."

"What does that mean?"

"You have a history of bad decisions," she says. "Look at all the terrible boys you dated in high school. Look at *B-R-I-A-N*. And what about that guy last year who you thought was the One after your first date?"

"Maybe I inherited my decision-making skills from the woman who followed a guy to another country."

Mom shoots me a murderous look—one I deserve—and points her knife in my direction. "This is not about me."

"No, this is about my career," I say. "I stayed on the night shift at Aquamarine when I had the chance to switch to days so I wouldn't have to sacrifice my time with Maisie. I juggled college, a full-time job, and parenting. I may suck at dating, but I have *always* made good choices when it comes to my career. Don't you dare try to conflate them."

We sit in silence as a space battle plays out in the background on TV. The scrape of silverware across our plates seems amplified.

"I'm sorry for what I said," I say. "It was disrespectful."

"But also true," Mom says. "I was like you when I was young, which is why I've always worried more about you than Anna."

"I really want this job, but I'd rather go with your blessing than without."

Mom smiles as she uses her knife to push a bit of casserole onto her fork. "I guess I wouldn't mind getting a smaller place with no yard to worry about. I've always hated cleaning up after that tree."

• • •

The next two days rush past like time-lapse film as I separate Maisie's and my belongings—keep, donate, trash—and prep the car for a cross-country trek. I sell my bedroom furniture and Maisie's old crib on Craigslist. I buy winter coats and accessories because my weather app shows temperatures in Ohio ranging from freezing to balmy in the span of a single day. And when I can't drag my feet any longer, I call Brian and ask him to meet Maisie and me at Lester's.

"I knew you'd be back." He aims his dimpled grin at me as he drops into the booth across from us. Maisie is drawing a picture of a fish on the place mat, and my heart gives a nostalgic tug as I watch. My feelings may have changed, but Brian and I had some good times. Together, we made a beautiful child.

"So, um—I wanted to tell you in person that Maisie and I are moving to Ohio," I say. "I've accepted a job as the manager of a specialty hotel, and I start next week. We leave the day after tomorrow."

"Wait." His eyebrows climb his forehead. Clearly not what he expected. "For real?"

"Losing my job was a wake-up call," I say. "I'm too old to be living at home with my mom and I'm tired of waiting around for you. This job is a chance for me to finally get ahead."

"But what about—" Brian points to himself, then gestures at Maisie. "I mean, how's that going to work if you're living in a different state?"

Brian and I never had a formal custody arrangement. It's always been a loose agreement that Maisie would live with me and visit him whenever he wanted to see her—which hasn't been as often as it should be. I've never asked him to help support Maisie financially, either.

"You're not exactly a functioning parent when you flake out on visits and invite your girlfriends over when you should be spending time with your daughter," I say. "So, until you get your priorities straight, you and Maisie can video-chat anytime you want."

He drums his thumbs on the tabletop, not looking at me. "This really sucks."

"I'm sorry."

"You know, I just remembered I've got a, um—a shift at work," Brian says, sliding out of the booth. "Come here and give me a hug, little pea."

He lifts her into his arms, and she hugs him tightly around his neck. I blink to keep from crying.

"Be good for your mama," he says. "And send me some drawings for my fridge, okay?"

"Okay, Daddy. I love you."

"Love you too."

As Brian puts Maisie down, he glances at me, and in his eyes, I see everything—confusion, anger, sadness, regret—and I understand because I feel it all too. "I guess I'll see you around, Rach."

"Take care of yourself, okay?"

Our server passes him—three glasses of water on her tray—as he leaves the diner.

"He, um—he's not staying," I tell her. "It's only the two of us now."

· · ·

We leave before sunrise. Maisie falls back asleep in her car seat, Fred tucked under her arm, and I've got a tall tumbler of cold-brew coffee to keep me alert. We said our goodbyes last night, but Mom comes outside, wrapped in her bathrobe, and kisses my cheek through the open car window. "Be careful and call me when you get to Savannah."

"I will."

"Ich liebe dich," she says, stroking my cheek.

"I love you too."

Fort Lauderdale is too sprawling to have a real sense of community, but I'm battered by memories as I make my way out of town: going to concerts at the Culture Room with various boyfriends, skipping school with the girls to hang out on the Hollywood Beach Broadwalk, and making out in Brian's car at the plane-spotting lot at the airport. I've lost touch with all my old friends—I'm not sure liking posts on Facebook counts as real interaction—but as I merge onto I-95, I'm forced to put away the past and pay attention to the road. Even at 4:30 A.M., the highway can be a white-knuckle adventure.

When Anna and I were little girls—about a year before our parents got divorced—Dad decided to take us on a family vacation to the Grand Canyon. He had a limited amount of time off work, so he pushed himself to reach Arizona as quickly as possible. We slept in the car, ate our meals in the car, and we only stopped when we needed gas, Dad was too tired to drive, or one of us had a bladder about to burst—because Mom drew the line at making her children pee in a coffee container. We reached our motel outside Grand Canyon National Park in less than two days, but Dad was so exhausted, he immediately collapsed on the bed, and Mom ended up taking Anna and me to see the canyon without him.

Neither Maisie nor I can handle that kind of marathon drive to Ohio, so I divided the trip into three manageable days. We'll have plenty of time to eat, stretch our legs, and maybe see a little of the country on our way.

Five hours, two potty breaks, and one accident in Maisie's Pull-Ups later, we cross the state line when we go over the St. Marys River. This is the first time in twenty years that I've left Florida, so I pull onto the shoulder of the highway to take a picture of the "Welcome to Georgia" sign.

We arrive in Savannah right before lunch.

Hotel snob that I've become after working at Aquamarine, I opt not to spend the night in a cheapie near the interstate. Instead I book a room in an old brick hotel overlooking the Savannah River. Maisie and I take a walk along the waterfront as a huge cargo ship loaded with containers steams upriver. We eat waffles for dinner at the Little Duck Diner. And I sleep most of the night on a sliver of the bed as Maisie stretches out in all directions.

We're on the road the following morning by first light.

From Savannah we head into mountain country through North Carolina, the skinny western end of Virginia, and West Virginia. It gets colder as we drive north. First I need to turn up the heat in the car, then we need to wear our new winter

gear whenever we get out. I take pictures at all the border cross-
ings and Maisie claps with wild delight when we go through the
mountain tunnels on our way to Charleston, West Virginia.

Our only option in Charleston is a chain hotel, but I choose
one with an indoor pool and we spend the afternoon swimming.
We splurge on room service for dinner and fall asleep to the
sound of rain splattering against the hotel room window. The
rain continues through the night and into the next morning,
when we leave.

The last day of the trip is the shortest, a deliberate choice
so I won't be completely wrecked when we reach the island. We
cross the Ohio River at Marietta, skirt the western suburbs of
Cleveland a few hours later, and finally arrive at the village of
Marblehead on the end of a peninsula jutting out into Lake Erie.

The ferry dock is on a smaller street off the main road. Kelleys Island is visible, straddling the distance between near and
far, but there's so much more lake beyond, I can't see the other
side. Even though it's right there in the name, I never realized
the Great Lakes were so large.

The dock is fairly deserted as I park the car and walk to the
ticket booth. Maisie skips alongside me. "Are we going on a boat
ride, Mama?"

"Yes." I point to a red car ferry tied to the dock. The lake is
murky brown, like coffee with cream, and the sky is the color of
steel. I feel a pang for the golden sunshine and the deep blue of
the Atlantic back home. "Probably that boat right there."

We reach the booth and there's an older lady inside wearing
a dark green puffer coat and gloves. Hot air from the space heater
behind her hits me in the face.

"One adult with a car," I say. "And my daughter is three."

Maisie lifts onto her toes and rests her chin on the window ledge. "I'll be four in May."

"Then you get to ride for free." The lady smiles at Maisie, then looks up at me. "Round trip?"

"Oh, um—no. One way, please."

Her gray eyebrows arch, and for the first time in days, I worry that I've made a terrible mistake. Is a one-way ticket to Kelleys Island in early April so unusual? I fight the need to explain myself as she hands me the tickets.

"Pull your car into the boarding line." She gestures toward a Budweiser delivery truck and a panel van with an HVAC repair logo on the side. "Once you're on the ferry, you'll need to stay in your car at all times, so if you have to use the restroom, you should probably do it now."

Maisie and I take her advice, and afterward I position my car behind the panel van. A few minutes later, a deckhand comes off the ferry and directs the beer truck up the ramp onto the deck. The panel van maneuvers on beside the truck. Next it's our turn. The ramp makes a metallic clunk under my tires and I feel the sway of the boat. Another deckhand guides me into place alongside the van and motions to kill the engine. With the car in park, I release Maisie from her car seat and let her climb up front with me.

We leave the heater running and sing along to the *Moana* soundtrack as the ferry churns across the choppy lake. To the east, we pass what looks to be an amusement park, and I make a mental note to find out more about it. To the north is Canada, but it's too far away to see. I don't know what lies to the west. More islands, I think. Michigan, maybe? This trip happened so fast, I didn't have time to study up on the geography.

Twenty minutes later, the ferry lands at the Kelleys Island dock.

The deboarding process works the same way, so I follow the HVAC truck off the ferry and onto the island.

Following Mason's directions, I drive along East Lakeshore to downtown Kelleys Island, which is little more than a T-junction of two roads. There's a small market, a few restaurants, a couple of seasonal gift shops, a small marina, and a second ferry dock. I turn onto Division Street and keep going—making note of the library—until I spot the cemetery on the right. There's no sign to mark the hotel entrance, which is a gravel driveway that ends beside a white two-story farmhouse with a wide front porch and dormer windows. It's old-fashioned and charming, and I can imagine it on a warm summer night with a porch swing and planters filled with . . . Well, I guess I have no idea what kind of plants thrive in Ohio, but I'm sure they'd be beautiful.

From the house, the driveway fades into a pair of wheel ruts in the grass, leading to a wooden building seamlessly incorporated into the ruins of a limestone block building. The words O.E. BROWN WINE COMPANY are carved into the stone face above the door.

I double-check my GPS.

Even though Mason mentioned the old winery, there is nothing else here that resembles the property he described, and a swirl of unease rises inside me.

Not wanting to risk my car's suspension on those bumpy ruts, I get out to take a closer look. At that moment, a man comes out the side door of the farmhouse and down a set of short steps. He's wearing faded jeans and a heathered charcoal-gray

Henley shirt that hugs his broad shoulders. His hair is black and cut short, swooping up and away from his face. His eyes are dark, and his jawline looks like it was chiseled from the same limestone block as the building. He's older than me by several years, maybe a decade.

"This is private property," he says, crossing the grass to my car. I haven't spoken to so many men in the past week that I don't recognize his voice. Mason Brown. "Unless you're here on official business—"

"I'm Rachel. You *hired* me to manage this property, but . . ." I throw out my hands at our unkempt surroundings. "Where the hell is the hotel?"

CHAPTER 5

Jobbig
Swedish
"an all-encompassing word that means troublesome or
trying, annoying or difficult"

"Sorry, I, uh—lost track of the days and wasn't expecting you."
Mason rakes his fingers through his hair and his jaw flexes. "I
can explain."

"Oh, I think you'd better." I cross my arms over my chest.
My earlier anxiety blooms wider and my heart rate begins to
climb. I really don't want to have a panic attack in front of a
stranger in the middle of nowhere, Ohio. "Because I drove almost thirteen hundred miles to get here and it's starting to look
like I've been misled."

"It's cold. Come inside."

I'm about to refuse when Maisie sings out, "Mama! I need
to go potty!"

"Fine." My breath is visible as I unfasten the car seat buckle and lower Maisie to the ground. She breaks away from me and walks beside Mason as he heads toward the house. He's not wearing shoes, only white athletic socks. His feet must be freezing.

"I'm Maisie Beck," she says in her chirpy little voice. "What's your name?"

"Mason Brown."

"Like Charlie Brown?"

"Yeah." By contrast, his voice seems bottomless. "Just like that."

"Maisie and Mason sound the same," she points out, exaggerating the letter *M*.

"I guess they do."

"Who do you like better, Snoopy or Woodstock?"

Mason glances back at me, and the last time I saw someone look that miserable was after Anna lost Ben. Before I can tell Maisie not to bother Mason with questions, he says something to her in a voice too low for me to hear, and she beams. He must have chosen Woodstock.

"Me too," she says happily.

Mason's expression doesn't change. He looks like he'd rather be anywhere else right now. The wooden screen door creaks as he pulls the handle, holding it open so Maisie and I can go inside first.

The kitchen is updated and modern, with thick butcher-block countertops, stainless-steel appliances, and a white subway-tile backsplash. The room is spacious and cozy at the same time. My mom would love cooking in this kitchen. It even makes me want to be a better cook. Beyond the island, an archway opens to a living room that's startlingly different. More like frat house meets garage sale, with a worn brown couch and an avocado-green

armchair. Like Mason's not fully moved in yet . . . or like someone has recently moved out. This house feels like one more piece
of a large, confusing puzzle.

We shed our coats and after they're hung on wooden pegs
next to the side door, Mason shows Maisie to the bathroom.

"Most people who applied for the manager position were
scared off by the idea of winter on the island, but you were un-
fazed," he says, coming back into the kitchen. "So when you said
you wanted the job, I didn't tell you the hotel was unfinished
because I didn't want you to change your mind."

"Why would you do that?"

"Because I'm completely in the weeds when it comes to running a hotel, much less building one," he says. "I thought . . .
well, I hoped . . . that if you saw the place and understood the
vision, you might want to stay and oversee the construction."

My brain has a whole argument prepared about false pre-
tenses and pulling up stakes, but—"Wait. What?"

"You worked at one of the best hotels in the country," Mason says. "I figured you'd know better than anyone what quality
looks like and the amenities that guests really want."

"Why didn't you say all this in the first place?"

"Probably because I'm an idiot."

"Not going to correct you," I say. "Lying was shitty and
underhanded."

Mason nods. "I know. I'm sorry."

"It was a major decision for me to uproot my life and take
Maisie away from her father, and that can't be brushed aside with
a simple apology."

He pushes away from the counter, shoves his feet into a pair
of suede desert boots, and grabs a navy down vest off one of the

pegs. "Here's my proposal. Come look at the property first. If you decide you don't want to stay, I'll reimburse the money you spent to get here and pay for your trip back to Florida."

Maisie comes into the kitchen lugging a giant tortoiseshell cat. A gorgeous *angry* cat whose legs dangle almost to the floor as Maisie hugs it against her chest. "Mama, look what I found!"

Mason's eyes widen with alarm. "Please put the cat down."

"I don't know if it's a girl cat or a boy cat," she continues. "But we're friends now."

"Put the cat down." There's a definite note of panic in Mason's voice, and both man and cat look on the brink of freaking out.

"Maisie, remember what I said about picking up animals that don't belong to you?" I say. "Please put down the cat."

She bends over and places the cat gently on the hardwood floor. It bolts almost immediately, and Maisie's eyes are glassy with tears as she waves goodbye.

"See you later, friend," she says, then bursts into giant sobs.

Mason scrubs a hand down his face and looks up at the ceiling as he blows out a long, slow breath.

"I'm sorry," I say, lifting Maisie, who buries her face against my shoulder. "She didn't know any better. And she's overly emotional because we've been driving for days and she hasn't had her nap."

"No, it's okay," he says. "Yōkai is a nightmare, so I'm relieved—and kind of shocked—she tolerated any of that. It could have gone very, very badly."

"Would you, um—would you mind if I let her take a nap on your couch?"

His mouth twists a little, like he wants to say no. "I guess."

I settle Maisie on the couch and cover her with the dark

green fringed throw blanket folded across the back. Her eyelids are already half-closed. "I'm going to go outside with Mason for a few minutes, but I'll be right back. If you wake up, stay on the couch, and don't touch anything. Especially the cat."

"Okay, Mama."

She's asleep before I've even buttoned my coat.

I follow Mason out the back door and we walk in the wheel ruts to the brewhouse, passing an older pickup truck on the way.

"I tried to keep as much of the old winery intact as possible," he explains. "Some of it wasn't structurally sound, but I built around it wherever I could, which is why some of the brewhouse is the original limestone and the rest is wood."

He opens the door and we're greeted by the scent of natural wood and warm barley. Or maybe hops. Either way, it's inviting and delicious.

"This is where the magic happens," he says, and for the first time since I arrived, Mason smiles. His face lights up. Softens. It feels like I've gotten a peek at something I'm not meant to see. Under any circumstances he's a handsome man, but his smile makes my knees go weak.

Oh shit.

I try to turn off the thought as he switches on the lights.

The brewhouse is huge, with soaring ceilings and skylights that flood the space with light. The wood floors are dark and polished, and the creamy white walls are bare. A blank slate. A bank of beer taps has been plumbed through a wall with a metal drain tray beneath, but there's no bar yet, no other fixtures, no furniture.

Along one wall, a set of wooden stairs leads up to what appears to be a loft.

"What's up there?" I ask.

"Come look."

As we reach the top step, I realize the upper level is an observation platform overlooking an array of gleaming stainless-steel vats and tanks, as well as racks of wooden barrels. Sacks of grain are stacked along one wall and the other has buttons and digital gauges.

"Most people, including me, have no idea how the brewing process works, so this is really cool," I say, leaning my forearms on the railing. "It might be nice to have some infographics up here with the different steps involved."

"That's—" He looks at me. Blinks. "A really good idea."

We go back down the stairs together and he stops at a spot beside the front door.

"Eventually this will be the lobby," Mason says. "When guests arrive, they'll check in at a reception desk right about here. Then they'll be offered a sample flight of our beers and decide which one they'd like on tap in their cabin for the duration of their stay. But there will also be a bar open to the public, with traditional tables and lounge-style seating."

"I love that idea."

He opens the door and we head outside. Set about a hundred yards into the woods is a small clearing where a cabin is under construction. Concrete slab. Scaffold of wood framing.

"There are ten of these around the property. Some closer to the brewhouse, some more remote," Mason says. "They'll be self-catering and eco-friendly, but I don't want them to be too rustic."

"More like . . . glamping?"

"Ugh." He grimaces and pinches the bridge of his nose, but nods. "Yeah, maybe?"

Unable to stop myself, I laugh.

"I was hoping to be open before the summer season," Mason continues. "But I got slowed down by some personal shit and then winter set in. Now I'm sort of flying by the seat of my pants with a loose goal of Fourth of July weekend."

"That's not much time."

"I know," he says. "So, here's the deal. If you stay, you'll have carte blanche over the design and functionality of the cabins and lobby, including the bar. I'm fucking tired of thinking about it."

"I really don't understand."

His sigh sounds like it's made of lead. "I bought this property as a project for my wife and me to build together. Instead our marriage imploded, so it's only me."

And suddenly the frat boy furniture makes sense.

"I'm sorry."

He shrugs like it's nothing, but the crease between his eyebrows says otherwise. "It is what it is."

"I, um—I'm going to need some time to think about this," I say. "I've always wanted to own a hotel, so being given this much latitude is . . . Well, it's practically a dream come true. But this whole situation has been kind of a bait and switch."

"I know, and I'm sorry I did that to you," he says as we walk back toward the house. "I can book you a room at a hotel closer to the ferry, or you're welcome to stay upstairs. It's intended to be an apartment, so I won't be in your space."

Once inside, I check on Maisie. She's sound asleep on the couch. Fred the Giraffe has fallen to the floor, and tucked under her arm is the giant tortoiseshell cat.

"Holy shit," Mason says, his voice low. "Yōkai hates every-one, including me."

He pulls up the sleeve on his shirt, displaying a razor-thin scar that runs up the side of his forearm from wrist to elbow. "She did this to me when I was trying to *feed* her, so I don't even know what to make of this."

"They must see something in each other that no one else can see."

Mason's dark brown eyes meet mine and linger. His expression is softer, less guarded, and heat rolls through me. I blink and the softness disappears, shuttered away like a house in a Florida hurricane. He turns and fixes his gaze on Maisie and the cat. There's a huskiness in his voice as he says, "Maybe so."

• • •

Maisie snores softly beside me as I lie awake in a bedroom on the second floor. The upstairs—like nearly everything else on this property—is not exactly what it was purported to be. There are three bedrooms and a bathroom, but there's no kitchen. It's not even close to being an apartment—it's the second floor of Mason Brown's house. And I'm certain my room is meant to be the master bedroom.

The furniture still has that fresh-from-the-IKEA-box smell, but the room is warmed by old-fashioned radiators—another thing I've never experienced in real life before—and the hard-wood floor is darkened with age. Like the kitchen, it's spacious and cozy, and for the first time in my life, I have a room I don't *have* to share with my sister or my daughter.

Maisie shifts positions and her leg flops across mine.

She tried sleeping in the other bedroom, but she's used to sharing a room with me. It's a hard habit to break. Yōkai is curled on the floor beside the bed like a furry throw rug, unwilling to be parted from her new—and apparently only—human friend.

At home, the hum of traffic was incessant, so *quiet* had a different definition than it does here. Kelleys Island is utterly still, and I can't sleep. Anna would say this job is too perfect to pass up. Mom would point out that Mason made a mistake and his apology was sincere. Both would be right, but he seems scattered. Lost. And fixing him is not my responsibility. Especially not when I'm trying to get my own shit together.

What am I doing here?

A tear slips down my cheek. I'm homesick. I'm farther away from my sister than I've ever been. And, even though I shouldn't, I miss Brian. Maybe I'm not the kind of person who can run away from home. But when I close my eyes, I can picture the cabins so vividly. Exteriors painted navy blue, forest green, and cranberry red. Interiors that are Hudson's Bay blanket meets Provence, maybe with a splash of flokati. I imagine the disgusted flare of Mason's nostrils at the description, and a smile tugs at the corners of my mouth.

I ease myself around Maisie to get out of bed, pull on my jeans, and slip a cardigan over my tank top. It's so much colder here than in Florida. The back stairs creak as I make my way down to the kitchen. I nearly jump out of my skin at the sight of a dark form outlined by the moonlight streaming in through the kitchen window.

"Sorry," Mason says. "Didn't mean to scare you."

"I didn't need those extra years of my life anyway."

His laugh is short and deep.

"Can't sleep?" he asks.

"The quiet here is so dense. Like nothing I've ever experienced," I say. "But I bet the stars are amazing out here with no light pollution."

"They are," he says, crossing to the coat pegs. He's not wearing a shirt, only a pair of green plaid pajama bottoms, and even in the shadowy kitchen, I can see the definition in his shoulders and chest. Not cut like a bodybuilder, but solid. Strong. He takes my coat and holds it out to me. "Come on."

Bundled in our coats, we head outside and take a few steps away from the house. Our breaths steam in the chilly air. When I tilt my head back to look at the night sky, it's as if the entire galaxy is on display. Like the night after my encounter with Blackwell, I sink to my knees, spreading out on my back in the grass. The ground is cold under my bare feet and dampness seeps through my jeans, but the sky is so vast.

Mason doesn't lie down, or even sit.

"So, uh—have you made a decision?" he asks.

On Kelleys Island, I'd hoped to find a hotel where I could step behind the front desk and be myself again. I'm tired from driving and thrown by the unexpected state of the hotel, but I thought this would be easier. I wish I could say yes, but I want to go home. Before I can answer, the stillness is broken by a series of hoots that remind me of a child playing a repeating note on a plastic recorder.

"Is that . . . an owl?" I ask.

"Northern saw-whet."

"I don't think I've ever heard a real owl before."

Something shifts inside me. This property is filled with *possibility*. A bubble of excitement wells up as I imagine capturing the magic and giving it to our guests. I'm going to say yes. I'm going to transform those concrete pads into little pockets of wonder, where people can look at the stars, listen to the owls sing their night songs, and feel at home. And it's going to be perfect.

"I've decided."

A shooting star comes into view and disappears almost as suddenly.

It feels like a sign.

Mason clears his throat. "Any chance you might share the answer with me?"

It's my turn to laugh. "Before I say yes, there's one more thing you need to know. It's important."

"Okay," he says warily.

"The Limestone Inn and Public House is the worst name I've ever heard," I say, pushing up off the ground and getting back to my feet. I brush my hands off on my jeans. "I mean, can you imagine having to spit out that mouthful every time you answer the phone?"

"Fuck. I never considered that."

"What about . . . the Limestone?"

He sighs, then extends his hand. There, in the moonlight, I take it and we shake. He offers me the ghost of a smile, something I'm already discovering is a rare thing for Mason Brown. "Welcome to the Limestone."

CHAPTER 6

Dépaysement
French
"a feeling of restlessness that comes with being away
from your country of origin and feeling like a for-
eigner; a mix of disorientation and culture shock"

A few days later the sky is mostly clear, and the lake is calm
and blue as Mason drives the pickup onto the deck of the ferry.
I rest my arm on the open window frame, enjoying the hint of
warmth in the air and the morning sun on my face. I was going
to take Maisie to the mainland to pick up some groceries and
a few things for our new rooms, but Mason offered to drive us
on his every-other-Sunday supply run. When I suggested we'd
slow him down, he scoffed and said it was ridiculous to make a
special trip when he was already going. Which is how I ended
up heading to Sandusky with a man who doesn't listen to the
radio.

"This pickup is nearly fifty years old." He looks at me around

Maisie, who is strapped in her car seat between us, munching her way through a baggie of Honey Nut Cheerios. "The radio's been busted for decades."

"This might come as a shock to you, but they make all manner of devices nowadays that let you listen to music wherever you go," I say. "You probably have one in your pocket right now that you also can use to make phone calls."

"What?" Mason slaps a hand to his chest. "Next you're going to tell me this gadget can give directions, too."

I laugh. "You really don't listen to anything?"

"I listen to podcasts."

"What kind of podcasts?"

His eyebrows raise slightly, and he cocks his head like I should already know the answer.

"Oh," I say, connecting the dots. "You listen to podcasts about beer, don't you?"

"Yep."

"That sounds . . . boring."

"It's not."

"Okay, then," I say. "Let's listen to one."

He scratches behind his ear. "So, um—they're not really—they're kind of—"

"Boring?"

Mason digs his phone out of his coat pocket and thrusts it at me. "Just play some music."

I cue up a premade playlist from one of his music apps, and as the beginning strains of a song begin, a text pops up from someone named Jess: I think I left my pearl earrings at the house. If so, send them to me.

I quickly hand the phone to Mason. "I didn't mean to see that. Sorry."

"Not your fault," he says. "Jess is my ex."

"It's none of my business, though. You're my boss."

The cab descends into quiet, making it feel like we're surrounded by Bubble Wrap. I've crossed too many lines today. I shouldn't have teased him about his podcasts. Touching his phone was far too familiar. Our relationship is only days old—certainly not mature enough to be this informal. We make the rest of the crossing in an awkward silence, broken only when Maisie starts singing a made-up, off-key song about Barack Obama riding a dragon. Mason and I laugh, and the tension eases.

"So, I assume you were being hyperbolic when you said I have carte blanche with the hotel," I say as we roll off the ferry deck onto the road in Marblehead. "Surely you have a budget in mind. I mean, the mattresses in the bungalows at Aquamarine were custom made for the hotel. Our guests claimed it was like sleeping on a cloud, but that kind of comfort comes with a very hefty price tag. Do you want that? Are you looking for high-thread-count sheets and L'Occitane minis in the shower? I need a baseline."

"Those kinds of decisions were supposed to be my wife's realm," Mason says. "But we couldn't agree on *anything* because her vision and mine were not aligned."

"What was her vision?"

"Custom mattresses. And if L'Occitane is fancy soap, then yeah, she wanted that, too."

"When I first landed on Kelleys Island, the first thing I

noticed was how unspoiled by civilization it is," I say. "I can understand how she might have wanted to surprise your guests with unexpected luxury. And having high-end clients would help the local economy."

"That was exactly her point."

"But there's not a lot for high-end guests to do," I continue. "People seem to come to the island for low-key activities like fishing, camping, and kayaking."

"Exactly."

"So you're looking for something more laid-back. Like maybe . . . summer camp without the terrible metal bunk beds and having to wear flip-flops in the shower."

Mason laughs. "Nailed it."

"What I'm going to do is put together some design ideas—along with different price points for key items like mattresses and sofas and bathroom fixtures—and you can choose the one you like best," I say. "From there, we'll plan a budget, then I won't have to constantly bother you for opinions."

"Okay. Yeah." Mason nods. "Perfect."

As we drive along a waterfront road, I can't help noticing that the view is not obstructed by condos and high-rise hotels. It's almost startling to see normal houses—not multimillion-dollar mansions—with waterfront views. There are no intersections where Walgreens and CVS battle for dominance. No strip malls with vape shops or payday loan stores. We're on the main highway I took to get to Marblehead and there's barely any traffic. I can't stop myself from laughing.

"What's funny?" Mason says.

"I don't know if you've ever experienced I-95 between Fort Lauderdale and Miami, but it's a nightmare," I say. "During rush hour, it's eight lanes, bumper to bumper, and even the middle of the night is busier than this."

"Well, it's Sunday morning and people are in church," he says, which makes me laugh harder. "But I get your point. The only time Route 2 ever really gets backed up is when there's an accident or Cedar Point is open."

"What's Cedar Point?"

Without warning, Mason's hand shoots out and catches Maisie's sippy cup the moment it slips from her fingers. Her eyes flutter closed and her head flops slowly sideways, resting against her car seat, as she tips into sleep.

"Did you notice the amusement park from the ferry?" he asks, handing me the cup without missing a beat.

"I . . . meant to ask about that," I say, mystified by the stealth move I just witnessed.

"Cedar Point has been around . . . I don't know . . . a long time," he says. "It started out as a bathing beach in the 1800s, but now they regularly break world records with their roller coasters."

"Do they have rides for tiny kids like Maisie?"

His expression turns inscrutable and . . . what just happened? He clears his throat. "Yeah, uh—they do. Even a little roller coaster with a Woodstock theme."

"Oh my gosh, she would *love* that!"

Mason doesn't respond. The Bubble-Wrapped awkwardness closes in again, and we drive the rest of the way to Sandusky in silence.

•   •   •

At the home improvement store, Mason rushes into the building before I even have Maisie unbuckled from her car seat. I don't need any hardware, but I let her help me choose a couple of plants for my new bedroom. When we return to the truck with a snake plant and a golden pothos—both common outdoor plants in Florida—Mason is already waiting in the cab. Listening to a beer podcast.

Our next stop is Target, where I buy a small TV, some new bedding and rugs, along with a waterproof mattress pad for Maisie's bed and a couple of new toys from the dollar section to distract her on our return to the island. Mason helps me load my purchases into the truck, but he's detached and polite. Like the stranger he is.

Finally we go to the grocery store. Mason separates from us almost immediately with his own cart. Maisie, who is starting to get tired of riding around in shopping carts, refuses a free apple that the store has on offer for children. She tries to grab a tin of Altoids and a package of emery boards in the checkout line, and when I won't let her have a *Moana* balloon, she bursts into tears.

"I'm sorry to ask," I say, over a wailing child, as I wheel the cart toward the pickup. Mason's groceries are already neatly stowed. "But is there somewhere I can take her to blow off a little steam?"

He scratches the back of his neck and it looks like he wants to refuse. Instead he says, "I have an idea."

Mason takes us to a small park in downtown Sandusky that's right beside the water. There are no other children at the playground, but Maisie rushes happily toward the swings, screaming, "Push me, Mama! Push me!"

"Be right back," Mason mutters, but I don't pay attention to which direction he stalks off in because Maisie's meltdown is over.

Across the bay, roller coasters rise out of the trees. A

freighter steams toward the mouth of the lake and seagulls catch rides on the breeze. Downtown Sandusky is old and charming, with restaurants and wide sidewalks where they probably have outdoor dining in the summer. Cars drive past frequently, but unlike at home, it's not an incessant, noisy flow.

Dad took a job with an insurance company in Fort Lauderdale after he was discharged from the army. Mom told me later that she always thought the city felt soulless. But after he walked out, the rest of us were too settled to move. We already had friends and Anna was on a rec league soccer team for little kids. Later, I was first clarinet in the marching band. Anna made the JV soccer team. Mom got promoted at the bank. I met Brian. Anna lost Ben. Noisy, fast-paced Fort Lauderdale was home. But now that I'm getting used to the quiet, I've never slept as soundly as I do on Kelleys Island.

Maisie has moved over to the slide when Mason returns, carrying a stack of Styrofoam takeaway boxes, a couple cans of soda, and a carton of milk balanced on top. I grab the drinks, and he spreads the boxes on a nearby picnic table, identifying the contents as he points to each.

"Fries. Fish. And a hot dog for Maisie, in case she's not a fan of fish."

He opens one of the boxes to reveal a pile of thickly breaded, deep-fried butterflied fillets. "Lake Erie yellow perch is a local delicacy. Best in the world."

"That's a bold claim to make. Especially to a girl from Florida."

He shrugs a shoulder. "I stand behind it."

I reach for a piece of fish, then take a bite. Inside, it's firm, yet flaky. It's not meaty like mahi or tuna, but it doesn't fall apart like tilapia or pompano. The taste is a little sweet and very mild. "Wow. Okay, so . . . you might have a case. This is incredible."

"We're lucky it's early in the season." Mason picks up a plastic knife and cuts Maisie's hot dog into three smaller sections. The motion seems practiced. Experienced. "In the summer, the line for perch is out the door."

"I want ketchup," Maisie says.

Mason tears open a packet and squeezes the ketchup on only one section of hot dog. Somehow this man understands that a toddler at a playground is unlikely to eat more than a few bites of anything—and uneaten buns covered in ketchup are soggy and undesirable.

"Do you have kids?"

His hands go still. "Why do you ask?"

"You're really good with Maisie," I say. "And because every time I mention kids, you get this deer-in-the-headlights look."

He looks beyond me. "Yeah." He blinks. "I did."

"Divorce?"

"No." His voice is quiet, low. For the longest time, that's all he says, and I wonder if he's going to elaborate. Finally he clears his throat. "I, uh—I'm going to wait in the truck until you two have had enough playground time. Stay as long as you like." He gets up from the picnic table and grabs a can of Pepsi before walking away.

"Maisie," I call out, closing the takeaway boxes. "It's time for us to go."

"I'm not ready," she calls from the swing set, where she's got her belly draped over the seat of one of the swings. "I'm playing."

"Mason has to get back to the island for work, so we need to leave."

"But, Mama—"

"Now, please."

• • •

The return trip to Kelleys Island is excruciating. Mason gives off a boiling kettle vibe the whole way and even Maisie must sense it, because she plays with her new pack of little plastic dinosaurs without the usual narration, which typically involves mermaids and at least one Disney princess. Without having to focus on driving—or talking—I notice things I didn't see before. Pizza places. The local farm stand still closed for the season. And a giant fiberglass waiter standing on the side of the road. He's wearing a black jacket and red bow tie, with metal framework where his hands should be—like there was once a sign or he was holding something. It's probably some retro roadside attraction with a fun backstory and I'm desperately curious, but the quiet, devastating way Mason said no when I asked if he'd lost custody of his child in the divorce still haunts my heart.

Back at the house, I give Mason a wide berth as we stash away our groceries. Afterward I unload the plants and other purchases, and put Maisie down for a nap. Yōkai slips into the room as I shut the door. Downstairs, Mason isn't in the kitchen or living room. And when I check his bedroom—which turns out to be a converted sunroom with French doors—I discover a desk drowning in paperwork and a futon made up for sleeping. It doesn't make sense to me that he owns this big, beautiful old house and relegates himself to the tiniest space. What the hell has he been through?

I find him in the brewhouse, pouring a bit of beer from one of the large tanks into a small glass. He sniffs. Takes a sip. He startles a little when he notices me. "Oh," he says. "Hey."

"I'm beginning to think this arrangement isn't going to work."

Mason's eyebrows pull together. "Why?"

"You are clearly uncomfortable around kids," I say. "I told you I had a child. I gave you an out—even if I didn't know it at the time—and you still offered me the job."

He stares at me and seems to decide something. He walks past, beckoning me to follow. We go out into the taproom, where he grabs a couple of glasses. "Do you like beer?" He gives a short laugh. "That probably should have been my very first question, huh?"

"I do like beer," I say, watching as he fills the first glass from one of the taps. "I prefer pilsners and lagers, and I really like a good Berliner Weisse."

He moves on to the second glass. "Any special flavor?"

"Not really. Raspberry and woodruff are traditional, which . . . you probably already know, don't you?"

"Yeah."

He hands me a glass of beer, and I follow him outside, where we sit on the low front stoop of the building.

"This is my eighth attempt at a lager," Mason says. "I can't quite nail it down, and it's been driving me up the fucking wall."

I take a sip. "I don't have anything constructive to offer because I'm not an expert. It tastes fine to me."

"'Fine' is not great."

"True."

He takes a long swallow, draining half the glass in one go. "Ever hear of Fish Brothers?"

Fish Brothers is a brand that popped up seemingly overnight. One minute, no one had ever heard of it; the next, it was being served in every bar in town. The TV commercials usually featured two cartoon fish heads talking in thought bubbles about random stuff. Every time a new one came out, it would go viral and wind up as a meme. "Is this a trick question?"

Mason laughs. "Is that a yes?"

"I think most people have heard of Fish Brothers."

"That was me."

"Wait. Really?"

"I mean, not only me," he says. "My college roommate and I were a couple of dipshits who thought it would be cool to brew our own beer so we wouldn't have to pay for it. Matt was already majoring in marketing, so I went from undecided to fermentation science major. Long story short: we landed on a few 'thirty under thirty' lists, our little operation blew up, and we sold the brand to a global brewing conglomerate about five years ago."

"That's incredible, but . . . why would you sell a brand that's so ridiculously popular?"

Mason fidgets with his glass, swirling the beer up the sides. "We'd already been approached to sell when my daughter, Piper, was born with a heart defect. She was going to need surgeries and hospital stays, and I didn't want Jess to carry that weight alone, so I cashed out and Matt stayed on. Piper had three operations in the first two years of her life, and her prognosis was great until she had an allergic reaction to one of her medications.

She died a couple of weeks before her fourth birthday. The anniversary of her death was . . . recent."

"Oh God, Mason. I'm so sorry."

He scrubs a hand across his face and closes his eyes for a beat, then two.

"Working on the hotel together was supposed to help Jess and me reconnect, but it made things worse, and she finally had enough," he says. "Not many people on the island know this, and the only reason I'm telling you is because it concerns you as my employee. If you were less observant, I wouldn't have said anything. I'm sure Maisie is a great kid. She seems great. But I guess I'm not in a place where I want to be around children yet."

"Do you want us to leave?" I ask, pressure tightening in my chest as I wait for his answer. It's not an oncoming panic attack, but I'm anxious about what he will say.

"It's not that drastic." He swirls what's left of his beer and shrugs. "I'm just not where I thought I would be by now."

"Okay. Here's what I propose," I say. "I'll find a day-care situation for Maisie as soon as possible. She shouldn't be on the property when there's construction happening anyway. When she's home with me—or on my days off—we'll stay out of your way. And we'll make our own supply runs to the mainland going forward."

The line of tension relaxes between his brows. "Let me know when you're going. I'll pay for the ferry."

"You don't have to do that."

"I'm not going to make you pay your own way off-island when I'm the one asking you to be here," Mason says. "Consider it an employment benefit."

"Fair enough. For what it's worth, I'm sorry about Piper. And Jess."

"Thank you," he says. "Let's file this conversation as closed and build a hotel, okay?"

"Deal." I tilt my glass and we clink rims. I take another sip as he downs the rest of his beer.

"You're right," I say. "Fine is not great."

CHAPTER 7

Voorpret
Dutch
"the unique sensation of the pleasure of anticipation"

It's a warm Friday in late April when I take the golf cart to the general store to splurge on a candy bar. Ordinarily, I wouldn't make a special trip downtown for a single item, but I've spent the past few weeks building a website and assembling ideas for my cabin design proposals, so today I decided to knock off work early and treat myself.

Working for Mason is nothing like handing out extra pillows or arranging wake-up calls, but I love flexing different mental muscles. And I love sneaking out to watch the progress on the cabins. It's slow going because the weather is unpredictable, and I have private doubts that we're going to make the Fourth of July opening deadline, but the project is exciting. And oddly calming. I haven't had a full-blown panic attack since the night I left Aquamarine.

I drive past Maisie's school, an old-fashioned redbrick building next door with only seven students currently enrolled. Maisie is one of two preschoolers, and she shares a teacher with a kindergarten class of one.

On my way into the store, I pause at the notice board beside the steps. There's a printed sheet listing the worship times for the churches on the island, along with a flyer for a beginner's yoga class and another for the "Hooked on Books" monthly book club. I snap photos of the flyers with my phone, as well as the church list. I don't remember the last time I went to church, but it's good information to have . . . just in case.

Inside, I grab a Snickers and a can of Diet Coke and head to the cash register, where a young woman with hot-pink hair is ringing up a pile of snacks for a guy wearing shorts too early in the season. He's got a beanie pulled low over his ears.

". . . you could join us if you want," I catch him saying, but the cashier scrunches her nose unapologetically and says, "Yeah, no. I'm good."

Ahead of me in line is a white woman around my age. She's wearing navy yoga leggings with a trio of white stripes running down the sides like track pants, a long-sleeved beige crop top, and a pair of flat red shoes with toe pockets. Her dark brown curls are held away from her face by a wide red tie-dyed band. Visitors have started trickling in on the weekends, but her outfit seems a little too hard-core yoga to be tourist-wear. She glances at me. I smile, and she smiles back.

"Are you the new manager at the brew hotel by any chance?" she says.

"I am. I'm Rachel."

"Hi. I'm Avery. I'm the yoga instructor at the wellness center. I've been meaning to come up and invite you to join our book club."

"I read the flyer out on the notice board right before I came in."

"The name is kind of cheesy, but it was started in the eighties and a lot of our members are sixty-plus," she says. "It's a fun group, though, and we read pretty diversely. It hasn't always been that way, but the past couple of years we've been committed to reading books written by women and writers of color. Often both. And no genre is off-limits."

"Reading is one of my favorite things. I haven't done much since I got here because I've been pretty busy," I say. "But I'd like to make time for that."

"Cool," Avery says, handing me her phone. She's wearing a silver band engraved with coordinates on her left ring finger. "We meet the third Thursday of the month and if you give me your contact info, I'll text you the details. Even if you can't finish the book in time, we'd still love to have you come meet everyone."

"Sounds good. I'll be there."

I program my name and number into her phone as Beanie Guy moves on and Avery pays for her Kind bar and a bottle of water. As I hand her phone back, Avery says, "Rachel, this is Tori." She gestures toward the cashier. "She's in book club too."

We exchange greetings and Avery waits for me to pay for my candy bar and soda. The cash register line cleared, Tori walks with us as far as the front door. "See you at book club."

"Looking forward to it," I say.

"I should also mention, every month we each kick in ten bucks and make a donation to a charitable cause," Avery says as we step outside. "It's not a requirement, so don't feel obligated."

My first paycheck had been larger than I'd anticipated. When I got it, I sought out Mason in the brewhouse to double-check that he'd done the math correctly.

"Don't question it," he said.

I laughed. "Have you met me?"

The corner of his mouth twitched, like he wanted to laugh. "It's a raise."

"But—"

"Look, if Jess had stuck around, she'd have done everything for the love of it," he said. "But it's not fair to expect you to be a Web designer, interior decorator, project manager, accountant, and all the other random tasks that will fall to you when we open, and not pay you accordingly."

"Oh." My previous employers paid as little as they could and our yearly raises were never enough to really make a difference, so Mason's generosity was unexpected. "Thank you."

He nodded. "You're welcome."

I sent a portion of my check to my mother to help with the mortgage until she can sell the house, but with a lower cost of living and a higher paycheck, I have enough left to contribute to a charitable slush fund.

"I'd be happy to help," I tell Avery. "Will you be teaching the beginner's yoga class I read about on the notice board?"

"Yeah," she says. "You're welcome to join us for that, too."

Even though my anxiety has been held at bay since I've been here, yoga might help it stay there. And it's been a long time since I've connected with people who weren't family members or coworkers. Since I've had friends.

"I think I will."

"Good. I'll text you soon."

I get into my golf cart and Avery into hers, and we both turn onto Division Street. I realize we're heading to the same place when she pulls into the school parking lot. She grins as we park next to each other. "Are you stalking me?"

"Absolutely. Next I'm going to assume your identity and steal your husband."

Avery laughs. "I give it about six hours before you're begging me to take him back."

"So much for my evil scheme."

"I assume you're picking up," she says.

"Yes. My daughter, Maisie, is in preschool."

"Oh, I have heard *all* about Maisie. She's from Florida, she has a real giraffe called Fred and a giant cat who sleeps in her room."

I laugh. "All true, except Fred is plush and the cat is just big. It's Mason's."

"Wait, Yōkai sleeps with Maisie?"

"Yeah, we don't understand it either."

"That's incredible," Avery says. "Anyway, Daniel usually picks Leo up from school or we'd probably have met by now."

"Your son is Leo?" I say. "According to Maisie, he looks like Flynn Rider and they're getting married on July thirty-ninth."

Avery cracks up. "Flynn Rider? From *Tangled*?"

"She's not quite four, so her knowledge of hot guys is basically limited to Disney," I say. "But congratulations, I guess."

The kids come out of the building—all seven of them at

once—and Maisie flings herself into my arms. She cups her hand around my ear and whispers loudly, "Mama, that's Leo."

"I know."

Leo's shaggy haircut is more surfer boy than Flynn Rider, but with brown eyes and the same dark hair as Avery, I can see why Maisie would reach for the comparison. Even though she's probably played with Leo all day, she turns shy, burying her face in my neck.

"We should probably coordinate," I say to Avery as I strap Maisie into her car seat, "so we don't wear the same color at the wedding."

She's laughing as she backs her golf cart away from the building. Leo and Maisie wave wildly at each other, screaming "Bye! Bye! Bye!" until Avery turns left out of the parking lot, heading toward downtown, and we go the other direction to the hotel.

• • •

Most mornings, Mason has already gone to the brewhouse by the time Maisie and I come downstairs for breakfast. I can tell how early he leaves by the temperature of the blue teapot on the kitchen island. If it's warm to the touch, we've missed him by minutes. If it's room temperature, he left the house before sunrise. If there's no teapot, he probably spent the night in the brewhouse, fretting over beer recipes.

The following Monday morning, after I drop Maisie off at school, Mason and I meet in the brewhouse office to discuss my design ideas and their corresponding budgets. The teapot was warm, so I'm hoping that's a good omen.

"So, what have you got?" he asks.

I hand him the first design board, covered in magazine clippings and fabric samples I ordered from vendors. It leans toward modern, with neutral tones on the floors and walls, and textiles in pale shades of woodland colors. The design is copied almost straight from the bungalows at Aquamarine, and I know Mason hates it by the tiny shift of his eyebrows.

"This is too fancy."

"I know," I say. "But is there anything you like from this design?"

"Not really."

"Okay."

I hand him the second board. This design resembles the inside of a Bass Pro Shops store, with lodgepole pine, striped wool blankets on the bed, and a campground vibe. It's more outdoorsy than the first one, but I think he'll find it too rustic.

"This is more deer camp than summer camp," Mason says. "But I like this direction a little better. The bedding is cool."

The third design is an eclectic mix of tile, wood, and textiles meant to feel like the first day at a lake house that's been in the family for generations. The ceiling lights are chandeliers, but the bedding is the same Hudson's Bay style as the last design. The sleeper sofas are made from durable fabric with throw pillows that look like they were made by someone's grandma. The lamps are mismatched, and the artwork looks like it might have been unearthed from someone's attic. It's not even remotely summer camp, but as his eyes rove the design, I find myself holding my breath.

"This is not what I was expecting," Mason says, and I'm

afraid that I've struck out until he looks up and gives me the biggest smile. "But this is exactly right."

Hearts don't literally skip a beat, but I do feel a sensation in my chest. Less anxiety, more kick drum. A visceral response to that smile. To him. I sit down suddenly, hoping none of this is being telegraphed across my face. I do not want to be attracted to my boss, but I am. "I, um—I thought this would appeal equally to men on fishing trips and women doing girls' weekends with friends. I wanted it to feel like—"

"Home."

I nod, feeling the thread of excitement that connects us. "Exactly."

"It reminds me of when my grandparents owned the house," he says. "They had stacks of old *National Geographic* magazines everywhere, board games from when my dad was a kid . . . How do we make this happen?"

"Well, I don't think we need custom beds." I circle some prices on my budget sheet, happy for the distraction. "But we should prioritize quality mattresses, sleeper sofas, and blackout curtains, because this *is* a hotel and not someone's guest room."

"I agree."

"Since all the cabins will be different, we can probably get deals on discontinued kitchen cabinets and maybe granite remnants for countertops. And as far as the decorating goes, I figured I would spend the next couple of months scouring thrift stores, estate sales, antique shops, and eBay for unique pieces."

Mason nods, studying the design. "Okay. Yeah. I like that."

"I know the industrial look is kind of a trend in taprooms," I continue. "But if the cabins are the bedroom of the property, then the taproom should be an extension of that. It should feel like the living room. People should want to sit. They should want to stay."

"That makes sense."

"And while we're on the subject, you should seriously reconsider putting beer taps in the cabins."

His head jerks up, his eyes registering surprise as they meet mine. "That was the whole point of the hotel."

"I know," I say. "But what do you think is going to happen when a bunch of people have a keg in their bedroom?"

Mason is quiet for a beat. Then: "It's going to end up . . . everywhere."

"Bingo."

"So what do you propose?"

"Wristbands," I say. "If someone is wearing one in the taproom, we know they're a guest of legal drinking age and their drinks are free. We could incorporate an RFID chip that also unlocks their cabin doors, but a plain waterproof wristband would work as well."

He blows out a slow breath as he runs his fingers up through his hair. "I need some time to think about this."

"I really don't mean to be a killjoy," I say. "But instead of holing up in their individual cabins, our guests should be encouraged to congregate in the taproom, where they can meet one another, get to know the locals, and have a good time without ruining the rooms. We'll save money on cleaning and on beer, because only the most hard-core drinkers would ever be able to kill a keg. Instead of tapping each cabin, we'll tap only what we need."

"Those are all solid points," Mason says. "But you just torpedoed my dreams, so I'm going to need a few days to get over it."

"That's fine," I say. "Book club is Thursday and I'm a few chapters behind."

CHAPTER 8

Merak
Serbian
"the pursuit of small pleasures every day, which all
add up to a feeling of contentment, fulfillment, and
oneness with the larger purpose and the universe"

My relationship with my body is complicated, and I'm fully aware that relationship doesn't make me special, unique, or unlike millions of other women in the world. I *want* to embrace body acceptance, but sometimes I also want to be thinner. It's comforting to know I'm not the only woman who feels this way, but it's still complicated. Especially having grown up with Anna for a sister.

As a little girl, I wanted to be as noticeable as her. She was this little pixie of a person with nearly white hair, freckles, and big blue eyes. She looked like she could grant all your wishes if you believed in her hard enough. Mom was careful not to compare us, but Dad would brag about his beautiful baby girl and joke how lucky I was to be the smart one. Except, Anna is every bit as smart as I am, and I don't need to lose weight to be beautiful. Admittedly, our dad was kind of a dick. He may have left a long time ago, but his small damages have endured.

As the minutes tick toward Avery's yoga class, I start getting cold feet. All I can picture is a room filled with agile, slender women dressed in expensive workout wear, while I'm wearing a pair of old gray leggings that are pilled where my thighs rub together. Throw in a black sports bra that might be a size too small and my only "sporty" tank top—pink, with the words YES WAY ROSÉ printed on the front—and I'm ready to change into my pajamas and curl up with a book.

Maisie and I reach the kitchen as Mason comes in through the side door. He pauses in the doorway, giving me a quick once-over before his eyes meet mine. "Oh, um—hi. You look—"

"Like a wine mom," I say, filling my water bottle at the sink. "I know."

He scratches behind his ear, a crinkle of confusion forming between his brows. "A wine mom?"

"You know, the stereotypical woman who drinks a lot of wine and wears clothes with cutesy sayings like . . ." I point to my shirt and as his gaze drops, I realize I've guided his attention straight to my boobs.

Mason's eyes meander back to my face slowly, his cheeks coloring. "I was going to say you look ready to take on warrior pose."

"Oh." I smile bigger than I should, pleased at the compliment and maybe also a little pleased that he was checking me out. "Thanks."

He glances at Maisie, who is trying to tie her own sneaker even though she has no idea how. "She's going with you?"

I can't read his tone, so I don't know how to take the question. "Yeah. You don't have to worry about her being underfoot."

"I wasn't—I'm not—" He opens the fridge and dips his head in to survey the contents, his face hidden behind the door. "I didn't know the wellness center offered childcare."

I forgot to ask Avery about babysitting, so I'm flying on a wing and a prayer to keep Maisie out of Mason's way. "I think they do."

"Huh. Okay."

Except when I get to the wellness center, there are no other children. No babysitting. There are women of all ages and a variety of sizes. That part is a huge relief, but without a sitter, I won't be able to join.

"I'm so sorry," Avery says. "Maybe Daniel could come get her and—"

"It's really not a problem," I say. "I should have asked. I'll figure out something for next time."

Tori, the cashier from the general store, comes out of the bathroom wearing yoga pants that match her brightly colored hair and a Hello Kitty tank top. She's younger than I initially thought. Maybe a high school senior or a freshman in college. "What's going on?"

"Rachel needs a babysitter," Avery says.

Tori shrugs. "I only came to pad your numbers in case no one showed up." She turns to me. "You should stay. I'll hang out with Maisie."

"Are you sure?"

"Never give a babysitter a chance to have second thoughts."

I laugh. "In that case, yes, and I'll pay for your time."

"Now you're speaking my language," she says, looking down at Maisie, whose eyes are practically heart shaped as she stares up at the hot-pink girl. Tori resembles Maisie's favorite Barbie doll. "Hey, kiddo, let's go do some kids-only yoga."

"What's that?" Maisie asks as she leaves the lobby holding hands with a stranger. I feel a little guilty, but as we head into the yoga room, Avery assures me Tori can be trusted.

"She was enrolled in an early childhood education program at vocational school and has already earned college credit for the fall," Avery says. "Tori is basically the official island babysitter, and those of us with kids are going to be up shit creek without a paddle when she leaves for Bowling Green."

"I've never really had to think about childcare because I've always relied on my mom," I say. "And I didn't feel comfortable asking Mason."

Avery nods knowingly, and I get the impression she might be one of the few people on the island who knows his secrets.

She assigns me a green yoga mat between Ruth, an elderly woman in a wheelchair, and Walt, a middle-aged man with a bushy beard, wearing a Led Zeppelin T-shirt. He's the only man in the class, but as we begin, it's clear he's a lot more flexible than I am. I use all the accessories available—block, strap, and modified poses that are easier for a beginner to maintain—and yoga still kicks my ass. I thought I was in moderately good shape, but as we finish in relaxation pose, I nearly fall asleep. I'm exhausted and sweaty. But I also feel an internal quiet that I've never experienced.

"I'm guessing it's not a permanent thing; otherwise, every-one would be doing yoga," I say when I share with Avery after class. "But it makes me want to come back next week."

"It can be a permanent thing, and everyone should be doing yoga," she says. "Just give me a heads-up next time and Daniel will take both kids."

"Are you sure?"

Avery waves me off. "Please. He goes to his parents' house and watches sports on TV with his dad while his mom spoils Leo rotten. I'm sure she wouldn't mind adding Maisie to the mix."

•   •   •

The Thursday morning of book club, Maisie wakes up on the wrong side of the bed. She cries because she wants to wear yellow socks, but after they're on her feet, she cries because they're not purple. She refuses to brush her teeth, then cries when I do it for her. And she cries more when Yōkai darts under the bed to avoid being cuddled by a cranky toddler. As I carry her down the back steps, I'm relieved Mason won't have to be party to any of Maisie's nonsense. I stop short when we reach the kitchen and he's there, pouring spring water from a gallon bottle into a stainless-steel teakettle.

He's dressed in a pair of threadbare Levi's and a flannel in varying shades of brown, sleeves rolled up, and hanging open over a T-shirt that's faded to a soft red. He usually wears a variation of this outfit every day, but the weather has been warm enough lately that he usually sheds the shirt by midday. I hate that I know this, but whether it's a coping mechanism or an idiosyncrasy, Mason Brown is a creature of habit.

"I thought you'd be at the brewhouse already," I say. "We'll just grab some Pop-Tarts for the road."

"You, um—you don't have to rush on my account." He

turns a knob on the stove and a blue flame springs to life under the kettle. "You live here."

For the past month, our arrangement has worked out well. Mason is typically still at the brewery when Maisie and I eat dinner, and by the time he comes home, we're upstairs for the night. I've run into him a couple of times in the kitchen when I've come down for a late-night snack, but usually we only see each other at work.

"Are you sure?" I ask.

He nods. "Rough morning?"

"You heard?"

"Kinda hard to miss."

"Sorry."

"I remember those days." There's a wistful note in his voice, then he clears his throat as if he can swallow the memories. He crosses to a cupboard and takes out the blue teapot, along with a matching bowl that has a tiny spout. Up close, the edges of the bowl are uneven, like they were handmade, and the color graduates from robin's-egg blue at the top to midnight blue at the bottom.

I place Maisie on a counter stool and go to the fridge for a carton of blueberry yogurt. Like in the pantry, Mason cleared space in the refrigerator. When I turn around, he's popping the top on an airtight metal cannister.

"What are you doing?" Maisie asks.

"I'm making tea," he says to her, before looking over at me. "I spent a lot of my youth rejecting Japanese culture because I didn't want to be different from my friends. My mom is thrilled I've been making up for lost time."

He shifts the kettle on the stove, as if that will make it boil faster. "Last Christmas, she had this *houhin* tea set made for me and bought a packet of *gyokuro* green tea to go with it. I've never been much of a tea drinker, but there's a whole process to *gyokuro* that appeals to me as a brewer, and now I kind of just enjoy the routine."

"I have to confess: my only experience with green tea is Arizona iced green," I say as I hand Maisie the yogurt and a spoon. "I practically lived on the stuff back home."

"My mom would consider that an abomination, but on a hot day . . . I get it." He gives me a tiny half grin and my stomach dips.

"Is your dad Japanese too?"

"He'll tell you he's German, Scottish, and Irish," Mason says. "But he was born and raised in Cleveland."

The teakettle whistles, and he pours the boiling water into the teapot but doesn't add any tea.

"It's time-consuming," he explains. "You don't want to steep the leaves in boiling water, so you start the cooling process in the teapot, transferring it first to the *yuzamashi* bowl, and then to the teacups until the water is nearly lukewarm. After, it's back to the teapot, at which point you add the leaves to steep."

"What do you do while the water is cooling?"

Mason shrugs. "Wait."

"In my world, when the kettle whistles, you dump the water into a mug and dunk a tea bag until the water turns brown," I say. "I had no idea tea could be so complicated."

"I didn't either," he says. "But at my first sign of wanting to engage more with my culture, my mom got very carried away. She spammed me recipes and boxes of ingredients started showing up in the mail, and every couple of weeks we have a Skype conversation strictly in Japanese. I dropped out of language school when I was twelve, so I'm struggling with level three on Duolingo and it's . . . not pretty struggling for words I used to know."

"That's really sweet, though."

Mason doesn't say anything, but I can almost see him trying to decide on a response. Before he can answer, Maisie asks, "Can I see the tea?"

He reaches into the metal container and brings out a few leaves. They're long and needle shaped. Even though it's a disruption to his ritual, he pours a bit of water from the teapot into the bowl, explaining that the water softens the leaves until they unfurl.

"What's *unfurl*?" Maisie asks.

"It means 'open up.'"

Their heads nearly touch as they watch together, her yogurt forgotten, and I get an airy feeling in my chest. Despite his reluctance, Mason *is* very good with Maisie.

He touches his hand to the side of the teapot, testing the temperature. "Now we'll put the water into the *yuzamashi* bowl so it can cool more. While we wait, you can eat your yogurt, okay?"

She picks up the spoon and digs in. No argument. No tears.

We all wait together as Mason transfers the water into the tiny cups, then back into the teapot. Finally he pours a cup of *gyokuro* and slides it toward me, then pours a second for himself. The tea is pale green, and smells a little like grass, a little like the ocean.

"Can I have some?" Maisie says, reaching for his cup.

Before I can remind her that she should wait to be offered a drink, Mason says, "You can, but remember that even though it's warm, it's not sweet like cocoa. You might not like it."

Maisie takes the tiniest of sips and her nose crinkles with distaste. "Mm. It's good."

Mason fights a grin. "You sure?"

She nods. "But maybe I'll save some for later."

"*Gyokuro* is an acquired taste," he says.

"What does that mean?" Maisie asks.

"It means sometimes you have to try it a few times before you like it."

She attempts another sip, then hands the cup to Mason. "I think I'll like it better next time."

I pick up my cup and drink. Even though I know better, I'm expecting the ginseng and honey sweetness of Arizona iced tea, but *gyokuro* is savory and briny and almost mushroomy. Nothing like any tea I've ever tasted.

"Is this what they mean by umami?" I ask.

Mason nods. "What do you think?"

"I wouldn't want to drink a lot—"

"No," he says. "Small cups, small servings."

"But I think I might like it better the next time too."

"You will." His gaze meets mine, then skitters away, and I wonder if those two words are a promise that we'll meet in the kitchen and drink tea again. Hoping for a next time is a bad idea, but I can't help myself.

"I'm sorry we interrupted," I say.

"You didn't."

"I was planning to check out the thrift stores and antique shops in Port Clinton today," I say, changing the subject, as Mason gathers the cups and *yuzamashi* bowl and carries them to the sink. "If I find anything that won't fit in my car, I'll see if I can have it shipped over on the ferry."

He digs into the front pocket of his jeans, pulls out his keys, and tosses them from across the room. "Take the truck."

"Are you sure?" I ask as the keys narrowly miss my fingertips and land on the floor.

"Hope you're better at driving than you are at catching."

When I stick out my tongue, he laughs. And I feel it all the way to the tips of my toes.

CHAPTER 9

Arbejdsglæde
Danish
"the heightened sense of happiness, fulfillment, and
satisfaction you get from having a great job"

After a soft-boiled egg and toast soldiers—not to mention being
mesmerized into a better mood by Mason and his tea ritual—
Maisie goes willingly into school and I head for the ferry dock
in the pickup.

There's a weird intimacy to driving someone else's car. The
seat is adjusted for their legs. Mirrors positioned the way they
like them. The radio buttons preset to their favorite stations. Or
not, if the radio has been broken for decades. The truck—an
International Harvester—smells old and dusty, and Lord knows
~~what~~ vintage sins are concealed by the colorful Mexican blanket
~~over~~ the bench seat, but it's not unpleasant. I kind of like
~~a veh~~icle with a deep history. And I feel my skin grow

warm as I think about sitting where Mason's butt—his incredibly nice butt—has been.

As the ferry churns across the lake to Marblehead, I stretch out in the seat and listen to a beer podcast called *Brewing 101*. The process is simpler than I imagined, but there's a whole science behind the types of malt and hops used to make specific kinds of beers, and an alchemy in combining them to achieve the desired flavor. As it turns out, brewing podcasts are not boring, and I wonder if Mason would consider adding a hotel package that would let guests take part in the process. I laugh, imagining him sharing his workspace with strangers. Maybe he wouldn't object to tours. I make a note to ask.

• • •

If someone had asked me to close my eyes and describe a small midwestern town, Port Clinton is what I'd have envisioned. Old-fashioned brick and stone buildings arranged in a neat grid of locally owned shops, restaurants, salons, pubs, boutiques, and—what I came for—antique stores. A bell jingles on the door handle as I step into a shop called Very Vintage Vivian, and from somewhere in the jumble of old furniture and décor, a voice calls out, "Hi! I'll be with you in a second." Followed by a small crash. "Maybe make that two seconds."

I wander through the shop, hoping something will catch my eye. After about five minutes, a woman around my age emerges from behind a china cabinet. Her long hair is dyed black on one side, platinum on the other, and her arms are covered in colorful tattoos from shoulder to wrist. She looks spectacular. "Can I help you find anything?"

"I'm just starting to look for lamps, artwork, and possibly some vintage beds for a specialty hotel on Kelleys Island," I tell her. "I can't pinpoint exactly what I want, but I'll know it when I see it."

"What's the vibe you're going for?"

"Kind of like . . . lake house." I laugh when she recoils, her nostrils flaring. "I didn't mean it that way. I'm not looking for themed stuff. No oars. No anchors. No cutesy lake house sayings. I want things that are nostalgic, interesting, and fun."

"Now *those* are words I understand."

"Oh, and I need crystal chandeliers."

She points up. Overhead are dozens of hanging light fixtures, among them five crystal chandeliers. "How many do you want?"

"I'll take them all."

"I'm Vivian, by the way," she says, leading me deeper into the shop.

"I'm Rachel."

There are several unassembled beds leaning against the back wall. Some look thrift shop old and are not quite what I'm looking for, but I find a cream-colored iron frame tucked behind a wooden cannonball bed.

"How big is this one?" I ask, touching the iron bed.

"Looks like a double, but we can measure to be sure."

She digs into a pocket on her leather tool belt and pulls out a measuring tape. Together we verify the size, and I steal a peek at the price tag. It's marked $550. I'm no expert on antiques, but I'd rather pay that amount for a vintage bed than the same amount for a modern replica with lesser quality, even if it has a few chips in the paint.

"It's going to need to be refinished," I say. "Would you take four hundred dollars?"

"I'd settle at four hundred and fifty dollars."

"Yeah, okay. Thanks."

While Vivian puts a sold sign on the bed and brings out a ladder from the back room to take down the chandeliers, I meander through the store, past an old hutch stacked with Fiestaware and bins filled with vinyl records. None of the furniture jumps out at me, but on a mid-century end table I spy a lamp with a base shaped like three fish, one atop another. It straddles a fine line between vintage and kitsch, making it perfect. On another table, there's a lamp from around the same era, with an iridescent green base shaped like tropical flowers and topped with a tiered lampshade. I take both to the cash register.

"Just got that green lamp in last week," Vivian says from the top of the ladder. "I've been debating whether I want to keep it."

"If you want it—"

"Nope," she interrupts, unhooking one of the chandeliers from the ceiling. "If I kept every piece I loved, I'd go out of business. I tend to trust these decisions to fate. If someone buys it, it's not meant to be mine."

"Good." I walk over to the ladder and reach up to take the light fixture. "Because I want that lamp."

The front door jingles and a blond woman steps inside carrying a couple of to-go coffee cups and a waxed paper bag bearing a doughnut logo. Vivian's face visibly softens as they smile at each other, making me think they're in love—or at least want to be.

"Perfect timing, babe," Vivian says. "I need help getting the crystal chandeliers down. Rachel, this is my girlfriend and business partner, Lucy."

"Hi, Lucy. Nice to meet you," I say. "Is there anything I can do to help?"

"You just keep shopping." Vivian leans down to kiss Lucy. "Rachel will be paying our shop rent and electricity this month."

I laugh. "Do you have any old board games?"

"We try to stay away from those because they don't sell unless they're in mint condition," Lucy says. "Are you thinking about using game boards as art?"

"Yep."

"Go on Etsy. Someone there can paint and age a Parcheesi board to look like it's a century old for a fraction of what you'd pay for vintage."

As Lucy and Vivian take down the rest of the chandeliers, I rummage through a bin of old paintings. There are a couple of pastoral scenes, some seascapes, a few flowers in vases, but the one that grabs my attention is a quirky painting of a gathering of bears dancing in the woods in the moonlight. It's whimsical, but not like something meant for a child's room.

"What's the backstory on this painting?" I ask.

"It's a print I picked up on half-off Wednesday at a thrift store in Sandusky because I liked the frame," Vivian says. "The original was done by William Holbrook Beard, an Ohio artist who was known for putting animals in humanlike situations. If you like his style, you can easily order prints of his other work online."

I'm not sure how Mason will feel about the bear painting, but I like that it doesn't take itself seriously and the frame is ornately carved and painted gold. I decide to buy it. If Mason doesn't like it, I can always hang it in my bedroom.

Next, I find a pair of wooden badminton racquets and an old croquet set. I don't know how to play either game, but when I ask Lucy for her opinion about buying them, she nods vigorously.

"My mom and her cousins used to play badminton every summer. Back in the day, everyone had a net," she says. "I feel like badminton and croquet have been replaced by cornhole, but the nostalgia factor is high."

An hour later—after the breakables have been secured in Bubble Wrap and I'm full of guilt for spending so much money—we load my purchases into the back of the truck. I hand Vivian one of my brand-new business cards. "If you get any more chandeliers or anything else I might like, please let me know."

"You got it," she says. "You might already be aware, but Milan also has a few great antique shops. And I've heard that one of the resorts over in Huron is renovating and will be selling off all the old stuff."

"Thanks for the tip," I say. "If you ever come to Kelleys, look me up."

"Same. Don't be a stranger."

On my way out of town, I stop to buy a bottle of wine for book club and grab a perch sandwich from a restaurant called Jolly Roger's before heading to the island. I leave everything in the truck and go to the brewhouse in search of Mason. I find him in the office.

"I'm going to need—"

"Wait," he says, a smile lighting up his face. "Come with me."

I follow him to the brewery, where he pours two small glasses from one of the tanks. Correction: one of the maturation tanks. Which I know from listening to that brewing podcast. I take a sip. Even though I still don't know what I'm supposed to be tasting, this beer is better than his last attempt.

"This is—"

"Great, right?"

"Better than great."

"I knew it," Mason says, more to himself than to me. "This is the one."

"Hope you saved the recipe."

"Crap." His smile slips and I feel a shot of disappointment drop into my stomach. Until he bursts out laughing. "Of course I saved the recipe."

"Jerk." I punch him lightly on the shoulder. "That was not funny."

"It was a little funny."

"Fine," I say as we return to the office. "It was . . . a little."

At his desk, he folds his laptop into a tablet and holds it up so I can see the label for the new beer. It's oval-shaped with a navy border. In the top part of the border, it says LIMESTONE BEER COMPANY, and at the bottom, KELLEYS ISLAND, OHIO. In the middle is a fish with bluish-silver scales and orange spots, intersected by an orange banner that says LITTLE FISH LAGER.

"I used to call Piper my little fish."

His smile isn't quite so wide as it was. It's softer. Sadder. There's no one on the planet more in need of a hug than Mason and I'm tempted to give in to the urge. But I'm afraid he'll curl up emotionally, like an armadillo sensing danger, so I leave him alone. "It's perfect. Fitting for the first beer of your new brand."

"Thank you."

"I bought a bunch of stuff today," I say. "But there's no rush to unload."

"We can do it now."

It takes us a few trips to carry everything into the tap-room, and we agree to leave the lamps and chandeliers wrapped until the cabins are ready for them. Mason brings in the bear painting.

"Where did you find this?" he asks, holding it up for a closer view.

"At an antique shop in Port Clinton. What do you think?"

"It's weird, but . . . I kind of love it?"

I smile. "I'm glad. Me too."

The truck bed is empty, and it's nearly time to pick Maisie up from school, but neither of us leaves the taproom. We stand there in silence and it feels like something more is supposed to happen. Like maybe, if he were someone other than Mason Brown, we'd be kissing each other's faces off. But he's him, and I'm me, and that doesn't happen.

"I should go get Maisie."

"Oh. Right."

"Thanks for helping me unload," I say, lingering at the door. "And the beer is . . . it's really great. You should be proud."

• • •

Mason is still at the brewhouse when Maisie and I are preparing to leave for book club. On impulse, I leave a foil-wrapped plate of cheesy orzo with asparagus and sun-dried tomatoes in the oven for him, along with a note on the counter. I grab the bottle of wine from the fridge on our way out the door.

"Mama, you look fancy," Maisie says as she climbs into her car seat.

Every day at the Limestone feels like casual Friday, so I opted to go a little dressier for book club. I'm wearing a pair of rust-colored corduroy pants with a white tank top and a denim jacket. For the first time in weeks, I used a blow-dryer and put on makeup. Also, I'm wearing dangly earrings, which is why Maisie thinks I look fancy. I rub my nose against hers. *"Ich liebe dich."*

As I climb into the golf cart, I notice Mason approaching the house, carrying a brown glass beer growler.

"There's a plate in the oven for you," I say, immediately realizing how weird that sounds. How weird it *is* when I've never done that before. We're not a family. I'm not his wife making sure he's fed before I go off to book club. Especially when he clearly knows how to take care of himself. My face is on fire. My whole body is on fire. I wish I could fall into a hole and stay there forever.

"Thanks," he says. "You, um—you look nice. Not that you don't normally look nice, but you look . . . extra . . . nice." He thrusts the growler at me. "This is for book club."

His clumsy sweetness does nothing to cool the flames. This is terrible. "Thank you."

"Have a good fun," he says, and his jaw twitches when he realizes what he's said. "I mean, have a good time."

Biting back a smile, I press the gas pedal. As Maisie and I bump down the gravel path to the road, I steal a glance in the rearview mirror. Mason is standing in the same spot, watching us leave. Right before I look away, he face-palms himself.

CHAPTER 10

Samar
Arabic
"staying up late after the sun has gone down and having an enjoyable time with friends"

"I'm so glad you could make it." Avery hugs me on the front porch of her cottage overlooking the lake, then takes the bottle of wine. As I follow her inside, Daniel whisks Maisie and Leo away to a sleepover at his parents' place before Maisie has a chance to register the separation. She's usually pretty chill about being away from me, but this is the first time she's slept at a stranger's house. Unless you count Brian.

"Everyone, this is Rachel, the new manager up at the brew hotel." Avery pauses just inside the front door. The members of the book club are seated around the living room, their ages ranging from mid-thirties to somewhere near ninety. "Rachel, this is Rosemary, Gail, Virginia, Diane, Courtney, and Pat. Tori is our ninth, but she's running late."

Their responses are a mixed bag. A few say hello, a couple offer a little wave along with it. The Baby Boomers of the group glance at one another as if I've been a recent topic of conversation—and might be again. There's some judging going on, but I get it. Kelleys Island is a tiny village and I'm the new girl.

"It's nice to meet you all," I say before following Avery to a table in front of the windows that's spread with a variety of appetizers, including chicken wings, a Crock-Pot of cheese dip, a second Crock-Pot of meatballs, guacamole, and a foil tray of stuffed mushrooms.

"We haven't had a new book club member in a couple of years," she explains, plunking down the bottle of wine amid a selection of beers, other wines, and a pitcher of margaritas. Candles flicker on the mantel and tables around the room, and soft indie music plays in the background. There's even a pink tinsel curtain hanging in the archway that's so thick, it obscures the room on the other side. "Plus, everyone is curious about you, living out there with a hot single man."

"You mean my *boss*? The one who pays me to work there?"

"That's how it is?" She sags slightly. I could share that Mason is a human hedgehog who's prickly on the surface with a soft underbelly, but then she might guess my feelings for him are in a weird place. And I don't want the island thinking I got my job by sleeping with my boss. "We're dying for fresh gossip around here, Rachel."

"Sorry to disappoint," I say, holding out the growler. "But Mason did contribute an exclusive sample of his first batch of beer."

Avery's eyes light up. "Oh, we're definitely trying that."

"This feels like a party." I spoon a little cheese dip on a paper plate with some tortilla chips and remind myself not to eat dinner next time. "But I've never joined a book club and it's been a very long time since I've been to a party, so I might be wrong on both counts."

She laughs. "Well, the first thing you need to know about book club—"

"It's never really about books," Rosemary interrupts from her seat beside the table. She's the one who looks like she might be in her nineties, with pure white hair that's swirled around her head like cotton candy. "It's an excuse for us to get away from our families for a night and kick up our heels."

"We do talk about books, though," Avery adds.

Virginia, the other elder stateswoman of the club, giggles. "Sometimes."

"Come sit," Rosemary says, patting the ottoman beside her chair.

I take a seat, and for the next ten minutes or so, we discuss the book, a popular romantic comedy that sat at the top of the *New York Times* bestseller list nearly all last year. Pat, one of the Boomers, is complaining that it was unrealistic right as Tori sweeps in the front door.

"Sorry I'm late," she says. "There's a group of wilderness weirdos camping up at the state park this week and they came into the store at the last minute while I was by myself. I can't wait for the Bulgarians to get here."

"The Bulgarians?" I ask.

"Most of the summer employees on the island are from other countries," Avery explains. "Cedar Point started hiring foreign kids in the late nineties to work at the park and it eventually spread out to the islands. They come from all over the world, but we get a lot of Eastern Europeans, especially Bulgarians."

"That's really good to know," I say. "At some point I'll be hiring staff."

"When are you planning to open?" Pat asks.

"Well, Mason's goal was Fourth of July, but the cabins aren't under roof yet, so we may have to open the taproom first and hope we won't completely miss the summer season."

"Ooh, speaking of which," Rosemary says. "I'd like to try that beer."

Avery pops the swing top on the growler. The bottle doesn't hold enough for everyone to have a full glass, but it's enough for a taste.

"Oh, I like this," Diane says. "Is it a lager?"

"Yes," I say. "It's called Little Fish."

"That's adorable," Tori says as the group sips and nods their approval. Even Pat, who doesn't seem to like much of anything, says, "Gotta hand it to him. The kid knows how to make a good beer."

I'm so excited for Mason that I want to text him with the rave reviews, but Avery hops up from her seat. "I'm sure you're all wondering what I have planned for tonight, and it was *tough* following Rosemary's boozy milkshakes last month, but if you'll follow me . . ."

She strides across the living room and disappears through the tinsel curtain. The rest of us follow, and on the other side of the archway, we find her dining room transformed into a karaoke bar. There's another tinsel curtain as the backdrop for a tiny stage, a microphone stand, and a karaoke machine. It's not a cheap setup either.

"Welcome to No Limits Karaoke," Avery says, holding up a straw fedora. "I've put all your names in this hat. You'll each take a name and choose the song that person will sing tonight. No passes. No exceptions. Not even you, Pat."

Avery makes a circuit of the room and when she gets to me, I draw a name from the hat. Rosemary. Oh God, how am I going to choose a song for a stranger who also happens to be the oldest person in the room? My panic must show on my face because Courtney leans over and says, "It's okay. This is how book club works. We all signed on for this."

"Avery never mentioned *any* of this to me."

Courtney laughs. "First rule of book club."

"You have five minutes to choose your songs," Avery says, distributing a list of available songs. It's not a binder, like at karaoke lounges, but there are still a lot of potentially embarrassing options. "And in the spirit of being welcoming, Rachel gets to sing first."

Back before I had Maisie, my friends and I used to go to a karaoke lounge in Fort Lauderdale and choose the most annoying songs we could find. The serious karaoke singers hated us, but it's made me bulletproof. There's nothing these ladies can pick that will throw me. Problem is, I don't want to choose anything too physically strenuous for Rosemary. But eventually a fun song jumps out at me. One she might not know. I write it down on the paper and Avery comes around to collect them.

"Okay, Rachel, you're up," she says.

I step up behind the microphone and study the eight women looking at me, wondering which of them chose the song I'm about to sing.

"Your song"—Avery presses a button—"is this."

The synchronized beats of "Holding Out for a Hero" fill the room. Thankfully, it's the original—not the *Shrek 2* version I've heard too many times to count—and I know it by heart. I don't have an amazing voice, but this song leaves so much room for showmanship.

"Bold choice," I say into the microphone. "But I have a toddler. I could sing this in my sleep."

The women laugh as I launch into the song, and for the next four minutes I'm Bonnie Tyler, stalking the stage and clutching my chest. As the song fades away, I take a deep, dramatic bow. They all clap wildly and someone even whistles.

"I never expected you for a ringer," Avery says.

"Yeah, well, you never told me book club might include karaoke."

Pat goes next and, up there onstage—wearing mom jeans and New Balance sneakers—she surprises me by singing "You Need to Calm Down" without needing the lyrics, and it's a complete delight. Courtney belts out "Jolene," Diane blushes deep pink as she giggles her way through the dirty parts of "You Oughta Know," and Gail manages a surprisingly good rendition of "Don't Stop Believin'." Virginia shocks everyone when she knows all the words to "Livin' on a Prayer," Tori has us clapping along as she sings "Hey There Delilah," and Avery channels Kurt Cobain with "Smells Like Teen Spirit."

Finally Rosemary takes the stage, using her cane for leverage as she steps up.

When the familiar strumming begins, I hold my breath. She leans toward the microphone and says, "Anyway, here's 'Wonderwall.'"

We all break down laughing, and tears are still trickling

from the corners of my eyes as Rosemary completely nails the song.

Some of us sing a second song of our choice, and Avery and I team up for "Summer Nights" from the *Grease* soundtrack. We drink, talk, and laugh a lot. Even though I don't know their in-jokes and local references, I feel included. Like I'm part of their community.

"How are you getting along out there with Mason?" Rosemary asks as we return to the living room.

"He's, um—kind of reserved, but we're getting things done."

"He wasn't always like that," she says. "The Brown family has owned that property since the early days of the island, and when he was a boy, Mason used to spend the summers with his grandparents. He and some of the other kids from the island, including Daniel, were as wild as could be."

"*Wild* is not the word I'd use for him."

She offers a soft smile and a knowing look. "Well, he's had a difficult time."

"I know."

"Keep that in mind," Rosemary says before letting out a small yawn. "And now I think it's time for me to head on home."

"Do you need a ride?"

"You're a dear for asking, but I only live a few houses down."

The book club members trickle slowly home until it's just Avery and me, cleaning up the mess. She doesn't send me home when I offer to help, and I appreciate the honesty. When the dishes are washed and her dining room is a dining room again, we pour some wine and sit in the yellow Adirondack chairs on her front porch.

"I covet these chairs," I say as she lights up a small joint and takes a long drag. "I have some like them on a Pinterest board for my someday house."

She offers me the joint. For years I've been the responsible one while Brian has smoked weed, played video games, and generally acted the fool. But tonight Maisie is happy and safe, so I don't overthink it. I take only a small hit, though.

"Look," Avery says. "I've seen Mason's place. All you need to do is tell him what you want and let him pay for it. He's not going to complain when his house stops looking like the front window display of a thrift store."

"What if he hates it? Or starts dating someone who hates it?"

She cracks up laughing. "Where is Mason going to meet someone to date? He never leaves the brewery. He's like . . . Miss Havisham. Which is why I'd hoped maybe the two of you might—"

"My sister lost her fiancé to suicide a couple of years ago," I interrupt, not wanting to go down that road. "I used to get so irritated with her because it seemed like she wanted to be miserable. Until one day when she packed up everything she owned, moved onto their sailboat, and left. I was so mad because I thought it was a selfish thing to do. But she got better because she was ready to get better. Mason will too."

Avery sighs. "I know."

"But I'll see what I can do about getting rid of that hideous couch."

"Hey, do you want to spend the night? We have a guest room."

"I'd say yes, but I also love the idea of sleeping all night in my own bed knowing Maisie will not be there when I wake up."

She laughs. "I don't remember the last time Daniel and I slept without Leo. He's the best birth control."

"Thanks for inviting me to book club."

"You're welcome," Avery says. "For what it's worth, I'm glad you're here. And I hope you don't mind that I basically forced you to be my best friend."

I nudge her elbow with mine. "I can think of worse things to be."

• • •

It's nearly eleven by the time I get back to the house. I'm not wasted or stoned, but I'm feeling just tipsy enough to want to look at the sky. I lie back on the grass and watch the stars grow denser as my eyes adjust to the darkness. After a bit, I hear the creak of the screen door and Mason's footsteps on the stairs. He lowers himself down beside me, not so close that we're in danger of touching, but not so far away that I'm not extremely aware of his body next to mine. "This is the time of year we start getting ticks, so you might want to consider spreading a blanket or—"

"Or maybe you could buy some chairs."

"Or that," he says quietly. "How was your night?"

"I'd tell you, but then I'd have to kill you."

"Must have been a wild time."

"It was a good fun," I say, teasing him about his earlier word gaffe.

Mason groans. "You're fired."

Laughing, I take my phone from my pocket and use the night sky app to identify the constellations. Leo. Virgo. Both the

Ursas. The planet Venus is particularly bright. "Speaking of wild times, Rosemary tells me you were quite the feral child."

"Pretty much," he says. "There was a whole gang of us—including Avery's husband, Daniel—and we built tree forts in the woods. Rode our bikes to the beach and stole grapes from the vineyard. Pulled pranks on the kids at the 4-H camp. And went swimming in the quarry even though it was strictly off-limits. Our parents never had to worry, though, because we always turned up in time for dinner."

"Sounds idyllic."

"It was," Mason says. "And even though my family lived in Cleveland the rest of the year, coming to Kelleys for the summer always felt like coming home."

"Is it too late to turn the cabins into tree houses?"

He laughs. "I've already considered it, but beer plus rope bridges equals a liability nightmare."

"Good point."

"Thanks for dinner, by the way."

"You're welcome," I say, tucking my phone back into my pocket. "You know, Avery is kind of worried about you. She calls you Miss Havisham."

"*Havisham?* I'd say I'm more Boo Radley."

"She thinks you spend too much time alone in the brewery, and that your house looks like a thrift store."

"Well, she's not wrong."

"People on the island care about you," I say. "You should probably check in with them occasionally. And . . . on that note, I will return to minding my own business."

"You're not telling me anything I don't already know. It's

just—never mind." He gets to his feet and the spot where he was lying feels conspicuously cold. "Night."

My heart aches for him. He's like a bottle of his own beer. Sealed up. Under pressure. How long before he explodes? Or makes himself sick? Or completely breaks?

"Good night, Mason."

May

CHAPTER 11

Forelsket
Norwegian
"the indescribable euphoria you feel when you start to
fall in love"

We're two weeks into May when I get a call from my mom.
We've spoken a couple of times a week since I moved to Ohio,
but today she's calling to tell me the house sold. Her new condo is
an adorable tiny one-bedroom unit with a canal view. It's within
walking distance to restaurants and shops, and she's transferring
from her bank branch to one closer to the new place. It's sad
to realize I'll never live in my childhood home again, but it's
probably harder for Mom. She hasn't lived anywhere else since
she left Germany. She raised two daughters and cared for her
granddaughter in that house.

"Do you need me to help you pack up your stuff?" I ask,
glancing over at Mason.

His eyebrows are furrowed as he looks at something on his

laptop, his head cocked. Considering. He rarely spends much time in the office, but he's been waiting for the label of his next beer to pop up in his inbox.

After Little Fish Lager, Mason dialed in on the formula for an India pale ale that he named Old Stone, but he's been more tight-lipped than usual about his current project. He's been staying late at the brewery every night, so leaving plates of dinner in the oven for him has become a habit. Each morning there's usually a little cup of warm green tea waiting for me on the kitchen island in return. Today I tasted a hint of lemon and honey that may have been added especially for me.

He looks up from his laptop. The crease between his brows relaxes and he gives me an encouraging chin tilt—Mason Brown shorthand for *go if you need to go*. I open a browser window to research flights.

"It's too expensive," Mom says.

"Flights are cheap right now," I say. "Tell me when you want me to come, and I'll be there."

"We could time it around Maisie's birthday next week. Anna will be flying home too, so we could celebrate both of their birthdays."

The tears that fill my eyes are unexpected, but I've missed my mom and I haven't seen my sister in more than a year. "That sounds great. I'll book a flight."

"How long will you be gone?" Mason asks after I say goodbye to Mom and disconnect the call.

"Three or four days," I say. "Long enough to pack up her belongings and hire a mover to do the heavy lifting. We'll have a birthday party for Maisie while we're there and give her a chance to see her dad."

He nods. "Better make it five."

"Are you sure? I haven't worked here long enough for vacation time."

"My hotel, my rules."

Mason might be Boo Radley, hiding in his brewery so he doesn't have to face the outside world, but his generosity never fails to blow me away. "Thank you."

"You'll need a ride to the airport."

"I can ask Avery."

"I'll drive you," he says. "I can visit my folks in Cleveland."

"Okay, thanks," I say. "Get the label for your new beer yet?"

The Old Stone label for the India pale ale features a drawing of Inscription Rock, a slab of limestone carved with Native American petroglyphs that was discovered on the island in the 1800s and has been a beloved tourist attraction for decades. The label has some of the same design elements as the Little Fish label and I'm dying to see this new one.

"Yeah."

"Can I see it?"

He shakes his head. "Nope."

"Why are you being so secretive?"

"Because I've never brewed anything like this before," Mason says. "I don't want to talk about it until I know it doesn't suck, so go do your job and leave me alone."

"Please?"

He rolls his eyes but, after a couple of moments, says, "Okay, fine. Come 'ere."

I wheel my chair across the room, and he moves to make space for us both behind his desk. This close, I catch a whiff of lemon soap and laundry detergent, and it makes me want to bury my face against his neck. It's been so long since I've felt a man's arms around me, and I can't help thinking that Mason's would be strong and warm and safe. The soft click of the trackpad brings me back.

The image opens and the label matches the others but features a yellow sun, blue water, and the name Sunshine Ale. Beneath the name, in smaller lettering, it says BREWED WITH JAPANESE GREEN TEA.

"It's, uh—I made it for my mom." He sounds nervous, which does absolutely nothing to dispel my unfortunate longing. His thoughtfulness reverberates through me like a bell. "Her name is Yōko. It can mean many things, but among them is sunshine, which is what my dad calls her."

"She's going to love this," I say. "I mean, how could she not? Thanks for letting me in on the secret."

He closes the image and I take that as my cue to roll back into my own space. I return to my search for flights when the question strikes me. "Is your whole name American or do you have a Japanese name in there somewhere too?"

Mason rubs his hand over his mouth like he doesn't want to tell me. "My middle name is Asahi."

"Like, the *beer*?"

"Unintentionally, but yes."

"Wow. Sometimes fate has zero chill."

His cheeks dimple as he laughs and the smartest thing for me to do is leave this office, pack up my belongings, and move back to Florida before this aching crush makes me do something foolish. Like tell him how I feel.

"What does it mean?" I ask.

I've always been interested in the meaning of words, especially words in other languages that aren't directly translatable into English. There's a Bengali word, *ghodar-dim*, that literally translates to "horse's egg" but conceptually it means "false hope" or "nothing."

"'Morning sun,'" Mason says.

The meaning makes me think of waking up—specifically, what it would be like to wake up to his face in the morning. It's another thought I have no business having, but I can't help thinking it would be a glorious thing.

"Rachel means 'ewe,' as in a female sheep," I say, redirecting my brain from that *ghodar-dim*. "And biblical Rachel was embroiled in a hot mess of a relationship, which—okay, never mind. That tracks."

"Maisie's dad?"

"Yeah. He was not my best decision." I realize we're veering into personal territory. I want to know more—everything, really—about Mason, but I already understand that if we continue talking about relationships, he's going to shut down. "Anyway, I found a flight for next week, so I'll book it if you're sure you can live without me for a few days."

"I'll try to manage."

•   •   •

On the drive to the airport, we listen to a podcast about brewing sour beers. I start off at a disadvantage because I don't know what a sour beer is, and it only gets worse. I know all the words the hosts are saying, but they're arranged in a way that makes me feel like I'm listening to another language.

"How do you understand this?" I ask when the end music fades away.

"It helps that I have an interest," Mason says. "But I've also been doing this for more than twenty years. I brewed my first batch of beer in my parents' basement during the summer between my freshman and sophomore years of college."

"Were you even legal to drink?"

"Nope."

"How'd that turn out?"

"It may not surprise you to know that the bottles exploded," he says. "Beer on the ceiling, glass all over the floor. My mom wanted to murder me but settled for banning me from ever making beer in the house again. She also made me clean up every last drop and shard. It took me a week."

"I bet she was proud when you got it right, though."

His eyes are shaded by sunglasses, but from the side I can see the corners crinkle as he smiles. "She was."

"Are you an only child?"

"I have an older brother and sister, Owen and Laurel," Mason says. "You?"

"My sister, Anna, is almost two years younger."

"Do you get along?"

"I don't really know," I say. "We were close when we were little girls. Constant companions, you know? But as we got older and our interests changed, we drifted. Then I got pregnant with Maisie and she met Ben—it's a long story. I haven't seen her in over a year, and I think we might be okay, but this trip will probably tell."

The conversation pauses when we pull into a toll plaza and Mason cranks down the window to pay the fifty-cent toll. Most of the toll plazas in Florida—at least in my part of Florida—have been replaced with toll-by-plate cameras, so having to stop is kind of charming.

"My relationship with my siblings has improved with time," he says, pulling away from the plaza. "Owen is older than I am by four years and Laurel by three. They were a unit and never wanted me around. One time, they locked me in the dog's crate—"

I burst out laughing.

"Oh sure, it's funny now," he says. "But I was in there until my dad got home from work and found me."

"You must have been terrified."

"I tried to convince the dog to let me out."

"Poor you."

"I'm traumatized," he says, but the corner of his mouth hitches up in a grin.

"How regularly does this memory come up at Thanksgiving?"

Mason laughs. "Every year, like clockwork, I remind them how terrible they were."

"When Anna and I were little, I tried to convince her that some cat poop in the backyard was candy," I say. "But that backfired when she picked it up and smashed it on my leg."

"As a younger sibling, I salute her."

"Mama," Maisie says, taking off her headphones. "I have to go potty."

"We're almost at the airport," I say, glancing over at Mason, who responds by pressing down on the accelerator. "Can you hold it?"

"Only a little bit."

A couple of minutes later, the airport comes into view and

Mason's attention is on the exit and departure signs, and I'm sad our conversation had to end. There was no awkwardness this time. No emotional retreats. I love his smile. And his laugh. And . . . oh, it's a good thing I'm getting on a plane.

Mason parks the truck in the unloading zone and while I'm taking Maisie from her car seat, he puts our suitcases on the curb.

"Where's your suitcase?" Maisie asks him.

"I'm not going to Florida with you," he says, but when her face begins to pucker into tears, he squats down to her level, a gesture that makes my heart feel like it's going to break out of my chest and offer itself to him.

"Hey, listen," Mason says gently. "I have to stay home and take care of Yōkai while you're hanging out with your daddy and your grandma—"

"She's called Oma."

"Right, Oma," he says. "You go visit Oma and I'll keep Yōkai company until you get back, okay?"

"Okay." Maisie flings her arms around Mason, nearly toppling him backward. He steadies them both and pats her gently on the shoulder.

Thank you, I mouth.

He gives me a thumbs-up.

I take Maisie's hand and she pulls her tiny suitcase behind her as we go through the sliding doors into the terminal. I glance over my shoulder. Mason is standing on the curb in front of the truck. He's still wearing sunglasses, so I can't see his eyes, but he lifts his hand in a wave before turning to go.

CHAPTER 12

Aspaldiko

Basque

"the euphoria and happiness felt when catching up
with someone you haven't seen in a long time"

Anna is waiting for us at the end of the concourse, and I almost
don't recognize her. Her pale hair is pulled back in a loose braid
and her fair skin is tanner than I've ever seen it. But more than
that, she looks . . . less fragile. She's still my tiny, beautiful sister,
but she's gained some necessary weight, and her smile is real.
She's happy. Maisie tugs her hand out of mine and runs straight
into her arms, screaming, "Auntie Anna! Auntie Anna!"

"Look how tall you are!" Anna exclaims. "You must be a
grown-up lady now, right?"

Maisie giggles. "I'm a little girl."

With my daughter clinging to her side like a limpet, Anna
reaches over the suitcases and hugs me. She smells like sunscreen

and a lemony soap that reminds me of Mason. "God, Rachel, I've missed you."

"I've missed you too."

Anna carries Maisie as I walk alongside her, pulling the suitcases.

"When did you get here?" I ask.

"We flew in yesterday."

"Keane came with you?"

"Yeah," she says. "I figured if I was going to keep circling the globe with the guy, it might be nice if you and Mom finally got to meet him."

I sneak a quick glance at her hand to see if there's an engagement ring there. "Is this your weird way of saying you're getting married?"

She laughs. "Maybe someday, but for now we're . . . us."

"Auntie Anna." Maisie touches Anna's cheek to get her attention. "I have a cat."

"You do?"

"Her name is Yōkai."

Anna gives me a quizzical look.

"The cat actually belongs to Mason, my boss," I explain. "She's a terror on four legs to everyone but Maisie and we have no idea why. They sleep together every night, and Yōkai waits for her to come home from preschool."

At the mention of preschool, Maisie launches into a run-on story that begins with school, bounces from Leo to riding the Kelleys Island ferry, and ends with a color-by-color description of the Mexican blanket in Mason's truck. By the time she finishes, we've arrived at Anna's rental car. I'm touched that she remembered to rent a car seat.

"How's Mom doing?" I ask as we leave the parking garage.

"I thought she'd be more nostalgic about leaving the house," Anna says. "But she says it feels like closure. Like, Dad is finally gone."

"But there are so many good memories attached to that house."

"You're right, but she still has *us,* and we can make new memories no matter where she's living. And I think that's where her head is right now."

"Have you seen the new place in person?" I ask.

"She wanted to wait until you and Maisie got here."

"God, that's so sweet."

"Before we get to the house and the hugging and the kissing and the Maisie-squeezing starts, I just wanted to apologize for . . . being such a brat," Anna says. "I know I got on your last nerve so many times after Ben died."

"Please don't apologize for that," I say. "I didn't understand until I got fired. And I know that doesn't compare to losing Ben, but it shouldn't have taken me losing *anything* to be better at empathy. So, I'm the one who's sorry."

"Thank you," she says with a small smile. "Now, tell me about the job."

"It's amazing," I say, and I feel like Maisie, babbling non-stop to Anna about having a hand in designing the hotel and my antique-buying excursions. I tell her about the island and book club. "I've even been going to yoga class."

"How do you like it?"

"I've only been a few times, but so far I love it."

"Mom said you live with your boss."

"Kind of."

"What does *that* mean?"

"Maisie and I live on the second floor of Mason's house, but it's not an apartment, so we share a kitchen," I say. "He's at the brewery practically day and night, and we hardly ever see him at the house. It's almost like having our own place."

"What's he like?"

"He's—" I drop my voice to a whisper so Maisie won't overhear. "God, Anna, he's so fucking hot."

She bursts into laughter. "Rachel! You can't say something like that when we're on 595 in a rental car!"

"I'm sorry, but it's true," I say. "And I can't confide in anyone on the island because it would get back to him in about four and a half seconds."

I pick up my phone and scroll through my camera roll until I find the photo I took of Mason for the website. He grumbled the entire time about wanting to stay behind the scenes, but when he smiled at the last second, I nearly dropped my phone.

I show Anna, who glances quickly. "Okay, I totally see what you mean. We definitely need to revisit this conversation over beers."

"Agreed."

"So, what's the story with Brian?"

"He's video-chatted with Maisie three times since we've been in Ohio, but he won't talk to me," I say. "He's supposed to come for cake tomorrow and then take her home with him for the night. Fingers crossed."

Anna takes the exit toward our old house and when we finally pull in the driveway, I notice the differences. The yard we never had time to beautify is spruced up with cocoplum shrubs and hot-pink penta flowers. The old painted house numbers have been replaced with modern-looking copper numbers. It looks like exactly what it is—a house in transition to a new owner—and I feel a little pang of sadness. Until Mom bursts out the front door and pulls me into the tightest hug. The kind of hug I've been missing. She kisses both of my cheeks and smooths back my hair. "I've missed you so much."

"Me too, Mom."

She gives me another quick hug, then practically dives into the back seat to liberate Maisie. As I open the trunk, Keane comes out of the house. I recognize him from the pictures Anna texted me over the winter, but he's taller than I imagined. Almost a foot taller than her. And I thought he was scruffy from being at sea, but even here on dry land his hair looks like it doesn't meet a comb on the regular. He's hot enough to pull it off, though. He goes to Anna first, draping his arm around her shoulders and dropping a kiss on the top of her head, as if they've been apart too long. He extends his other hand to me. "You must be Rachel. I'm Keane."

"It's nice to finally meet you."

He nods. "Likewise."

It's hard not to compare Keane to Mason, with his neat black hair and leaner build. Mason is taller than I am by a handful of inches, but not as towering as Keane. Mason is almost a decade older than Keane as well, and there's something reassuring about the subtle age lines at the corners of Mason's dark eyes. But more than the way he looks, being around Mason calms me in a way I've never experienced. Only now do I realize how chaotic and stressed out Brian made me feel.

"Let me take those bags," Keane says, scooping up the suitcases and carrying them into the house. Although I'm clearly partial to Mason Brown, Keane gets bonus points for the Irish accent. If I were Anna, I'd be under that all the damn time.

Anna and I follow Keane inside, and behind us comes Mom, with Maisie on her hip, listening intently to a revised version of the story she told Anna at the airport.

My heart is full.

•   •   •

We spend the next couple of hours sifting through memories as we start packing Mom's possessions into moving boxes. Mom and I frequently pause on items, considering the sentimental implications of getting rid of them, until Anna steps in like the tough-love guy on HGTV makeover shows.

"The memories are here," she says, touching her temple as she takes a plastic baby bowl away from Mom and puts it in the donation box. "This takes up space in your life that you need for other things."

Anna knows better than any of us how that works. The only physical objects she has left from her relationship with Ben are a couple of Polaroid pictures, his record collection, and his boat, but she says that's all she needs.

It's late afternoon when we haul the bags of trash to the curb and pack the rental car with boxes of Goodwill donations that Anna and Keane will drop off on the way to their hotel. After showers and a change of clothes, we all meet up at the pirate-themed restaurant where Anna used to work. It's never been my favorite place—even though the food is decent, the waitress uniforms are gross—but Anna is introducing Keane to her old haunts.

While the hostess—dressed in a sexy pirate costume with

petticoat ruffles and bodice lacing—leads us to our table, Keane leans toward Anna and quietly says, "Do you still have your uniform? Because I'd be happy to role-play the patriarchy and let you smash me."

She chokes on a laugh, then elbows him in the side, hissing, "Stop!"

No context was needed for that joke to land and as I try not to snicker, I feel an old familiar surge of envy. I want what they have. I want someone who looks at me the way Keane looks at Anna. Someone who makes me laugh out loud. Someone who makes me blush in public.

Someone like Mason.

Maybe I'm making too much out of a really good conversation. Maybe it's been so long since I've felt a connection with anyone that I'm creating one that doesn't exist. Maybe living in his house makes his distance feel near. I'm operating on autopilot as I take my seat, vaguely aware of everyone else at the table. Mom has commandeered my child, so I don't have to worry about Maisie, and it leaves too much space in my head for thoughts I shouldn't be having. I pick up my phone, toying with the idea of texting him.

"Rachel." Mom's voice penetrates my bubble. "Do you know what you want to drink?"

"Oh, um—a margarita, please, on the rocks with salt," I say, putting down the phone and pushing away thoughts of Mason Brown.

I tune back into my family for the rest of the meal, catching up on Anna and Keane's adventures in the tropics and Mom's plans for her new condo. After dinner, Mom takes Maisie home so the rest of us can hang out. We move to seats at the bar, where we order another round of drinks. Keane, I notice, is drinking Coke.

"Designated driver," he says.

"And . . ." Anna prompts.

"I have a murderous hangover." He aims his thumb at her. "This one introduced me to Carla last night at Waxy's Pub."

I let out a laugh because I know Anna's best friend and I've been to that pub. Both are dangerous and almost impossible to experience in moderation.

"In the thirty years I've inhabited this planet, I have never met *anyone* who could consume more Guinness than I and live to tell the tale," Keane continues. "Carla's ability to hold her drink is . . . supernatural. I'm not fully convinced she's even human. She's good fun, though."

As he takes a sip of soda, Anna leans toward me. "Okay, so spill the beans on your boss."

"I . . . he . . ." I stop, not knowing where to begin.

"That bad, is it?" Keane says.

"Yes."

I tell them everything I know about Mason. His wife. Piper's death. The unfinished hotel. The nonstop fixation on beer. The plates of food in the oven. The green tea on the kitchen island. Miss Havisham.

"Stall the ball a minute," Keane says, reaching for Anna's margarita.

As he downs it like a man who's been living on a desert island for years, she shakes her head. "I have no idea what's going to come out of his mouth next, so . . . be ready for anything."

"The green tea is a dead giveaway," Keane says. "But yer man's not going to make a move while he's all tangled up. He's grieving a child. He probably has lingering regrets over his divorce. And now he's caught feelings for someone who works for him, and it's likely he feels guilty for wanting to be happy. He has no idea what to do with any of that information, so he's a right fucking mess."

Anna blinks a couple of times. "He's . . . actually correct."

"Actually?" He slaps a hand to his chest like he's been wounded. "Of course I'm correct. Rachel, you need to understand that, at present, Mason might not have anything to give. When I met your sister, I was fully prepared to be nothing more to her than a friend, because that's what she needed. I mean, she was also a pretty shite sailor."

"Hey!" she protests.

Keane laughs and kisses her cheek. "I love you to the rings of Saturn and back, but you were very . . . not good."

Anna may as well melt right there.

"I hate you both so much," I say, laughing.

"Listen," Keane says. "Mason is not so much sending signals as he is lighting flares. But he doesn't know he's doing it, so you have to be patient."

"Thank you."

He gives me a little salute. "Always happy to help."

While Anna and Keane fall into a personal conversation about checking up on their dog—they left Queenie with friends in Montserrat—I send a quick text to Mason.

Arrived safely. Packing underway. See you in four days.

The reply bubbles appear on the screen, then disappear. They reappear and disappear again. I hold my breath, waiting for

his response. Wondering what he's typing and erasing. Finally
Mason's message pops up on the screen.

> If I don't starve to death first. There's no dinner in the
> oven.

His words are followed by a wink-face emoji. It's not a lot to
hold on to, but I grab it all the same.

CHAPTER 13

Tampó
Filipino
"when a person withdraws his or her affection or
   cheerfulness toward someone who has hurt them"

The next day is a continuation of the first as we finish sorting,
packing, and making donation runs. When the movers come, we
leave them to pack the truck, and head to Mom's new condo,
taking her most personal possessions with us. The condo is larger
than it looked in the online listing, and because it's on the third
floor, the cathedral ceilings make it feel more spacious. There's
also a generous lanai that could be used as an extra room.

"You're going to have incredible sunrises," Anna says, opening the sliding door. We all crowd out onto the lanai, which
overlooks a wide canal lined with powerboats and sailboats of
various sizes. The complex grounds are neatly landscaped with
yellow hibiscus shrubs and palm trees. "And you'll never have to
mow the grass or pull weeds again."

"I love it here," Mom admits. "I'm going to have the movers put the dining room furniture out here so I'll have more space inside. And I bought a new living room set with a sleeper sofa for when you girls come visit, or for guests." She laughs. "Like I ever have guests."

"Fire up Tinder, Mom," I say. "Find yourself a silver fox."

She wiggles the tip of her nose with her middle finger, cracking us all up and making Maisie demand to know why we're laughing without her.

When the movers arrive, Mom stays behind to direct them where to put her furniture, while the rest of us go to Publix for birthday cake and decorations. Usually we bake homemade cakes, but since Mom's new kitchen isn't set up yet, I buy a chocolate sheet cake with white frosting, blue icing, and *Moana* decorations. We pick up some frozen pizzas, paper plates and napkins, red Solo cups, and two jugs of cheap sangria for post-birthday drinking. On our way through the checkout, Keane gifts Maisie with the Mylar *Moana* balloon she cried about at the grocery store in Ohio. By the time we return to the condo, the movers have arranged Mom's furniture and sorted the boxes into their proper rooms.

We set up the party on the lanai and, as the minutes tick closer to dinnertime, my stomach ties itself into knots, worrying Brian won't show up. Worrying that he will. Finally the security system beeps, and his face pops up on the video monitor. Mom quickly buzzes him in. By the time he reaches her front door, a fist of anxiety has closed around my chest.

"Daddy's here!" Maisie sings out, running to greet him. He looks as adorable as ever in his favorite orange track jacket and loose-fitting jeans, but he behaves differently, his attention focused solely on Maisie as he puts down a wrapped present and scoops her into his arms. She holds his face in her hands and rubs her nose against his—a trick she learned from Leo, apparently.

"Happy birthday, little pea," Brian says. "How ya doing?"

"I have a cat now. Her name is Yōkai."

"That's so cool." Unlike Anna, Brian doesn't look to me for an explanation. His gaze skitters around the room and he says, "Hi, um—thanks for inviting me."

Mom ushers him through the condo and out onto the lanai. Anna fetches a couple of pizzas from the kitchen, while Keane pours cups of sangria for the adults. I bring the present from the living room. It's wrapped in paper that looks like purple mermaid scales. I want to believe that this is Brian trying, but we've been down this road before. Never with purple mermaid scales, though.

Brian looks nervous as he takes a seat at the table—he should, given that he's facing a wall of Beck women—but Keane presses a cup of sangria into his hand and says, "Take the edge off, mate."

Keane deftly steers him into small talk, and Brian shares that he recently started a new job at a cell phone store and plans to enroll in an air traffic controller course in August. I want to drag him out of the room and demand to know why he couldn't have done these things when we were together. But my family is here, and Maisie is listening.

"That's so great, Brian." Despite how angry I am, I mean it. "Congratulations."

"Yeah, um—thanks." He looks beyond me again. Something is incredibly off. Brian isn't being flirty and charming. I don't need that from him, but he won't even make eye contact.

I wonder if he's planning to flake out on Maisie and doesn't want to admit it in front of everyone. Or . . . A new fear rises in me that I've never considered. What if he takes her tonight and doesn't bring her back? There's no way to ask him that question without it sounding like an accusation.

I choke down a piece of birthday cake and put on my biggest smile as Maisie opens her gifts. Anna brought her a blue batik dress and a little steel pan drum from Grenada, as well as a tiny straw purse from St. Lucia. Mom loaded her up with Shopkins collectibles. And inside the mermaid box from Brian is a modeling sand kit with molds to make shapes. It's a thoughtful gift, and I hate how my first assumption is that someone else picked it out. Like Brian's mother, Rosalie. Or Eden. If she's still in the picture.

None of this makes sense.

Maybe I'm overreacting. Maybe I've turned Brian's awkwardness at being in the same room with me into a full-blown conspiracy theory. But when I hand him Maisie's backpack before they leave, I memorize what she's wearing.

·   ·   ·

I don't sleep. The panic in my chest is alive and writhing as I pace the condo from kitchen to lanai, and back. I sit down on the couch. I turn on the TV. I get up again. Turn off the TV. Mom has been in bed for hours, and Anna and Keane left for their hotel not long after Brian took Maisie. I consider driving to his apartment to get her. I even put on my shoes. Shouldn't I trust him? He's never done anything to hurt her, but I can't shake the fear. Instead I go outside and walk along the seawall until light breaks the horizon. When I return, Mom is on the lanai having her morning coffee.

"You're up early," she says with a frown. "I saw you walking. Are you okay?"

"No. I've spent the whole night terrified that Brian won't bring Maisie back."

"Why didn't you say something?"

"How do you accuse your ex-boyfriend of attempted kidnapping without sounding unhinged?"

"I meant to me, Rachel," Mom says. "You didn't have to spend the night alone."

"I didn't want to worry you."

"Well, I'm worried now, so you didn't spare me anything."

"I'm sorry."

She pulls me into a hug, rubbing my back like she did when I was a little girl. I break down, sobbing against her shoulder.

"I know you've always hated it when I say you can do better than Brian," she says. "But regardless of how I feel about him, I don't believe stealing Maisie would ever cross his mind. Long-range planning and execution are not in his skill set."

"But you heard him: he's going to college and got a decent job."

"You told him he needed to get his shit together," Mom points out. "Seems to me that he listened."

"That doesn't explain why he was acting so sketchy last night."

"Brian was comfortable with your relationship because you never challenged his behavior. When you moved to Ohio, you broke the cycle. I suspect he's hurt and angry, and has no idea how to manage that," she says. "Not making eye contact and refusing to speak to you makes perfect sense for someone who has the emotional depth of a teaspoon."

She takes my chin firmly in her hand. "And if you had come to me with this last night, you would not have spent the night worrying about something that Brian Schroeder is not smart enough to pull off."

When I laugh, it's wet and snotty from crying. "You're right. I let my fears get away from me."

"You're a mother," she says, kissing my forehead. "It happens."

Mom goes into the kitchen to start breakfast and I nap on the couch until the security system beeps and I see my daughter on the video screen.

Maisie comes bursting into the condo, hopped up on pancake syrup and orange juice, Brian on her heels. His sunny smile fades and he averts his eyes. Maybe Mom was right.

"Hi, Brian," I say, but his gaze won't stick. "Do you have a minute? We need to talk."

"I, uh—I really don't have time right now," he says. He hugs and kisses Maisie. Tells her to be a good girl for Mama, like he always does. Then bolts like a scared rabbit, without a backward glance.

• • •

Mom insists on coming inside the airport with Maisie and me, instead of simply dropping us at departures. Anna and Keane have already left for Antigua. From there they'll take a ferry to Montserrat, where their boat is moored. That kind of vagabond lifestyle is too unpredictable for me, but it seems to work for them.

Mom waits with us in the check-in line and hugs us one last time before we go through the security checkpoint. She watches until we're through to the other side, then waves until she can't see us anymore.

Maisie falls asleep on the plane, her head on my thigh, and three hours later we're in Ohio. As we taxi down the runway, I turn on my phone to find a text from Mason.

I'm in the cell lot. Let me know when you're out front.

A bubble of happiness rises inside me, and I smile at my phone, knowing full well I look ridiculous. I can't wait to get back to Kelleys Island. I can't wait to see Mason.

Our seats are in the bulkhead row behind business class, so Maisie and I are among the first people off the plane. I want to race through the airport, but I can only move as fast as Maisie can walk, so by the time we get to the arrival doors, my anticipation level is through the roof. I need to pump the brakes on this, but when his green pickup pulls up to the curb, I can hear the blood rushing in my ears, and it sounds like *hope, hope, hope.*

Ohio must have been experiencing a heat wave because when Mason comes around the back of the truck, he's dressed in a pair of olive-green shorts and an untucked plaid shirt that is not flannel, sleeves rolled to the elbows. He's even wearing brown leather flip-flops. The whole package makes me a little dizzy. Like when he dropped me off, his sunglasses block his eyes, but he offers me a cockeyed grin. "Glad you're back."

"Oh really?" I try to play it cool. I hope I'm playing it cool.

"The construction manager keeps asking questions that I can't answer," Mason says, hoisting the suitcases into the truck bed, and my heart does a little dip. "And being alone in the house was weird."

And after the dip comes the swoop. "It was?"

"A little." He shrugs, which is definitely not a declaration of his undying love, but it's Mason Brown sweet. "Your mom settled in?"

"Pretty much," I say. "She has to figure out where everything goes, but that's the fun part."

"I most definitely do not agree."

"I wish I could say I'm shocked, but no . . . that's very on-brand for you."

He gives a short laugh and . . . God, I didn't realize how much I missed that sound. How much I love that sound.

"Did anything exciting happen while I was gone?" I ask.

"The mattresses and bedding for the cabins arrived a couple days ago," Mason says. "The taproom looks like a warehouse, so we might have to rent a storage pod or something if we're going to open the brewery on time."

"Mason," Maisie pipes up. "My auntie Anna gave me a drum for my birthday."

"What kind of drum?"

"It's a steel pan."

He glances over her car seat at me for clarification.

"My sister lives on a sailboat in the Caribbean." I tell him about Ben's death and Anna's subsequent sailing adventure, how she met Keane.

"Keane is like a pirate," Maisie says. "But he doesn't wear the black thingy on his eye."

"Oh yeah?" Mason says carefully.

She nods. "One of his legs only has leg on the top part. The bottom's not real."

"He wears a prosthesis," I explain.

"Okay, I follow that logic."

Maisie launches into one of her monologues about her birthday party, and I clock Mason to make sure she's not stressing him out, but he nods and makes appropriate noises in all the right places.

We stop for pizza in Sandusky, and when we finally reach Kelleys Island, it's dark and Maisie is crashed out in her car seat, well past her bedtime. Mason grabs the suitcases as I carry her into the house.

When I switch on the kitchen light, I see it.

The frat house is gone.

Instead there's a plush goldenrod-yellow micro-suede couch tossed with colorful throw pillows, an armless leather chair the color of whiskey, and a teal velvet armchair. There are end tables and lamps. Plants and artwork. A large area rug that ties together the colors of the furniture. A bookshelf with not enough books. And in the space between the kitchen island and the living room, there's a wooden dining table with ladder-back chairs.

"What—" I stop abruptly, shocked speechless.

"Do you like it?"

"It's—How could I not? It's beautiful."

"I've been thinking a lot about how I've been living on hold for the past year," he says. "Like there was a chance Jess would come back and fill the place up again. But that's never gonna happen. I've also been thinking that it's selfish to expect you and Maisie to steer clear of me. You shouldn't have to confine yourself upstairs because my head is a mess."

"Are you sure?"

"After Jess left, I completely shut down," he says. "Which is why the hotel isn't finished, the beer didn't get brewed, and the upstairs apartment never happened. Trust me, I know this arrangement is not normal, but we can't keep living like it's a temporary situation. If you don't want to do this anymore, I can—"

"I want to stay."

He nods. "Okay, then. Welcome home."

I push away a tear with the heel of my hand. "Thank you."

"You should probably get Maisie to bed."

"Yeah, you're right," I say, impressed at how far out onto an emotional limb he's gone. I don't press him to go further. "I'll leave the suitcases for the morning. Good night, Mason."

"Night."

• • •

In the morning, the suitcases are in the hallway outside my bedroom door and there's a warm cup of green tea on the counter. I sip slowly as I walk around the new living room. It feels like every detail was mined from my own brain, or—

I call Avery. "Did you have anything to do with this living room transformation?"

"I might have stalked your Pinterest account and offered suggestions *that had absolutely nothing in common with your preferences.*"

"You knew?"

"Mason asked for our help, which he hasn't done in an awfully long time," Avery says. "So I went on a wild spending spree with his credit card and the three of us did all the work. It was like being part of the behind-the-scenes crew on a home make-over show."

"Why would he do this?"

"That's what we've been wondering," she says. "For the past year, Mason has walled himself off from almost everyone. Then you show up and blast a hole in the brickwork, and things start getting done. But when we asked, he just shrugged and said the house needed to be finished."

I can't tell her what Mason told me about living on hold and hoping Jess would come back. It's not my story to share.

"He wasn't wrong about that," I say.

"I know," Avery says. "But we're still hoping you two are having some sort of secret affair."

"We're not. I swear. I'm just as surprised as you."

"Well, it was nice to have the old Mason back for a little while."

If this Mason—and the Mason who picked me up at the airport yesterday—is what he's really like, I'm in bigger trouble than I thought.

"I know there aren't a ton of kids on the island, but how do people handle day care after school lets out for the summer?" I ask, changing the subject. "I don't know what I'm going to do with Maisie."

"I'll take her," Avery says. "She and Leo get along so well, and it would be great for him to have someone to play with. And since my classes are in the evenings and on weekends, I'd be happy to have her."

"How much?"

"Nothing."

"Really?" I say. "Are you sure?"

"She'll be doing me a favor," Avery says. "I can only take part in so many LEGO spaceship battles before I lose my mind."

I laugh. "I can't say no to that."

"We'll work out the details at book club."

June

CHAPTER 14

Ailyak
Bulgarian
"the subtle art of doing everything calmly and
without rushing, while enjoying the experience and
life in general"

By the second week of June, it's crystal clear—and not at all
unexpected—that we will not be opening the hotel in time for
the Fourth of July. Despite the incessant buzz of saws and the
thwack of nail guns echoing around the property, only the first
cabin is under roof. We might be able to offer tours when we
open the taproom, but there's no point in trying to rent out the
cabin when there's still so much construction underway.

The taproom bar arrives on the first Tuesday ferry. The top
is made from repurposed bowling alley lanes with a dark mahog-
any front, all varnished to a glossy shine. Under Mason's direction, the delivery guys move it into place and bolt it to the floor.
Later in the day, we accept a delivery of twelve swivel barstools,

half a dozen tables, and twenty-four metal tub chairs—and the taproom starts looking like a real bar.

On Wednesday the tile layers arrive to install the floor in the first cabin, and I slip out of the office to have a look. The cabin is built from the same natural wood planks as the brewhouse, with limestone fascia concealing the concrete pad foundation. It has a small verandah—just big enough for a couple of chairs—and the drywall inside has been covered with white shiplap. The effect is timeless, like the cabin could have been standing here for a century.

I'm watching the floor progress when Mason comes up alongside me.

"I'm really sorry we're not going to meet our goal for opening next month," I say. "But it's going to be beautiful."

The past couple of weeks have been a frenzy of orders and deliveries. Sleeper sofas, Pendleton wool blankets, and bathroom fixtures from a hospitality wholesaler. I found several vintage Persian rugs on Craigslist and picked up a couple more beds at an antique shop in Milan. I also bought discontinued cabinetry from several different home improvement stores and worked with a local granite dealer to get remnant pieces of countertop at a discount. Each cabin will have a different color and style of cabinets in the efficiency kitchen.

"Missing the deadline is on me," Mason says. "Without you, none of this would be as far along as it is."

I think it's a compliment. It feels like a compliment, but I don't know how to accept it with grace. Instead I deflect to updating him on the construction.

"The landscapers should be here early next week to build the patio behind the brewhouse and lay paths from each of the cabins," I say. "We should consider building a firepit, too. I was thinking we could use the back of the building to host outdoor movie nights."

Mason studies me a long moment and I feel my cheeks grow warm. I want him to press me against the side of the cabin and kiss me. I moisten my lower lip with the tip of my tongue, willing him to do it. But he just swallows noticeably and says, "You're . . . really smart."

I can't stop myself from smiling. "Yeah, well, you hired me."

• • •

Thursday evening I'm making lasagna for dinner when I get a call from Vivian at the antique shop in Port Clinton.

"Remember that resort I told you about?" she says. "The auction is Saturday morning at eight. The old décor was modeled on a Western ski lodge, so they might not have the kind of things you're looking for, but it's a high-end place, so it won't be tacky. It's probably worth checking out."

"Definitely. Thanks for the reminder."

"I'll text you the details," she says, and then she's gone.

Her text message appears shortly after, and a few minutes later Mason comes into the kitchen from outside. He doesn't normally finish working this early in the day, so I'm a little surprised when he kicks off his brown suede sneakers at the door. I tell him about the upcoming auction.

"It might be a chance for us to find some interesting pieces for the taproom," I say as I chop an orange bell pepper for the salad. "I know you trust me, but the brewery and taproom are your domain, and I wouldn't mind your input. If you can spare a day off."

"Okay." Mason stares into the fridge as if he'll manifest his own dinner with enough concentration.

"I thought you'd be a harder sell."

"The beer is coming together," he says. "The lager, the IPA, and the green tea ale are ready. I have a Kölsch in the fermenter, with another experimental brew ready to go into the mash tun."

As he takes a glass storage container of leftover chili from the fridge, I set another place at the dining room table, where Maisie is drawing a picture with a blue crayon.

"I'm working with the orchard on Catawba to make a peach wheat beer for the summer and I've got some stout aging in rum barrels from Grenada that will be a good fall seasonal," Mason says. "I've also reached out to the other brewery on the island and another on the mainland for guest taps."

"This is really exciting," I say, taking the pan of lasagna from the oven.

"The lager and green tea ale are probably the best I've ever made."

"Better than Fish Brothers?"

"Feels like I got my mojo back," he says as he watches me peel the foil away from the steaming cheesy dish. He looks down at his chili with a slight frown, and I hide a smile.

"Do you want to join us for dinner?"

"If you don't mind."

I meet his eyes. "If I minded, I wouldn't have asked."

Mason quickly returns the chili to the fridge, then takes a seat at the head of the table. Maisie holds up her drawing for him.

"Do you like my porcupine?"

"I've never seen a blue porcupine before," he says.

"That's because she lives in the ocean."

"Can she breathe underwater?"

"Yes," she says. "She wears a snorkel to swim down to her house."

"Where's her house?"

Maisie puts the paper down in front of Mason. "Can you draw it?"

As he picks up the crayon, I ask, "Are you planning to grow this brewery into a national brand?" I'm hoping the question will keep him from thinking too hard about what he's doing.

"Nah." He sketches a few crude lines. "Matt was the master-mind behind Fish Brothers becoming a household name. For me, it's always been about the craft and the science."

"Have you considered offering brewing classes?"

"Not really."

"You could do a weeklong seminar," I say, cutting the lasagna into squares. "Participants would take part in the brewing process and leave with a sample of the beer they made. If you offered the seminar only once a year, you'd sell out the minute the reservations became available, and you could feature the resulting beer as a limited release."

"That's a really great idea. How do you come up with this stuff?"

"I'm always thinking about it." I bring the salad bowl to the table, then go back for the lasagna. "I mean, the point of hospitality is keeping your guests entertained, whether they're family and friends or paying customers. The more activities we offer, the more likely it is they'll return or tell other people."

Mason puts down the crayon and slides the picture back to Maisie. Drawing is not one of his best skills, but the porcupine's

house bears a resemblance to a pineapple—not unlike Sponge-
Bob SquarePants's house.

"A prickly porcupine should have a prickly house," Mason
says, making Maisie giggle. He looks at me. "Is there anything
I can do to help?"

"You just did."

Mason plates the lasagna while I fill our individual bowls
with salad, and we eat together. Like a family.

Stop it, Rachel.

Like friends.

• • •

The resort auction is scheduled early on Saturday morning—
and I don't want us to miss out on anything good—so we drop
Maisie off at Avery's house on Friday afternoon. On the ferry,
Mason and I sit in the truck, listening to a podcast about hops.

"I had no idea there were so many varieties," I say. "I thought
hops were hops."

"This is what makes brewing complicated and exciting.
Every hop has a different flavor profile and there are so many
other ingredients you can add during the process that will affect
the outcome."

"How do you know what to add?"

"Some things are traditional, and you learn as you go," he says.
"But mostly it's about experimenting. There's a brewery in Cleveland using seaweed from the northern coast of Ireland in one of
their stouts, which lends a briny umami note to the beer, and I *hate*
that I didn't think of it first."

"Do you experiment more now than when you were at Fish
Brothers?"

"Definitely," Mason says. "Busting out of the gate with our amber ale set the tone for the rest of our beers. We wanted to appeal to the masses, so I played it pretty safe. We did the things big breweries were doing, like a Mexican-style lager meant to be served with a lime wedge."

He rolls his eyes, like maybe making that particular beer wasn't completely his decision.

"Even the smallest breweries need some standard ales or lagers for people who aren't interested in green tea or seaweed or fruit in their beers," he says. "But without the pressure of a buying public, I can brew whatever I want."

I tuck my legs up beneath me on the bench seat as I shift to face him. "How did your parents react when you told them you wanted to make beer for a living?"

"Growing up, I was the nerdy kid who—Okay, did you ever see the movie *Up*?"

"Yes."

"Russell is basically nine-year-old me."

"Aww, that's so cute."

"I was the kid who asked for a chemistry set for Christmas, won first-place ribbons at the science fair, and did not flinch when dissecting things in biology class. So I'm sure my parents assumed I'd pursue something STEM," he says. "I'm not sure they'd have ever guessed fermentation science, but they've been surprisingly chill about it. Especially when I started getting good at it."

The lake is shimmery and blue, and with the windows down we can hear the faint screams of roller coaster riders at Cedar Point. I fiddle with the fringe on the edge of the Mexican blanket.

"We went on a family vacation once to the Grand Canyon,"

I say. "I don't remember much about the actual canyon, but I have vivid memories of the motel."

"Yeah?"

"There were these desert landscape paintings hanging above the beds that—I realize now—were objectively terrible, but I thought they were beautiful. And it was so glamorous that they *gave* you shampoo and soap."

Mason laughs.

"I'm not saying that's where my desire to work in hotels began, but . . ." I give a little shrug.

"What was your go-to response when people asked what you wanted to be when you grew up?" he asks.

"Usually whatever my Barbie was doing at the time." I tick them off on my fingers. "President. Ballet dancer. Polar marine biologist."

"That's . . . oddly specific."

"I know, right? At one point I wanted to be an aerobics instructor because of Barbie, but not once did I ever say I wanted to scrub hotel toilets. I only ended up doing that because I graduated from high school without a plan."

Mason clears his throat. "I called Cecily after you sent me your résumé. She said your talents were being wasted as a night desk manager."

I slap the dashboard. "I knew it! You *did* call my references."

"Only her."

"Still, I knew you couldn't be that trusting."

"I trusted Cecily, though," he says, his eyes fixed on the horizon. "And she wasn't wrong."

CHAPTER 15

Mamihlapinatapai
Yaghan
"a meaningful, but wordless, exchange between two
  people who both desire to initiate something but are
  hesitant to act on it"

I'm still feeling the warmth of Mason's compliment when we
park along a block-length row of shops and restaurants in the
historic section of downtown Sandusky, where he's booked a
couple of rooms in a boutique hotel overlooking the bay. The
hotel has only nine guest rooms, along with two bars—including
one on the roof—and an adjoining taco restaurant.

After checking in, we take the elevator to the second floor.
It's a brief ride, but being enclosed in a small space with Mason
makes me jittery. This is a business trip, and we have separate
rooms, but when we make eye contact, I feel like I might spon-
taneously combust.

Our rooms are at the back of the building, across the hall from each other, and when I step inside, my hotel nerd heart swells with joy. The room is modern, with an exposed brick wall and white subway tiles in the bathroom. Through my window is a view of Jackson Street Pier—part ferry dock, part city park. Thanks to the warm weather, Sandusky is bustling. Cyclists pedal past the hotel on a bike trail. A busker plays guitar in the park on the pier. And a couple holding hands buys ice cream from a tiki-themed cart.

I take a quick shower and swap my jeans and T-shirt for a coral-colored wrap dress and leather sandals, then head downstairs to meet Mason at the hotel bar. He's not there yet, so I order a glass of rosé and head out onto the narrow back deck. I'm leaning against the railing when he comes up alongside me.

"Hey." He places a glass of beer beside my wine and rests his forearms on the railing. He smells like fresh soap and I'm almost afraid to look at him. When I finally work up the nerve, his hair is damp at the ends and he's wearing an untucked dark denim shirt with rust-colored chinos and white low-top Chucks.

"Hey yourself," I say, trying to keep my tone friendly, despite every nerve ending in my body lighting up with need. And desire. Definitely both.

"I like your dress."

"Thanks. What are you drinking?"

"It's a Dortmunder, which is one of my all-time favorite lagers," he says. "I've never been able to pin down a recipe that tastes great. I've brewed it dozens of times, and it's always completely drinkable, but—"

"Fine is not great."

The corners of his eyes crinkle as he smiles. "Exactly."

We fall into companionable silence as the sun sinks toward the horizon. The sunset is obscured by some buildings, so when our glasses are empty, we cross the street to the pier, where we can watch the sunset beyond the city coal docks. We both take pictures with our phones, and I text mine to Mom and Anna.

"Are you hungry?" Mason asks.

"I'm getting there."

"The taco restaurant connected to the hotel is really good," he says. "Usually when I come to Sandusky, I eat my weight in sushi to hold me over until the next time, but we can have anything you want."

"Sushi sounds great."

"The restaurant is in a taproom," he says as we walk back down the pier.

I smile. "Of course it is."

"You can take the boy out of the brewery . . ."

Which only makes me laugh. "Do you ever think about anything else?"

"There's a quote that's widely—and falsely—attributed to Benjamin Franklin that goes something like 'Beer is proof that God loves us and wants us to be happy,'" Mason says. "Beer makes me happy."

"I'm kind of surprised you didn't go into viniculture given the history of the property."

"The winemaking thing was another branch of the family tree," he says. "That line of succession died off in the 1950s, and the winery was already falling into ruin when my grand-dad had a chance to buy the property. It was just a summer place for our family until I bought it from my dad."

"Do you ever miss Cleveland?"

"Nah, Jess was always more social than me."

A tiny *ha!* escapes me, and I clap my hand over my mouth. "I'm sorry."

"No, I know," Mason says. "But, like I said, I was a nerdy little kid and I learned at a pretty young age that most people weren't interested in hearing the things I wanted to talk about. My interests have broadened since then, but I never completely got the hang of being social."

"My life is divided into before and after Maisie," I tell him. "I used to stay out all night partying with my friends, but when I got pregnant, everything shifted. I didn't have time for anything but work and Maisie, and my single friends stopped having time for me."

"That sucks."

"Yes and no. It hurt, but clearly they weren't particularly good friends."

"What about Maisie's dad?"

"I wanted to believe that Brian was the first guy who had any interest in me beyond sex," I say. "But he yanked me around for years because he knew I would always take him back."

"Why did you?"

"I didn't think I could do any better."

"That's ridiculous."

"Says the guy who looks like he fell off page twenty-four of the J.Crew catalog."

Mason snorts a laugh. "Someday I'll introduce you to my mom and she'll show you pictures of the braces and blond highlights."

"Oh God, you didn't."

"I did."

"With black hair? What were you thinking?"

"About getting girls."

"Did that work?"

He levels a look at me. "What do you think?"

"Well, time has been your friend," I say as we reach the entrance of the taproom/sushi restaurant. "Shouldn't have that problem now."

Mason holds the door open for me. "I hope not."

I'm not sure if that was an implication, but my cheeks are warm as we take seats at the bar. I hang my purse on the hook below the bar top and change the subject. "This is definitely something we need to install."

"Hooks?"

"A lot of women don't want to put their purses on the floor, so they end up holding them on their laps," I say. "Hooks are a convenience that cost next to nothing."

"Okay. Done," he says. "Do you want to try a flight of beer samples?"

"That sounds good, and since you're the expert, you can choose."

"Don't threaten me with a good time."

I laugh. "Just nothing with oysters in it, please."

"Fair."

He rattles off his choices to the bartender. She returns a few minutes later and places a wooden tray in front of us with five small glasses of beer, ranging from pale golden to a deep chocolatey brown.

"So this first one is a cucumber Berliner Weisse." Mason picks up the glass and offers it to me first. Cucumber is not a flavor I've ever tried. I take a tentative sip.

"The watery cucumber-ness softens the tartness of the beer," I say. "I like it, but I'm not sure I'd order it on the regular."

"Cucumber-ness? That's not an official beer-tasting term."

"It is now."

He grins as he puts the same glass to his lips, and an intense pulse of heat flashes through me, settling between my thighs. My throat dries up as I watch him swallow.

"You're right," he says. "It's refreshing, but I like a little more *oomph*."

"Yes. Oomph." The words trickle out, feeble and a little wobbly.

"Are you okay?"

"Perfect. What's the next beer?"

I attempt to stay present and offer relatively intelligent opinions as we taste a Czech-style pilsner, an amber ale, a Belgian double bock, and the seaweed stout Mason told me about. But it's difficult when we're facing each other at the bar. Anyone looking at us from the outside would think we were having a great date. It *feels* that way too. He's animated as he talks about top fermenting and dry hopping, and I don't understand everything he's saying, but his passion is overflowing.

Like he's held it in because no one was listening.

Losing Maisie would be unbearable, so I can't blame his ex-wife for not listening when she was grieving. But I also can't blame Mason for withdrawing into the one thing that brings him comfort when Jess was probably not equipped to offer it. No one is the villain here. They both deserve happiness.

"Sorry," he says. "I was on a roll and couldn't stop."

"I don't mind."

"We, uh—we haven't looked at the menu."

"What do you usually order?"

"An assortment of sashimi and an ichiban roll that has spicy tuna and salmon," he says, pointing out the roll description on the menu. "Seaweed salad to start."

I am not a woman who can't order her own food. And like Mason, I can eat my weight in sushi. But he's said more words in one night than he's spoken since I've known him. I don't want him to stop. "Let's do that. And whatever beer is best with sushi, which I'm guessing is something light like pilsner."

Mason's eyes widen and he nods his approval. "Nailed it in one. And if you're going to have pilsner, it might as well be the original."

He orders the food along with a couple bottles of Pilsner Urquell.

"One summer when we were in college, Matt and I did a backpack tour of European breweries," he says. "We went to Guinness, Carlsberg, Heineken, Chimay, Bitburger, and Weihenstephan, but Pilsner Urquell was the holy grail."

"I could not tell you where any of those—No, wait. Guinness is Irish and at least a couple of those are German."

"Ireland, Denmark, the Netherlands, Belgium, Germany, and Czechia."

"I'd love to go to Germany," I say. "My grandparents live in Berlin, but we've never met because my mom is estranged from them. They've sent birthday cards and Christmas gifts since Anna and I were young, but I don't really *know* them."

"You should go."

"I'll have to ask my boss for some time off."

The corner of his mouth hitches up in a half grin. "You might have to wait until winter, but the Christmas markets will make it worthwhile."

"Most bosses aren't so generous."

"Yeah, well, I learned the hardest way that life is too short." He looks down at the bar a moment, then clears his throat. "But even before that, our employees at Fish Brothers were productive and happy because we didn't suck the life out of them. There has to be space for more than just work."

"Funny how you don't follow your own policy."

"Hey, I'm sitting in a restaurant with a beautiful woman, eating sushi, and talking about beer." He goes completely still when he realizes what he said. "Which I hope you will take as the compliment it was meant to be, and not as, you know, sexual harassment."

My laughter begins with shaking shoulders and by the time Mason joins in, I've got tears trickling from the corners of my eyes. "No one has *ever* complimented me quite like that."

"I aim to please," he says. "Or, more accurately, to make things weirder than they need to be."

"A-plus effort."

We fall silent, and briefly I hope he'll double back to the compliment. Maybe he'll say all the things I want to say to him. But he doesn't. The bartender brings us a *how are we ever going to eat all this?* amount of sushi, and we eat every bite.

The beer flows. The conversation flows. And I have no idea how to turn off the tap of feelings I have for this man.

•　•　•

We wander slowly back to the hotel, lingering to throw pennies in the fountain at the bottom of Columbus Avenue. We keep our wishes to ourselves.

The hotel bar is crowded as we reach the back deck.

"Do you want to grab another drink?" Mason asks.

I'm stuffed with raw fish and beer, and it's been a long day, but I don't want the night to end. Tomorrow we'll be back to business and I'm not ready to let go of this version of Mason Brown, whose jaw never once tightened and whose shoulders never went up. I also really like this version of Rachel Beck, who had dinner with a man who doesn't send her into anxiety spirals. "I could have one more."

His fingertips touch the small of my back as he leans in. "Wait here." As he walks away, the warm imprint of his fingers stays with me.

Mason returns with two glasses of rosé. "It's standing room only in there, so we might as well stay out here." He lifts his glass to offer me a toast. "Yes way, rosé."

I laugh as we clink glasses. "I like it here."

"The hotel? Sandusky? Ohio?"

"All of the above."

"Good."

Despite what Keane said about Mason lighting flares, his signals have been all over the place tonight. Right now I get the feeling that I could take his hand and lead him willingly up to my room. But I'm not sure he knows what he wants. Especially when only a few days ago he admitted he'd been waiting for Jess to come back. After four years of nothing special with Brian, I want more than to be someone's rebound fling.

"I was thinking about trying out movie night on the back patio when it's my turn to host book club," I say. "We can work out all the hiccups before we have guests. And I have to basically go big or go home."

Mason shakes his head. "I would have lived in eternal ignorance about the true nature of book club if Avery hadn't asked to borrow the karaoke machine."

"Wait. That's *yours*?"

"I bought it for the taproom."

"Not gonna lie, I kinda love that you bought a karaoke machine before you even had a bar or . . . beer."

"What can I say? I'm an optimist."

"Yes. Like Eeyore is an optimist."

He laughs. "I'm not that bad."

"Not when you try."

Mason's face settles into a thoughtful expression, his eyes dark and serious. "I'm trying."

"I know," I say. "I, um—I think it's time to call it a night."

Without a word, he takes my empty glass and I follow him through the bar. He pauses to return the glasses and we walk in silence to the elevator. His expression is impenetrable as I press the button for our floor.

"Do you need a wake-up call?" I ask, desperate to return to some sort of equilibrium.

"I'm good."

The elevator reaches our floor at what feels like record speed, and in a matter of steps we're at the end of the hall between his room and mine.

"Thank you for dinner," I say, leaning back against my door. "And for the room."

"Maybe we'll find some good stuff tomorrow."

"I hope so."

"Rachel?" There's a question in my name, but I can't discern what it is.

"Yeah?"

"I would like to kiss you."

My breathing grows shallow, but not from panic. This moment is the penny at the bottom of the fountain. "You would?"

"I have for a while," Mason says. "But—"

"You don't have to give any reasons. I understand," I say. "And if you cross the hall and kiss me, I will kiss you back. But I'll mean it, and I'm afraid you won't. Not yet."

"Wow." His breath whooshes out like he's been deflated. "That's . . . not how I thought this might go."

"Me neither." I'm the one who closes the space between us, lifting my face to touch my lips to his cheek. "But it will be better for us both, when you're sure."

CHAPTER 16

Verschlimmbesserung
German
"something that is meant to be an improvement, but
actually makes things worse"

Between the noise from the rooftop bar and the persistent regret, I spend the better part of the night tossing and turning in
my bed. More than once I talk myself out of crossing the hall,
knocking on Mason's door, and telling him I've changed my
mind. Instead I take care of my own needs and fall asleep when
the bar finally closes.

A few hours later my alarm jolts me upright. I rush through
my morning ritual, twist my damp hair into a bun, and put on
a casual black dress with a denim jacket.

Mason is waiting for me in the lobby, looking as tired and
sheepish as I feel. He hands me a to-go cup of coffee.

"Thanks," I say lightly. "Good morning."

He harrumphs. "Debatable."

Not sure how to take this, I don't respond. I follow him out of the hotel and down the block to where the truck is parked. We stow our bags in the back.

On the drive to Huron, we don't listen to podcasts or talk about anything, and I don't know what to say that will erase the awkwardness between us. The only consolation is that the elephant in the room is a lot smaller than it would have been if we'd slept together. Then again, maybe there'd be no elephant. Maybe we'd be happy.

The auction site is a warehouse at an industrial park, rather than at the resort. Even though we arrive fifteen minutes early, there are already a couple dozen cars in the parking lot.

"Have you ever been to an auction?" I ask Mason as we join a line of people waiting to get into the building.

"No," he says. "You?"

"This is my first time too."

"Hopefully, it's not like in movies where someone inadvertently scratches their nose and ends up accidentally buying a million-dollar diamond bracelet."

"Pretty sure that doesn't actually happen in real life," I say. "But don't wave your paddle around unless you plan to use it."

"My dad told me the same thing when I was eleven and we had the sex talk," he says, and I bark out a loud laugh, making the people in line ahead of us turn around. Mason innocently sips his coffee, leaving me to catch their early-morning disdain. I elbow him in the side and when he grins, I feel the lift in my chest.

The doors open promptly at 8:00 A.M. and the line surges forward. At the door, a gray-haired man tells us the auction will begin at 9:00 A.M., and offers us paddles. Mason accepts one and waggles it at me, making me choke on my coffee.

Inside, the merchandise is divided into two rooms. The first is filled with folding tables, each one laden with textiles, small electronics, lamps, mirrors, artwork, artificial plants, metal luggage racks, and boxes of bulk hotel toiletries. All these items are marked for sale, and there is a line of red metal loading carts along the wall. The second room is arranged with folding chairs and an auctioneer's podium. This room holds the more valuable pieces, including all sorts of furniture, larger paintings, animal skins, tapestries, several chandeliers made from antlers, and a pair of enormous wooden doors, intricately carved with woodland scenes.

"How do you want to do this?" Mason asks, grabbing the handle of a loading cart. "Stick together or split up and regroup? Some of these people have a real Black Friday look about them."

"Let's do this together," I say. "If someone wants something that badly, they can have it."

"Fair enough."

We start in the sale hall, wandering the rows.

"A lot of these luggage racks are in great condition," I say. "Should we—"

"No," Mason says before I can finish the question. "I appreciate that you're trying to cut costs, but we don't need to do this when we can afford to buy brand-new for our guests. Let's focus on why we're here."

But the deeper we get into the resort's castoffs, the more I realize none of it works. Some of the artwork is too Western, while other pieces feel like they're appropriating indigenous culture. There are a lot of paintings of fish, and the bears are far too serious.

"Do your parents have any old photos of the winery when it was intact?" I ask, an idea forming. "Or maybe some pictures of the Brown ancestors who lived on the island?"

Mason picks up a wood carving of a black bear as if he's considering it. "Probably. Why?"

"I'm thinking some framed black-and-white photos might be kind of cool in the taproom," I say. "None of this feels right."

He puts down the bear. "I can ask my mom."

We manage to find a couple of Craftsman-style table lamps with blue stained-glass shades that will look great in the lounge area of the taproom, but the rest of the sale hall is a bust. Mason pays for the lamps and we stow them in the truck before returning to the auction room.

As soon as we're through the doors, Mason stops in his tracks.

"I want that," he says, pointing to the biggest of the antler chandeliers. It's about six feet across at its widest point with glass bulbs mounted among the branches of the antlers. It's more rustic than I would choose, but the ceiling of the brewhouse is extremely high and the chandelier would make a statement. "I'm winning it."

Many of the seats are already occupied, but we find two chairs together near the back. We sit through auctions for several animal skins that had been hung on the walls of the resort's main lobby, a series of woodland paintings, and a set of pendant globe lamps ringed with metal pine trees. Then the big chandelier comes up for bidding.

"All of the chandeliers were handmade by local craftsman Al Parkinson, using authentic elk horns sourced from Wyoming and Montana," the auctioneer says. "This largest chandelier features thirty-six bulbs and measures seventy-one inches in diameter by sixty inches high. Valued at ten thousand dollars, we'll start the bidding at five hundred dollars. Who'll bid five hundred?"

Several paddles—including Mason's—go up as the auctioneer launches into rapid-fire mode. Five hundred doesn't seem unreasonable, but less than a minute later the bidding has cleared a thousand dollars and Mason keeps raising his paddle. The field of buyers begins to thin at two grand. There are even fewer when the bidding reaches a ridiculous three thousand dollars. But Mason doesn't stop. He's one of the last two people vying for the chandelier when the high bid hits four thousand dollars. And less than five minutes from the opening bid, the auctioneer bangs his gavel and declares Mason the winner.

After years working at Aquamarine, I shouldn't be fazed by someone dropping an obscene amount of money on something so impractical, but Mason Brown being that someone is a shock to my system.

"Are you seriously going to spend that much money on a light fixture made from discarded animal parts?" I ask, incredulous, as we go to the cashier's table.

"Listen, I don't know how to say this without sounding like a privileged asshole, but the amount of money Matt and I made when we sold Fish Brothers was—"

He stops abruptly. Sighs. Runs a hand through his hair.

"It was enough to build a hotel and still have more than I'll ever need," Mason says. "Mostly I do good things with the money. I donate to children's heart foundations and dog rescues and Planned Parenthood, but occasionally I buy a giant fucking chandelier for fifty-five hundred bucks because I want it."

I don't know what to say. I know my feelings are coming from my own history of financial insecurity, which is not Mason's problem.

"Is it going to fit in the truck?" I ask.

He pulls on his lower lip, then releases it. Very quietly, he says, "Fuck."

"You pay," I say, digging through my purse for the tape measure I started carrying after my first visit to Very Vintage Vivian. "I'll measure."

Out in the parking lot, I quickly take the dimensions of the truck bed, then go back inside to compare them to the size of the chandelier.

"It will barely fit and only sideways," I tell Mason. "And we'll need something to cushion the antlers that will bear most of the weight. Like . . . polar fleece blankets. We could buy a bunch to protect the chandelier on the way home, then wash them up and keep them on hand for our hotel guests to use outdoors on chilly nights."

"You—" He shakes his head the tiniest bit, then leans in and kisses my forehead. "You're brilliant."

Swaddled in red polar fleece, the chandelier looks like an enormous badly wrapped Christmas present as we head west on Route 2. Mason's eyes go to the rearview mirror so frequently that I make him pull over to switch with me. While I drive, he spends the rest of the trip obsessing over every bump in the road until we finally reach the ferry dock.

• • •

"What's the story with Yōkai?" I ask, trying to distract him from the chandelier as we settle in for the ferry crossing.

"When I was a kid, my Japanese grandparents immigrated to Ohio to be closer to my mom. After my grandpa died a few years ago, my grandma decided to adopt a kitten for company." Mason leans against the door. "But when Obaachan went to the shelter, she ended up adopting the massive mean-spirited cat no one else wanted."

"Poor baby."

He snorts a little. "Yōkai means 'demon ghost.' Which . . . well, you've met her. But she was never mean to my grandma, because they understood each other."

"How did Yōkai end up with you?"

"Right around the time Jess and I were splitting up, Obaachan had to move into assisted living and couldn't have a pet," he says. "Mom decided I should take the cat so I wouldn't be alone. You've seen how well that's been working out."

"She seems to love Maisie."

"My theory is that Yōkai sensed my grandma wanted her— especially when no one else did—and she knows Maisie's affection has no reservations."

"Yōkai probably doesn't trust you, emotionally speaking."

Mason shrugs a shoulder and nods. "She came to me at a pretty low point in my life. I feed her and keep her litter box clean, but I haven't really given her many reasons to like me."

"Maybe you should."

He considers this briefly, before handing me his phone. "Help me?"

We spend the remainder of the ferry ride with our heads nearly touching as Mason orders Yōkai a cat tree, an array of toys, dried fish treats, and a fluffy antianxiety bed. I mention that he should keep the delivery box because she might like that, too.

"And you could turn the sunroom into a habitat for her," I suggest as the boat gently nudges the landing.

"That's . . . my bedroom."

"I know, and it's kind of ridiculous that you're sleeping on a futon in your own home, when there are three bedrooms upstairs."

"I didn't want it to be uncomfortable for you and Maisie."

"So you're uncomfortable instead? That's better?"

"No, but—"

"Mason, I appreciate everything you've done for Maisie and me, but you have to be comfortable too," I say. "I'd even be happy to give you back the master bedroom."

"You don't have to do that, but I'll think about making a habitat room for Yōkai."

I start the engine and drive off the ferry, following a car with an Indiana license plate. As I pull into the driveway at Avery's house, Daniel comes out onto the front porch, followed by Avery, Maisie, and Leo.

"What the heck is that?" Daniel asks.

"Elk horn chandelier for the taproom," Mason says. "Can't stay and show you. We're in the homestretch."

"I've gotta see this." Daniel opens the driver's door for me. "I'll take him the rest of the way. You, Avery, and the kids can follow in the golf cart."

"Mama!" Maisie wiggles her way around Daniel's knees, and I'm so happy to see her that I give up the driver's seat and scoop her into my arms. She's wearing glittery purple nail polish and there's a bright pink streak in her hair that gives me pause, until I notice Leo has a green braid hanging from the back of his head like a *Star Wars* Padawan and Avery is sporting straight blue bangs below her dark curls.

"They're clip-on," Avery explains as Mason and Daniel slowly back out of the driveway. "We were playing hair salon and I remembered I had a few color extensions from back in the day."

"Sounds like she had fun while I was gone."

With the kids buckled into their car seats, Avery and I climb into the golf cart.

"She was a little tearful at bedtime, missing her mama," she says with a smile. "But Daniel helped them build a fort with the couch cushions and they camped on the living room floor."

"Thank you for keeping her."

"How was the sale?"

"I found a couple of lamps," I say. "But the big score was the chandelier, which was all Mason's doing."

"Really?"

"He was like a different person."

Avery gives me a sideways glance. "In a good way?"

Everything that happened—especially the kiss that didn't—is sitting in my mouth, wanting to spill out, but she was his friend first. And the circumstances around last night aren't exclusively mine. I don't know how to talk about it without stepping on Mason's privacy.

"He was very enthusiastic about winning that auction."

"I can't wait to see the chandelier," she says. "Did you do anything fun last night?"

"We had drinks and sushi at a place in downtown Sandusky."

"Like a date?"

I laugh. "You are relentless."

"Like a date?" she repeats, batting her eyelashes at me.

For a moment I tumble back in time to the hallway, wondering if I should have said something else. Done something else. I shake my head. "Not a date."

We pull into the driveway of the hotel as Mason and Daniel are carrying the chandelier through the double doorway into the taproom. The kids run ahead of us.

"Oh! Hey! I meant to ask you if you could host book club this month," Avery says. "I know it's last minute, but Gail's mother needs surgery, so she can't host."

"Definitely. I already have something in mind."

While Maisie and Leo run in and out through the swinging staff door into the brewery, Mason unwraps the blankets from around the chandelier.

"Damn," Daniel whispers, then takes his wallet from his pocket, fishes out a dollar, and hands it to Avery.

"Swear jar," she explains. "We've been trying to watch our mouths around Leo, especially now that he's starting to ask what those words mean."

"I give thanks daily for the substitutes gifted to us by *The Good Place*."

"Can we hang it?" Daniel asks Mason.

"The wiring's ready."

"Do you have a ladder that tall?"

"Yep."

Daniel rubs his hands together. "Let's do it."

Avery and I take the kids to the house, where we clean the blue stained-glass lamps while the kids color at the dining room table. Yōkai slinks out from wherever she's been hiding and curls protectively around the legs of Maisie's chair. I share my idea to turn the sunroom into a cat habitat.

"Do it," Avery says.

"The problem is that Mason sleeps in there."

"Wait. What?" she says. "I thought that was his home office and the futon was just . . . junk."

I explain how he meant to make the second floor into an apartment, and how he's been sleeping on the futon so Maisie and I would have privacy. "If that were an issue for me, I wouldn't have agreed to move into a stranger's house, but he's been very . . . proper about it."

"We need to do what he did to you while you were in Florida," Avery says. "Move his stuff upstairs and build a cat habitat. Daniel could mount shelves on the walls for Yōkai to sit at different levels. I saw that on Pinterest."

"The difference is that this is Mason's house. I can't make decisions for him."

"You're just not bossy enough."

"My younger sister would like a word."

Avery laughs. "Oh, did I tell you about the fart?"

"I think I would have remembered," I say.

"Earlier this week, one of the ladies in my yoga class let out a massive fart," she says. "Which is . . . whatever. Our bodies make noises and I usually pretend it didn't happen, because no one should feel embarrassed by calling attention to it. But this time it smelled too terrible to ignore. I had to stop class and open the windows."

"Was it anyone I know?"

"Maybe."

"Pat?"

She laughs. "I'll never tell."

I'm scratching the side of my nose with my middle finger at her when my phone dings with an incoming text message from Mason. Light is hung. Come see.

• • •

The chandelier dominates the airspace above our heads, the elk horns adding visual texture and the glass bulbs throwing off a warm light. It fits the eclectic motif we've got going on. I glance over at Mason with a smile. "It's perfect. Worth every penny."

He nudges my elbow with his. "You should trust me more."

"I do."

"Was that a moment?" Avery eyes us with suspicion. "Because it looked like one."

"Not a moment." Mason's head pivots in a resolute no, but I'm not completely certain she's wrong.

"Babe," Daniel says, "you watch too many Hallmark movies."

"I know. Which is how I've learned to recognize a moment when I see one."

Mason clears his throat. "How about we all grab some dinner? Let's put this ridiculous conversation out of its misery."

But as we're gathered around a table at the Village Pump, eating walleye tacos and drinking beer, we don't look like a group of friends having dinner together. We look like two couples with kids. Some of the locals are eyeing us with curiosity—especially since many of them haven't seen Mason in months—and I wonder if the satellites will be rattling with gossip tonight.

"How long have you guys known each other?" I ask, pointing a french fry from Daniel to Mason.

"I must have been about eight when the Browns started coming to the island for the summer," Daniel says. "Mason was older than me, but when most of the other kids were teenagers or babies, two years wasn't much of a gap."

"Owen and Laurel ditched me immediately the first summer," Mason adds. "My dad gave me an old fishing pole and told me to go try my luck at the state park. When I got there, Daniel was mucking around in the water."

"I was trying to catch crawfish for bait."

"So I offered to help, and we used our bait to catch a few bluegills—"

"And then nearly burned down the woods behind the winery ruins when we built a fire to roast our fish," Daniel says, laughing.

The two of them take turns telling tales of growing up on the island, making Avery and me laugh with their childhood antics, until Maisie's eyelids begin to droop, and Leo falls asleep with his head on Daniel's shoulder.

"We should probably get these kids to bed," Avery says.

Mason settles the bill, then lifts Maisie out of her booster seat. She goes boneless in his arms, and he carries her outside the restaurant. He and Daniel do a complicated handshake as they say good night. Avery gives me a hug and I thank her again for watching Maisie.

Mason carefully buckles Maisie into her car seat, and she wakes for only the briefest moment before nodding off and sleeping all the way back to the hotel. He carries her into the house, up the stairs to her room, and deposits her gently on the bed.

"Thanks for, you know . . . everything," he says as we stand in the hallway. Maybe hallways are our thing. "I'm sorry I made it weird last night."

"I did that."

He laughs quietly. "Yeah, maybe you did."

As we stand there on the brink of something we both feel but neither of us is ready to identify, I slip my arms around his waist and hold on until I feel his arms encircle me. I don't kiss him. He doesn't kiss me. We simply hold each other for a few long moments, and when I let go, he does the same.

"Good night," I say, opening my bedroom door.

The little half grin he shoots me is nearly as devastating as his full-blown smile, and I wonder if not kissing him was a mistake. "Night, Rachel."

CHAPTER 17

Kilig
Filipino
"the feeling of blushing and getting butterflies in your
stomach when you see someone you love"

The next two weeks give me no time to think about hugs or sexy
smiles or anything other than opening the taproom in time for
the Fourth of July—and book club. We're flooded with deliveries: a pair of leather sofas for the taproom lounge area, a kilim-
style indoor/outdoor rug, a large old-fashioned map of Kelleys
Island in an ornate gilt frame, a beer menu board for behind the
bar, kegs of beer from other breweries, an outdoor movie screen
and projector, and twenty-four teal Adirondack chairs—twenty
for the cabin verandahs and the rest for the front porch of the
house. We also get a box filled with cat accessories.

A paving company comes from Oak Harbor to lay cement
for the parking lot and pave the gravel driveway. A sign company
out of Sandusky builds a beautiful wooden sign marking the

entrance to the Limestone. The stone patio behind the brew-house is completed, along with a firepit and walking paths to the cabins.

The Wednesday before book club, I'm buying more William Holbrook Beard prints online when the construction manager comes to the office to tell me the first cabin is finished. I drop everything and follow him out to the building site. The exterior of the cabin hasn't changed significantly since the last time I looked, but inside, the bathroom has fixtures and the kitchen-ette is complete. The first bed—the old-fashioned double from Vivian's shop—is assembled with the mattress and box spring in place, and there's a sleeper sofa in the middle of the room, waiting to be positioned.

"I'll make Keith available tomorrow and Friday to help with anything you need when it comes to arranging furniture and hanging pictures," he says. "And we're just about done assem-bling the chairs."

"I appreciate that so much. Thank you."

As much as I'd love to dive straight into decorating the cabin, I force myself to return to the office and finish up my artwork order before picking Maisie up from Avery's house. I'm serving up dinner at home when Mason comes in from the brewery. With the opening drawing near, we'd reverted to our plate-in-the-oven/tea-on-the-kitchen-island routine, so I'm surprised to see him.

"Smells great. What is it?"

"I just threw some orzo, black beans, corn, and green chiles in the Crock-Pot with a little enchilada sauce and spices," I say. "It's nothing special, but it's tasty."

He fills a bowl and joins Maisie and me at the table.

"I hired a couple of bartenders today," Mason says, dredging a flour tortilla through his bowl. "Tomas is from Slovakia, Lenna is from Estonia, and they both have bar experience. Once we're booking the cabins, I'd like to hire a couple more people for table service, but for now I think we'll be okay with just two. How was your day?"

"The Adirondack chairs are ready for book club," I say. "And I get to start decorating the first cabin tomorrow."

"Need any help?"

"Not from you. I want it to be a surprise."

He laughs. "Fair enough."

After dinner, he loads the dishwasher so I can give Maisie a bath. Once her wet hair is combed and she's in her pajamas, I let her watch *Moana* for the 6,521,943rd time.

"Do you have a minute?" Mason asks. "I want to show you something in the taproom."

"Yeah, sure."

The walk to the brewhouse is so different from when I first arrived on the island. The wheel ruts have been paved over, and the unruly grass has been tamed. There are flower beds along the driveway waiting to be filled with marigolds, red geraniums, and pink impatiens. Spotlights illuminate the front of the brewhouse and the sign by the front door that matches the one out along Division Street.

"That first day I pulled into the driveway, I would never have been able to envision this," I say. "But now . . . it's beautiful."

"You did this."

"We did this."

Mason opens the door for me and switches on the light. The chandelier illuminates, casting sparkles on the sloped ceiling. The leather couches have been arranged into a lounge area, with the kilim-style rug creating a kind of boundary. There's a wooden coffee table and a pair of end tables accented with the stained-glass lamps. Hanging on the wall over one of the couches is the old-fashioned Kelleys Island map.

"That looks so welcoming," I say. "I love it."

He grins as he gestures toward the bar. "There's more."

Attached to the wall behind the bar is the black menu board. Mason fishes his phone from the back pocket of his shorts and touches the screen a couple of times. Suddenly the menu board begins to move, shuffling the letters into place—like an old-fashioned departures board in a train station—until the names and prices of the beers are spelled out. Little Fish Lager. Sunshine Ale. Old Stone IPA. Porch Swing Kölsch. Stargazer Berliner Weisse.

"That is amazing, but—Wait. How did I not know about the Berliner?"

"Damn it." He runs his hand up through his hair. "You weren't supposed to see that. Can you pretend you didn't see that?"

"Did you—You made a beer for me?"

"Yeah."

"What's the flavor?"

He goes behind the bar, takes down a glass, and fills it from one of the taps. The beer that pours out is slightly pink. I lift myself onto a barstool as he slides the glass to me. "It's hibiscus."

"Really?"

The flavor of hibiscus is reminiscent of cranberry, both tart and sweet, followed by the puckery tang of the Weisse beer. Mason worries his lower lip between his teeth as he watches me. "Do you hate it?"

"I love it."

"I struggled to find the right flavor." He reaches beneath the bar and hands me a bottle with the label. In the center of the oval is a night sky with the familiar Y-shaped constellation of Cancer. My constellation. My sign. "Eventually I figured out that I needed something more unique. More . . . Floridian."

An ache blooms in my chest. Not painful, but warm and deep and possibly life-changing. "You did?"

"I do."

"Are you sure?"

He nods, his eyes locked on mine. "Absolutely."

I stand on the rung of the stool and lean across the bar. Mason leans from the opposite direction. But there's too much real estate between us. Our lips barely touch, and the edge of the bar is practically cutting me in half. We both burst out laughing.

"Worst first kiss ever."

"Definitely a contender," he says. "Should we give it another shot?"

"I think we should."

Mason comes out from behind the bar and stops in front of my barstool. With no preamble, he takes my face gently in his hands and the feel of his fingers on my skin sends a cascade of shivers down my spine. He grins, pleased with the effect he has on me, and leans in. This time, our mouths come together perfectly.

One kiss leads to another and another, each one hungrier than the last. Now that we've had a taste, neither of us can get enough. The back of his shirt is bunched in my fists as I pull him closer. He shifts me forward on the stool and I wrap my legs around his thighs. Even with our bodies touching in so many places, I want more of him. All of him. On the floor. On one of the new leather couches. On the bar. Anywhere. Everywhere.

Mason pulls back suddenly, his breathing ragged. "We forgot about Maisie."

"Oh God," I groan. "I'm a terrible parent."

He leans forward and kisses me softly. "Not even close."

"Do we have to go?"

"Okay, *now* you're a terrible parent."

I fake-punch him on the shoulder as I lower myself off the barstool. "I was going to invite you to my room after I put Maisie to bed, but now . . ."

Mason kisses me so thoroughly, my knees wobble. "Invite me."

"Are you sure?"

"I'm not in love with Jess anymore, if that's what you're worried about," he says, pausing to switch off the lights and lock the door as we leave the taproom. "I don't think I'll ever get over losing Piper, but you've pulled me out of a rut, so—"

"I don't want gratitude sex, Mason."

"Oh shit. No. I don't mean it like that," he says, taking my hand. "You've turned my life upside down in the best way, and I want you to stay for . . . as long as you want."

For a second it almost seemed like he was going to say *forever*.

We walk in silence until we reach the house. On the porch, right before he opens the door, I stop him. Kiss him. "To be continued."

"Count on it."

Inside, we find that Maisie has built a pillow fort with the couch cushions—thanks, Daniel—and she's lying inside with

Yōkai, the two watching *Moana* together. Mason sighs, and it's impossible to miss the sadness in his eyes, the way his shoulders sag.

"I know this is hard for you," I say. "I'm sorry."

"No. It's okay. Obviously, I didn't really consider what I was opening myself up to when I said you could live here," he says. "But getting the wind knocked out of me occasionally when Maisie does something that reminds me of Piper is all on me. It's not Maisie's fault. It's not your fault."

"What was she like?"

"She was this perfect blend of Jess and me," he says, fishing his wallet from his back pocket. He hands me a photo of his family. "Smart. Goofy. Soft. Brave. Headstrong. Piper loved to go fishing with my dad, but she usually wore sequins and fancy shoes while doing it. She was curious about brewing and one time I took her to this beer event, and she told everyone in the room that her favorite beer was Dortmunder. She was like, *three*."

The little girl in the photo has Mason's smile and the same black hair. And I can't help noticing that Jess is not perfect and thin, like I imagined someone as handsome as Mason might choose. She's beautiful, with long brown hair and green eyes, and she's bountiful like me, maybe even a little bigger.

"Piper is beautiful," I say. "Both of them are."

He smiles as he tucks the photo back into his wallet. "Thank you."

"You, um—you don't have a fat girl fetish, do you?"

"I've dated women of all sizes, so I wouldn't exactly call it that," Mason says. "But I'm not especially attracted to jutting hip bones and sharp clavicles. I tend toward soft and curvy. In general, though, I think having a type is limiting. I mean, sometimes I'm even a little hot for Pedro Pascal."

"Statistically speaking, everyone is a little hot for Pedro Pascal," I say. "So you're not that special."

"My ego says thanks."

"You and Pedro would make a cute couple."

He laughs. "What about you? Do you have a type?"

"I tend toward men who tend toward me."

Mason shakes his head. "You need to stop that."

"It's been my experience."

"You are beautiful and smart," he says. "And any man who doesn't appreciate all of you doesn't deserve any of you."

I want to kiss him. Or, better yet, grab his hand and drag him upstairs. But Maisie is right there, so I shift my hand enough to wrap my pinkie around his and give a little squeeze. "Thank you."

With no cushions left on the couch, we sprawl on the rug on either side of the pillow fort. Mason pulls a small plastic bag out of the front pocket of his shorts and takes out a tiny cat treat. He puts it on the floor near Yōkai. She waits until she's sure he's not trying to trick her into something, then darts out a paw and pulls it close enough to eat.

"Can I have one of those?" Maisie asks.

"They're cat treats," Mason says.

"I'm a cat."

"You're a dingleberry."

"What's a dingleberry?"

"It's a very silly person."

"I'm not a person," Maisie says. "I'm a cat."

"You're still not getting a cat treat. They're gross."

"How do you know?"

"I ate one."

Maisie falls sideways with laughter, causing the fort to collapse. Yōkai bolts into the kitchen, and our little moment of bliss is scattered all over the living room. We put the cushions back on the couch and settle down to finish the movie. Mason sits at one end while I sit at the other, Maisie snuggled against me. By the time the end credits are rolling, she's asleep with her head on Mason's thigh, his hand resting on her back. And the cat is perched on the top of the couch, watching over them both.

I turn off the TV.

"That's a pretty good movie," Mason says.

"Glad you like it," I say. "Be prepared to watch it at least a thousand more times."

"Oh God. I'd almost blocked that part of toddlerhood out of my brain."

I laugh, lifting Maisie from the couch. Mason switches off the lights and as I head up the front stairs, Yōkai streaks past to get to the bedroom first. I tuck Maisie into bed, then go out into the hall, where Mason leans against the door frame. He catches my hand and pulls me in for a kiss. It's sweet and short.

"Would you mind if we took a rain check?" he says. "Tonight was . . . a lot."

"It was, and it's fine."

"You're great."

"You're right," I say with a smile. "You're still welcome to join me, even if it's only so you don't have to be alone. But I won't take it personally if you say no."

"I'd like that."

"Come on in."

Mason steps into the bedroom and stops just beyond the doorway. "Wow. This looks great."

I've collected a few funky bits and vintage bobs from my antique shop treasure hunts, and some artwork from late-night scrolling on Etsy. A few more plants. Painted knobs to replace the drawer pulls on the IKEA nightstand and dresser. A cluster of paper star lanterns.

"Thanks," I say, going into the bathroom to change out of my clothes. It's not that I don't want Mason to see me naked, but this is new and I'm nervous. When I step out into the bedroom, he has stripped down to his boxer briefs—the body-hugging, heart-pounding, dry-mouth kind. It's a small relief that he doesn't have six-pack abs or an Adonis belt, but Mason's body is lean and fit. I want to run straight back into the bathroom and hide.

"You look cute in those pj's," he says, and I'm glad I chose the ones with pineapples on them. They're not exactly sexy, but they're my least schlumpy. "I'm guessing by the book on the nightstand that you like the left side."

"Thanks, and yeah, the left is mine."

"This is a little weird." Mason turns down the bedding on the right side. "I don't think I've ever slept with anyone I wasn't married to."

"Look at it this way," I say, slipping under the covers. "You won't wake up with anything to regret."

One corner of his mouth kicks up in a grin as he gets into bed beside me. "I mean, I might regret not making you come."

His words do absolutely nothing to kill the aching need between my thighs and my face flushes with heat, but I've gone so long without sex that a little longer won't kill me.

I hope.

He lifts his arm so I can settle against his chest. I haven't done this with anyone in a long time either. His skin is warm and comforting against mine.

"Any rules I need to know?" Mason asks.

"Spooning is welcome. Touching me under my pajamas without consent is not."

"Noted," he says. "And same."

I stretch my arm across his waist, snuggling in a little deeper. "Perfect."

"Can I kiss you good night?" He reaches up and turns off the light.

"I'd be offended if you didn't."

His mouth finds mine in the dark. The kiss is brief because neither of us can keep from smiling. He touches his lips to my forehead. "Night, Rachel."

"Sweet dreams."

I shift onto my side and Mason curls up behind me, his arm pulling me close. His mouth is beside my ear as he whispers, "They won't be nearly as sweet as this."

CHAPTER 18

Meraki
Greek
"when you pour yourself so wholeheartedly into doing something with soul, creativity, or love that you
leave a piece of yourself in your work"

I thought waking up in bed with Mason might be awkward, but no . . . it's every bit as glorious as I imagined. In sleep, his face is relaxed and beautiful, and it makes me want to figure out how to keep it that soft in the waking hours. I don't want to disturb him, and it feels creepy to watch him sleep, so I turn over and doze off.

The next time I wake, it's when my phone dings with a text message from Keith, the construction worker. I'm ready to start on the cabin. Where are you?

"Oh shit. It's after eight." I throw off the covers and scramble out of bed, my brain foggy and unable to figure out what I should do first. "I'm late."

Mason's laugh is deep and husky from sleep. "Call in sick. I'm sure your boss won't mind."

"I need to get started on the cabin and prepare for book club tonight," I say, rummaging through my dresser drawer for a clean pair of shorts. "And . . . God, I have to get Maisie to Avery's house."

"Rachel, relax." He gets out of bed. "You go do the cabin; I'll run Maisie uptown and do as much prep work as I can for book club."

"Oh no! What am I going to do about Maisie tonight? I completely forgot that Avery will be here with me at book club." My anxiety ramps up. "Maybe she—"

"Take a breath."

I pause and inhale deeply.

"Daniel and I will handle it," he says.

"I don't want you to have to do that."

"I'm offering," he says. "Let me help you."

"Okay. I'll go get Maisie dressed, and maybe she can eat a Pop-Tart or—"

"Rachel. Stop." Mason takes me by the shoulders and ducks his head until we're eye to eye. "Trust me. I've done this before."

"You're right. Thank you."

He gives me a fast kiss. "Go."

I dress quickly as he leaves my bedroom. Wash and moisturize my face. Brush my teeth. I go to Maisie's room, where I find her putting socks on Yōkai's paws.

"We have to move fast today because I woke up late," I say, praying this won't be one of Maisie's stubborn days. "Let's get dressed."

Five minutes later, we tramp down the back steps—with a

now sockless Yōkai—and into the kitchen, where Mason has made us egg-and-toast sandwiches, neatly wrapped in paper towels. There is no tea and I wonder how he feels about that.

"Do you want to ride to Leo's house in the truck today?" he asks Maisie.

"In the back?"

He laughs. "No, ma'am, but I'll carry you on my back to the truck."

Maisie scrambles up on one of the kitchen stools and launches herself onto his back, wrapping her arms around his neck. He grabs the egg sandwich, takes the keys for the truck from their hook by the door, and winks at me. "I'll see *you* later."

When they're gone, I slip on my shoes and head out to the cabin, where Keith is waiting. He's an older man with graying hair and work-worn hands.

"I'm so sorry I'm late," I say. "Thank you for the wake-up text."

"Where do you want to start?"

"Let's get all the furniture in place first, then I'll know where the artwork should go," I say. "Once that's done, I can do all the fluffy stuff myself."

I finish my breakfast sandwich on the way to the storage pod, where I have everything arranged by cabin. We make several trips, carrying furniture, artwork, lamps, rolled-up rugs, and boxes of textiles. Keith is patient as I consider and reconsider the placement of the sleeper sofa, coffee table, and chair, creating a small seating area within the larger space. Finally I'm satisfied. We break for lunch, and when we return, he mounts the curtain rods and installs one of the crystal chandeliers. We hang the dancing bears print above the bed and crisscross the badminton racquets over the sleeper sofa. I took Lucy's advice and bought a vintage-look Parcheesi board from an Etsy shop, which Keith mounts to the wall in the kitchenette. Once all the drill dust has been swept, I send him back to his regular job and do the rest myself—making up the bed, arranging throw pillows, stocking the kitchen drawers with utensils and appliances, hanging the curtains, and supplying towels and toiletries to the bathroom. When I finish, I head to the taproom to see how Mason is coming along with book club prep.

All the Adirondack chairs have been arranged in rows facing the outdoor movie screen that Mason set up at the back of the brewhouse. I go in through the brewery door and find him pouring a bag of malt into the gristmill, which is the first step of the process.

"Are you starting a new beer right now?"

"I think so?"

"What about book club?"

Mason finishes emptying the bag into the mill, then leads me through the swinging door into the taproom. The tables have been arranged buffet-style, waiting for everyone's food contributions.

"Red wine on the table," he says. "White and rosé in the cooler under the bar. Buffalo chicken dip in the Crock-Pot that's reputed to be as addictive as crack, so consider yourself warned. Box of crackers, right there. Celery and carrots, also in the cooler."

"You thought of everything."

He taps his temple, then points a finger at me.

"Daniel and I thought we'd camp in the woods and teach

the kids how to catch lightning bugs," Mason continues, "but if they get bored or scared or whatever, we'll bring them home."

"That's too much for me to ask of you."

"Volunteered, remember?"

"Are you going to be okay?" I ask.

"I don't know," he says. "But I'll deal with it."

"Thank you."

"What movie are you showing?"

"*Thelma & Louise*."

"That's cheerful."

I laugh. "It seemed like a movie the book club would appreciate."

"Oh, they will," he says, leaning forward to give me a quick kiss. "But if we find Rosemary and Virginia in a convertible at the bottom of the east quarry, that's on you."

• • • •

"Welcome to the Limestone," I say as the book club members gather around me outside the brewhouse. "This month's meeting is a two-parter. Part one is that you get to be our very first guests in the taproom, so come on in."

Everyone is talking at once as we shuffle inside the building. There are some *oohs* and *aahs*. A couple of *wows*. A breathless *whoa*.

"Beautiful," Rosemary says at the same time Tori says, "Awesome!"

"Thank you," I say. "We've got a few finishing touches yet, but I'm really pleased with how it's coming together."

"I didn't think Mason would ever get this place finished,"

Pat says, carrying a baking dish filled with fried mac-and-cheese balls to the buffet table. "But I love how he made the old winery part of the building."

"I've been dying to see it up close." Diane adds a bread bowl filled with spinach dip to the table.

"Me too," Courtney agrees.

"Grab a drink. Fill a plate. And you're welcome to have a look around," I say. "There's an observation platform up the stairs, but it's quiet in the brewery tonight."

"I was hoping we'd get to see Mason in action," Gail says, waggling her eyebrows in an *if you know what I mean* way.

"Gail!" Virginia exclaims, scandalized. "You've known him since he was a little boy, riding his bike around the island."

"If you haven't noticed," Gail says, "he's not a little boy anymore."

Avery looks at me, her eyes wide, and covers her mouth with her hand to keep from laughing out loud.

"Sorry to disappoint, but he's babysitting tonight." As soon as the words leave my mouth, I feel like I've said too much. Glances flutter around the room. Unspoken questions. Word travels fast on Kelleys Island. Surely they've heard about the night we were at the Village Pump together. They must be curious.

"Well, I'm delighted to hear that," Rosemary says. "He's spent far too much time holed up in this brewery."

"Anyway," I say, redirecting their attention away from my personal life. "I thought we could book talk for a bit while we eat, and then head out back for the second part of the night."

For the next thirty minutes or so, we have a lively discussion about the book—a young adult fantasy set in the Phoenician underworld—pausing only to refill our glasses and plates. For the most part, I keep my mind on book club, but when I pull the Stargazer tap handle, I'm reminded that Mason made it for me, and I'm warmed by the thought.

When the book discussion tapers off, I encourage everyone to refill their glasses before we go outside. We all top up our drinks and head out the back door onto the patio.

Even though the evening is warm, I draped a red polar fleece blanket over the arm of each of their chairs for effect and lit a fire in the pit. The projector is set up on a barstool at the back of the patio.

"We're hoping to make outdoor movie night a regular feature for guests and locals," I say. "So, once again, you get to be my canaries in the coal mine. Tonight's feature was selected especially for you . . . *Thelma & Louise.*"

I press play on the projector and settle into an Adirondack chair next to Avery.

"You did so good," she whispers.

"Thanks," I say. "But between karaoke and movie night, Mason knows too much about book club. We're either going to have to kill him or make him an honorary member."

Avery snickers. "I don't think any of them would complain about him being at book club every month, especially Gail."

•   •   •

Mason and Daniel emerge from the trees not long after Courtney's golf cart turns out of the driveway. Each man is leading a small child by the hand. Maisie is cuddling Fred against her neck, which means she's exhausted beyond measure, but Leo is practically vibrating with energy, a peanut butter jar of fireflies clutched in his hand.

"We . . . messed up," Daniel confesses. "Leo is high on s'mores and Maisie is amps-to-eleven cranky."

Maisie breaks away from Mason and runs to me. First she hugs my legs as if we've been apart for days, then begins to pummel my thighs with frustrated little fists. "I want to go home."

I pick her up. "You are home, baby."

"No. I want to go to our other house, where Oma lives."

"She has a new house, remember? We helped her move there. This is where we live now."

Maisie rubs her nose against my shoulder. "I don't like it."

"We'll talk about it in the morning, okay?"

"I don't want to talk about it."

Mason looks stricken. Like he did something wrong.

"This is normal for her," I say. "Don't take it personally. You did great."

"We've got cleanup," Avery tells me. "Get her to bed."

True to form, Maisie falls asleep in my arms on the way to the house. I don't bother undressing her or putting her in pajamas. I take off her sneakers and tuck her into bed. Yōkai leaps onto the bed and settles against Maisie's back.

"Thanks," I whisper to the cat, who responds with a baleful glare.

I return to the brewhouse, where Mason has dismantled the projector and screen, and Avery has collected the blankets to keep them from getting damp with dew. Daniel is washing the dirty glasses in the taproom while Leo runs in circles singing "ashes, ashes, we all fall down" before collapsing onto the floor.

"Chocolate after bedtime was not my best-ever plan," Daniel says. "But on the bright side, he'll probably sleep late."

I pour the dregs of the wine bottles down the drain. "Today

was a long day, and even best friends need to take a break some-times. I'll keep Maisie home tomorrow."

Mason and Avery come in from outside, and the four of us finish cleaning up the taproom. Avery scoops up Leo mid-spin. "Time to calm down, little man. We're going home."

After thanking them and saying good night, Mason and I are alone in the taproom.

"Hi," he says, catching my hand and reeling me in.

I smile, my heart taking flight. "Hi."

He takes my face in his hands and when he kisses me, it feels like a relief. *Finally.* I slip my arms up around his neck and his arms encircle my waist, pulling me closer. His tongue dips into my mouth and we kiss for ages.

"Oh God." We're interrupted by a voice. Avery's voice. "I'm *so* sorry. I forgot my purse."

It's too late to pretend like we weren't making out, so Mason holds me in his arms as she scurries across the room to where her small suede bag is lying on the couch, and back to the door.

"I didn't see a thing," she says, throwing an excited fist in the air. "But I knew it! I love you both. Bye."

Mason touches his forehead to mine when she's gone, laughing a little. "We are *never* going to hear the end of this."

"I know."

"But we were never going to be able to keep it a secret," he says. "When I'm with you, I remember what it feels like to be happy, and anyone with eyes is bound to notice."

"You are so good for my ego."

"Glad to hear it." He kisses the tip of my nose. "Your ego deserves it."

"We should go in the house."

He releases me from the circle of his arms and takes my hand. "That was subtext . . . right?"

"If you want it to be."

Mason grins. "I definitely do."

We pause to lock the brewhouse, then walk to the house. Thin, wispy clouds sail through the mostly clear sky. Stars are everywhere. And the air has just a kiss of breeze.

"Have you ever done it outside?"

"Done what?" he asks, despite shooting me a grin that tells me he knows exactly what I mean. "Fishing? Baseball? Mowing the lawn?"

I elbow him in the side, laughing. "Jerk. You know I'm talking about sex."

"I have never had outdoor sex," he says. "Have you?"

"No."

"Wanna try?"

"Yes."

"Wait right here." Mason sprints back to the brewhouse and returns with one of the red polar fleece blankets, then leads me to a small hollow at the back of the house between two over-grown lilac bushes. This time of night there's no chance anyone will see us, but I appreciate the tiny nod to privacy.

"If we didn't need to stay close to Maisie," he says, spreading the blanket on the grass, "I'd take you deep into the woods and do unspeakable things to you."

I kick off my sandals and lie down. "Ooh, like what?"

"They wouldn't be unspeakable if I told you, now would they?" Mason sprawls out beside me and lifts his arm for me to snuggle up against him. His T-shirt smells like woodsmoke from his campfire with Daniel and the kids.

"I don't believe you."

He laughs lightly. "You're very smart, because I have no idea what I'm talking about. My hottest take is that kissing is essential foreplay."

"A demonstration, please."

Mason shifts to face me and brushes his lips against mine. Featherlight, then gone. He kisses my cheeks, nose, forehead, and as he reaches the side of my neck, I feel the heat pooling between my thighs.

"I see what you mean."

"Oh, I'm just getting started."

The next kiss is long and slow, and I sink into the pleasure, surrendering myself completely to the feel of his mouth on mine. Time loses meaning and when I finally open my eyes, the stars have moved across the sky.

"Rachel," he says, his voice soft and low. "I want to kiss you everywhere."

The thought takes my breath away and I whisper, "Yes, please."

He unfastens the buttons down the front of my dress, and even the briefest touch of his hands on my skin is almost too much to bear. My dress falls open and I send up a silent prayer of thanks that I wore cute underwear. I reach for the hem of his T-shirt and Mason takes the hint, yanking it over his head. I unhook my bra as he removes his shorts, our clothes turning to piles on the grass. He slips off his boxer briefs, then kneels on the blanket to help me take off my underwear.

I feel so exposed. Not only because a man who has never seen me naked is witnessing every imperfection all at once, but because it feels as if my body is on display for the whole universe to see. My instinct is to pull the blanket around me. Hide myself. Until Mason breathes out a sound that's almost . . . reverential.

"You." He stops. Swallows hard. "Rachel, you are a fucking goddess."

He leans down and begins with my mouth.

This kiss is nothing less than the ones that have come before, but this time his warm bare skin is pressed against mine. With a soft sweep of his tongue, he coaxes a hungry moan from my mouth, capturing it in his. Heat rolls through me like a wave, tumbling my senses until I can't tell which way is up.

His lips move away from mine, grazing softly down my neck. Goose bumps spring up on the backs of my thighs. The pad of his thumb slides slowly across my nipple. My breath hitches, sparks dance behind my eyelids, and my back arches, greedy for more. He replaces his thumb with a swirl of his tongue, and I nearly levitate off the blanket.

"Mason." His name spills out like a plea, his mouth almost too much and not nearly enough.

"You okay?"

"Fine, but—" I gasp as he draws my nipple into his mouth, and the rest of the sentence is lost.

Mason was not embellishing when he said he wanted to kiss me everywhere. By the time his lips graze my inner thigh, I'm begging for release. By the time I cry out his name, the universe consists of only two.

July

CHAPTER 19

Liming
Trinidadian and Tobagonian English
"the art of doing nothing while sharing food, drink,
  conversation, and laughter"

The Fourth of July has always been one of my favorite holidays.
I love watching fireworks displays. Love dressing in red, white,
and blue. And I always loved helping organize the all-night barbecue at Aquamarine. Despite being an experienced hand, my
stomach is twisted in knots as I run a mental checklist for the
Fourth of July soft opening of the Limestone. Because most people
on the island celebrate the holiday with their families, Mason
and I decided to hold an all-day open house with free beer and
brewery tours, also providing visitors the opportunity to check
out the finished cabin. Everything is ready, except me. Mason's
family is coming from Cleveland and this will be the first time
we meet.

"What if your parents don't like me?" I ask as he comes out

of the bathroom wearing only a pair of navy shorts. I'm already dressed in a pair of brick-red shorts with a plain white T-shirt and navy low-top Chucks.

After our night under the stars, Mason moved upstairs into my room—our room—and we turned his office into Yōkai's cat habitat. Daniel is building her some wall shelves, but for now she's content to hang out on the top rung of the cat tree, where the sunlight lands exactly right. She and Mason aren't best friends yet, but Yōkai doesn't lash out quite so often.

"They'll like you," he says.

"How are you so sure?"

"I've known my parents for thirty-nine years." He moves up behind me in front of the mirror, where I'm tying a blue bandanna in my hair, and kisses my cheek. "You look so cute in this outfit that I want to take it off of you right—"

"Mason!" a female voice—his mother, I presume—calls out as the side screen door creaks. "We're here!"

He's buttoning his red-white-and-blue plaid shirt as we hurry down the back stairs into a kitchen filled with Browns. From the last step, I watch as he's enveloped in a cloud of hugs and kisses from his parents, siblings, in-laws, nieces, and nephews. Having come from such a small family, their presence fills the room and it's a little overwhelming. Hearing the commotion, Maisie comes running in from Yōkai's room and skitters to a stop when she sees so many people.

"Family," Mason says. "I'd like you to meet Rachel Beck. She started here back in April as the manager for the hotel project, but we're kind of . . . together now."

His parents share a quick glance, as if this is new information, and then his mother looks at me. Sizes me up. She doesn't offer a toothy smile, but the corner of her mouth hitches up in a startlingly familiar way.

"Rachel, these are my parents, David and Yōko Brown." Mason reaches for my hand, pulling me over and resting his arm around my waist.

His dad looks to be in his late sixties or early seventies. He's imposingly tall, with silver hair and the same chiseled jawline as his younger son. There's a green tattoo on the back of his forearm. Maybe something military, but time has faded it too much to tell.

Mason's mom is about the same age as her husband, with a gorgeous streak of white in her otherwise chin-length black hair and almost no wrinkles. She's wearing a blue skirt that falls to her ankles with a white tunic top and a sheer red infinity scarf. Very chic.

"Hi," I say, shaking hands with them both. "It's so nice to meet you."

"Mason has told us a lot about you," his dad says. "Just not this part."

"Well, it's a little new to all of us."

"And who is this sweetie?" his mother asks as Maisie creeps around the corner of the kitchen island and flattens herself shyly against my thigh.

"This is my daughter, Maisie." I crouch down to Maisie's level. "This is Mason's mama and daddy, and the rest of his family."

She stares wide-eyed at his parents, not saying anything as she tries to parse the relationships.

"That's my sister, Laurel, and her husband, Mike," Mason says, gesturing toward a woman whose features more closely resemble their dad. Her nose is more prominent, her eyes less angular. Laurel's husband is a handsome Black man, with dreadlocks bound in a bundle at the nape of his neck, and their three children are a beautiful blend of the two of them. "And that's John, James, and Lillie."

We exchange hellos as Mason points at the other group.

"That's my brother, Owen, and his wife, Didie."

Of the Brown siblings, Owen is the one who looks the most like their mom. His wife is also Asian, but with a rounder face, wider nose, and darker skin tone. I can't identify her specific ethnicity, but she is gorgeous and extra curvy, and I love that their family is so large, beautiful, and inclusive.

"And their kids are Keo and Mali," Mason continues.

Another round of hellos and welcomes, and finally we've all met.

"Mom and Dad, the guest room upstairs is for you," he says. "And the first cabin has a standard bed and a sleeper sofa. Daniel and Avery Rose have offered a room at their house if you don't want to share the cabin, so feel free to flip a coin or rock-paper-scissors your way to figuring out who gets what."

"There's plenty of space for kids in sleeping bags in Maisie's room too," I add.

Mason's nieces and nephews are all older than Maisie, but the youngest, Lillie, looks like she's only a couple of years older. She approaches Maisie. "Do you want to play Barbies?"

Maisie nods. "Do you want to see my room?"

The two of them drag Lillie's suitcase, bumping up the back steps, as the rest of Mason's family scatters. Mason, Owen, Didie, Laurel, and Mike go out to see the cabin, while the older kids find bikes in the shed and disappear down the driveway toward Division Street. Mason's dad follows the little girls, carrying suitcases up to the spare room, leaving me alone with Mason's mom.

"Has Mason asked you about getting some old family photos for the taproom walls?" I ask before she has a chance to bring up my relationship with her son.

"He must have forgotten," she says. "But that boy has been scatterbrained his whole life."

"That sounds about right."

She laughs. "How many photos do you need?"

"Can I show you the taproom?"

"I'd love to see it."

We walk slowly along the path to the brewhouse, newly bordered by sunny marigolds and velvety red geraniums, with solar lights scattered between the flowers. Mason's mom takes it all in. "I haven't been here since last fall. This whole area was a tangle of grass."

"It was the same when I arrived in April."

"Did you do all of this?"

"Yes and no," I say. "I think Mason knew he needed a push, but when he hired me, he had no way of knowing I would actually push him. I took some of the weight off his shoulders."

She's quiet for a moment, then nods. "Yes, I can see that."

We reach the front door. I hold it open for her and switch on the lights. Overhead, the chandelier sparkles and the stained-glass lamps spill blue patterns across the floor. Yōko's eyes wander over the room.

"I had the beer labels enlarged and framed, but there's a lot of leftover space," I say. "I thought that since Mason has a really rich family history, old photos—especially ones that are more candid, less posed—would look cool. And not just the Browns, but your family as well."

"We have an attic full of old photos," she says. "Come to Cleveland one day. We'll go through the boxes together and you can choose the ones you like best."

"I'd like that."

Yōko pauses in front of the label for Sunshine Ale. "What's this?"

"Oh! That was meant to be a surprise."

"Green tea," she says, covering her smile with two fingers. "He's always been such a thoughtful boy."

"He is."

"You love him," she says. A statement, not a question.

"I have made . . . mistakes when it comes to men," I say. "Choosing the wrong ones or jumping too soon, so I'm learning to not use that word frivolously. I care about Mason very much, but he's still working through some things, I think."

"David and I were shocked when he told us that Jessica left," she says. "We loved her. We still love her. But we understand that their marriage could not bear the weight of their combined grief. I want my son to be happy, and if you are part of that happiness, you are welcome in our lives."

"Thank you."

"Let's not tell him I know about the beer," she says conspiratorially.

"Deal."

• • •

As morning gives way to a sunny afternoon, Maisie and Lillie run screaming through a sprinkler that Mike set up for them in the side yard. Local folks come and go, stopping at the taproom to sample Mason's beer and sneak a peek at the first cabin. Daniel, Avery, and Leo show up with an American flag cake decorated with blueberries and strawberries, and not far behind are Daniel's parents, Fred and Betsy Rose. Vivian and Lucy bring canning jars of spicy homemade pickles and a giant bowl of potato salad. Mason's dad takes control of the barbecue, grilling hamburgers, hot dogs, and veggie burgers for Didie, who doesn't eat meat. As they get hungry, the older kids trickle in from biking around the island. And Rosemary swings by with a bottle of apricot cordial that she made herself from the tree in her backyard, the elders sipping it as they catch up on island gossip.

I'm watching Maisie play when my phone rings with a video call from Brian.

"Brian! Happy Fourth," I say.

"Yeah, um—can I talk to Maisie?"

"She's playing in the sprinkler. Maybe we can do this tomorrow instead?"

"You said I could talk to her anytime I want."

"I know," I say. "But she's literally dripping wet and she's not going to want to stop what she's doing."

"You can't keep her from me. It's not right."

"Brian, it's a holiday."

He's silent, and in the background I hear someone speaking. It sounds like his mother, but I can't make out what she's saying.

"I want to talk to Maisie," Brian says, a sharp edge to his voice.

"Fine." I cross the yard to where the girls, and now Leo, are sticking their faces directly into the sprinkler stream. There's no point in making small talk with him, so I don't. I turn the phone in Maisie's direction so she can see his face. "Maisie, Daddy wants to say hi."

She runs over and waves at him. "Hi, Daddy! I'm very busy playing with my friends! Bye!"

As she scampers back to the sprinkler, I turn the phone around. Brian's mouth is set in a hard line, and he looks angrier than I've ever seen him.

"You did this," he says.

"No, Brian," I say, keeping my voice level. "You did this. Every time you brought Maisie home early so you could play video games or hang out with your girlfriend, you sent the message that there were things more important than your daughter. And you called during a holiday celebration."

I hear Rosalie speak up again off-screen, but I can't understand what she says. He glances away for a beat, as though he's listening, and suddenly the screen goes dark. The whole conversation leaves me unsettled. Why would he choose *today* to kick up a fuss about not speaking to Maisie? What was he trying to accomplish? I try to call him back, but the phone goes straight to voicemail.

"Hey." Avery yanks me out of my head as she walks up with a red Solo cup in each hand. I've seen her briefly since the night of book club, when she caught Mason and me making out in the taproom, but I've been so busy getting ready for today that we haven't had many chances to really talk. She offers me one of the cups. "Brought you a beer."

"Thanks."

"What's going on right there?" she asks, touching her fingertip to the spot of tension between my eyebrows. "Everything okay?"

"Nothing worth talking about."

"Does Mason have anything to do with it?"

"No," I say, scanning the property until I spot him playing cornhole with Mike, Daniel, and Owen. "He's great."

"Not to put too fine a point on it, but I knew it."

I laugh. "You did."

"And I've been trying very hard not to ask you for details," Avery says. "Daniel keeps reminding me that it's none of my business."

"I haven't been in very many relationships, but in the past, I've spent a lot of time feeling stressed out because I wasn't getting what I needed in . . . any way," I say. "What I can tell you about my relationship with Mason is that he keeps my anxiety at bay, leaving lots of room for the good stuff."

"That's all I need to know," she says.

"The yoga helps too," I add, making her laugh.

"I don't need to be the consolation prize."

●　　●　　●

By dusk, the charcoal in the grill has burned down to a soft orange glow, and someone has built a fire in the pit. Mike and Owen break out boxes of bamboo sparklers for the kids. I hold my hand over Maisie's as we touch the tip of her sparkler to one of the charcoal embers. She squeals with delight as the sparkler bursts into blue light and together we wave it around. Mali writes her name in the air. Lillie swishes her wrist like her sparkler is a fairy wand. James and John have a lightsaber duel. Keo holds five burning red sparklers at once, declaring himself a fire lord. Leo extends his sparkler to arm's length and spins in a circle.

Maisie starts wearing down after eating a couple of toasted

marshmallows, so I take her to the house for a nap. Her sleep pattern is going to be thrown off, but she's never seen a fireworks display, and I don't have the heart to deny her.

As I reach the bottom step, I notice Mason standing at the kitchen window that overlooks the dark, quiet side of the yard. I stand beside him, and he drops his arm around my shoulders.

"Hello, stranger," I say. "You okay?"

"Mostly, but sometimes the memories come at me."

"Today has been a lot. Do you want to skip the fireworks and chill while everyone else is gone?"

"Nah," he says, kissing my temple. "That's my favorite part."

"I like your family."

"They like you."

"You've got your own little United Nations."

Mason laughs. "True. Mike's mom is Guyanese, and Didie's parents came to the States from Laos. Dad always wants traditional picnic food on the Fourth of July, but the rest of our holiday meals are amazing. Just wait until Thanksgiving. You'll see."

I love the way he's projected us months into the future, but I don't want to get ahead of myself. Don't want to get comfortable being this happy. "That sounds nice."

"Are *you* okay?"

"I had some unnecessary drama with Brian earlier," I say, not wanting to drag Mason into my domestic issues. But I can't shake the feeling that there was more to that weird conversation than Brian wanting to have a friendly chat with Maisie.

"Gotcha," Mason says. "And thinking about Thanksgiving is thinking too much."

"Yeah."

He faces me and rests his hand against my neck, his thumb

stroking my cheek. "For the record, right here, right now, I would rather be with you than anyone in the whole world."

"That's a lot of people."

"That's what I'm saying." The kiss he gives me is lingering and sweet. "We should probably rejoin the party, considering . . . it's our party."

Yōkai slinks into the room and jumps up onto the kitchen counter, something I've never seen her do. Even Mason looks surprised. She doesn't rub herself against him—she hasn't come close to that level of affection yet—but stares until he offers her a treat.

Outside, James, John, and Keo have graduated to setting off firecrackers, and I wonder out loud if we should confiscate them.

"It's a rite of passage," Mason says. "When Owen and I were their age, Dad gave us bottle rockets to keep us busy until the fireworks display."

We rejoin the rest of the Brown family around the fire-pit, where they're gathered in chairs, sharing family stories and laughing. Except for Avery and Daniel, the rest of the locals have gone home.

I take a seat beside Mason's mother, who leans over and places her hand on top of mine. "He showed me the sunshine beer. I pretended to be so surprised."

I laugh. "Did you taste it?"

"Oh yes," she says. "I like it very much, but I like your hibiscus beer better."

"This is the first Fourth of July I haven't had to work." I tell her about the all-night barbecue at Aquamarine. "Guests would go watch the fireworks on South Beach, and when they'd get back to the hotel, there would be a grill loaded with Kobe burgers and steaks, and a full bar until sunrise. Because I worked nights, I was never home to watch fireworks with my family."

"And are you having fun?"

"I am," I say. "Next year I might try to cook something."

"After we moved from Japan, David brought me to the island for my first Fourth of July," Yōko says. "If you haven't noticed, Kelleys Island is very white, so some people were scandalized that David Brown had married an Asian girl."

"I would believe that."

"It wasn't long after the war in Vietnam, so I kept having to explain that I wasn't Vietnamese. And one old man kept shouting at me because he thought I didn't understand English."

"Yikes."

She nods. "Most people were polite, if not nice, and we watched the fireworks on the same porch we'll be watching from tonight. Except back then, Fred Rose's father owned the house."

"The roots go deep here, don't they?"

"They certainly do," she says. "And it can take time for the islanders to warm up to new things. Rosemary Walcott helped break the ice."

"I like her so much," I say. "She and Avery were the first to make me feel welcome."

"I bet you miss your family."

I tell her about my mom—including her similar move to the States after marrying a military man—and about Anna's adventures in the Caribbean, until Mason's dad notices it's time to head to Carpenter Point for the fireworks. I go to the house to wake up Maisie and carry her out to where Mason is waiting with the pickup truck. His siblings, nieces, and nephews are all riding in the back, and when Maisie sees, she begs to join them.

"I'll hold her," Didie offers.

"It's a short drive and I'll take it slow," Mason assures me. "Promise."

I hoist Maisie over the side of the truck into Didie's lap and climb up into the cab. With two golf carts behind us, we form a small parade as we move through downtown and out West Lakeshore Drive. The Roses' house has an unobstructed view of the lake and it looks as if half the island has turned out for the show. They're spread out on blankets and seated in folding lawn chairs across the sprawling front yard.

Mason leads Maisie and me across the road, where we sit on a large rock beside the water, all nestled together like a set of spoons.

"This has always been my favorite spot. From here you can see the fireworks from Lakeside and Put-in-Bay." He gestures toward dark landmasses to the west. "And on clear nights you can see the show at Cedar Point, too."

Seconds later a rocket whizzes up into the night sky from Lakeside and explodes into a huge red burst. The whole crowd reacts with a collective *ooooooh!*

Maisie draws in a gasp of wonder. "Mama, did you see?"

"I did," I say as the next burst blossoms into shimmering green. Then, to Mason: "Thank you for sharing your favorite spot with us."

He answers with a kiss that walks a thin line between PG and PG-13. And leaves me a little breathless.

"Hey," Daniel says from the next rock over. "You two are supposed to be watching the fireworks."

Mason grins at me. "Who says we're not?"

CHAPTER 20

Natsukashii
Japanese
"a feeling that warms the heart because it brings back
  memories"

It's a blistering-hot day in mid-July when I drive my car onto
the deck of the ferry. Air-conditioning on full blast. Four more
cabins are finished, so I take the day off to go look through old
photos with Mason's mom in Cleveland.

The Browns live on the east side of the city, in an affluent
suburb with expansive lawns and big, shady trees. Their neighborhood is made up of McMansions, American ranch houses,
and century homes. The Browns' house is a redbrick colonial on
a huge wooded lot that reminds me of the property on Kelleys Island, and I can imagine Mason playing in the yard as a little boy.

By the time I reach the end of the long driveway, Mason's
mom is waiting on the front steps. She's wearing a beige tunic
dress with black leggings, and the combination makes me feel

like I left my A game at home. If she's this beautiful as a senior citizen, I can guess how breathtaking she must have been as a young woman. Probably as breathtaking as her son.

"I'm so glad you found us okay," she says. "Come on in."

Inside, the house is elegant, with a lot of floral patterns and curvy-legged furniture. There are photos of their children and grandchildren everywhere, and the side of the refrigerator is covered with children's artwork. Yōko pauses at the stove, picks up a pair of extra-long wooden chopsticks, and gives the contents of a pot a quick stir before leading me to a sunroom. Through the windows, the backyard stretches into the distance, ending at a river.

"I had David bring the boxes down here where it's not so hot and dusty," she says. "We can look for a bit and then have lunch. I'm making ramen."

"It smells delicious," I say. "I've only ever eaten the kind that comes in a packet."

"Those are fine, but homemade is so much better. I made *chashu* and *shoyu tamago* last night—"

"What does that mean?"

She laughs. "I forget that you're new here. *Chashu* is pork belly and *shoyu tamago* is a medium-boiled egg that's been marinating in soy sauce overnight."

"I've definitely never tried that."

"I'll tell you what I told my kids," she says with a laugh. "If you don't like it, we have peanut butter and jelly."

We sit in a pair of wicker armchairs with yellow floral cushions, and she opens the lid of the first box. "These are the oldest photos of David's family on Kelleys Island. Likely we'll find a nice picture of the winery in here. Most of the people will be very stiff and posed, but maybe we'll get lucky."

Yōko plops a thick stack of photos in my lap. "If you have any questions, David may know the answers, but I think we're looking for aesthetics rather than history."

"Right. The history is relevant to the extent that it's Mason's history," I say. "But I'm more interested in a sense of playfulness, I guess. Evidence that these people had lives outside formal family portraits."

Many of the early photos are sepia-toned professional portraits mixed in with slightly blurred home photos of people lined up in rows. Some of them have names written in cursive along the bottom. Some have identifiers on the back. Yōko sets aside a picture of the winery, but neither of our first two stacks yield anything else.

As we shuffle through our next piles, she tells me how Mason loved to play in the Chagrin River—the one behind the house—when he was a boy.

"We had a black Lab and the two of them would set off down the river in the morning," she says. "He came home soaking wet so often, I started keeping a towel and dry clothes outside the back door so he could change."

"He sounds like he was a handful."

She nods. "Owen and Laurel were active in sports, and Mason was not, but he was a curious boy, so he found many ways to occupy himself. Not always good ways."

"He told me how his beer exploded in the basement."

"Oh, don't even get me started," she says. "There was also a time when I was putting away laundry and found a plastic milk container filled with yellow liquid in his closet. I wondered if he was too lazy to walk down the hall to the bathroom at night, but when I asked, he told me he was trying to ferment hard cider."

"Sounds like he's always been a brewer."

"There was a time I hoped he might be a chemist or a pharmacist," she says. "But I'm enormously proud of his beermaking. Oh, look at this!"

She hands me a photo of a young white couple walking on a fallen tree that extends partially over a river. The young woman is wearing a belted dress with short puffed sleeves and Mary Janes with heels, her arms held out as she tries to keep her balance. Behind her, the young man wears a suit with a loosened tie. He has one hand in his pocket. Both are laughing and not looking directly at the camera.

"This is exactly what I was looking for," I say.

"Those are David's parents," Yōko says, holding up a second photo. It's the same couple, but in this one, the young woman is sitting on the log with the young man standing beside her. "This is their official engagement photo. That one was taken afterward."

"It's perfect."

By the time we finish the first box, it's nearly lunchtime. The only other photo I found was one of David's grandfather as a chubby-legged baby, sitting in the bed of a Radio Flyer wagon.

"Let's take a break and eat," Yōko suggests.

In the kitchen, she strains the soup base into storage jars as the ramen is boiling. I watch as she pours some of the soup into bowls and adds the boiled noodles. She uses the ramen water to hydrate a bit of dried mushrooms. From the fridge, she cuts slices from a roll of pork belly and halves the eggs, which have soft and creamy yolks inside. She arranges the meat, eggs, and mushrooms on top of the noodles, along with some green onions and small mounds of red seasoning. As the finishing touch, she adds small sheets of nori, which I recognize from eating sushi. Compared to the ramen packets I've eaten in my day, this lunch is positively gourmet.

Yōko hands me a pair of chopsticks and a flat-bottomed soupspoon like they provide in sushi restaurants. I watch as she stirs all the ingredients into the soup. She pinches a portion of noodles and folds it into the bowl of the soupspoon, then dips the spoon into the broth. I mimic her as best I can. My first bite is like no ramen I've ever tasted.

"Wow, this is amazing," I say. "I don't think I can ever go back to instant."

She laughs. "I'll give you my recipe. It's Mason's favorite."

"I'd love that. Thank you."

After we clean up the kitchen, we return to the sunroom and dig into the next box. This time we find a photo of Mason's dad as a little boy sitting on a shaggy pony at a carnival. In one of my stacks, I find a random shot of a collie-type dog standing alone in the grass.

"Oh, that was David's childhood dog, Angus," Yōko says as I add the photo to the keeper pile. "They grew up together."

She hands me an image of four teenage white girls holding hands on a beach. Two are wearing swimsuits with skirted bottoms while the others wear two-piece suits with high-waisted boy shorts, all of them smiling as the waves lap at their ankles. "I think this is David's mother and her friends. Maybe at Euclid Beach."

When we exhaust the Brown family boxes, Mason's mom opens a third box, this one filled with her family photos. The first picture is an unsmiling little girl around Maisie's age with blunt bangs and cheek-length hair, wearing a kimono and standing on the steps of a shrine.

"That's me when I was three years old at the Shichi-Go-San festival," Yōko says. "My memory is vague because I was so young, but my mother said I was upset because I wanted to stay home and play. Not even the lure of candy could make me crack a smile."

She picks up the next photo and her face softens with love. This one is clearly from around the time she met David. He is young and lean, wearing a white button-down shirt. She's a straight-up hottie. His arm is draped around her shoulders, and they're looking at each other as if no one is watching. She touches her husband's face.

"When I met him . . . Well, I wouldn't call it love at first sight, because I had a Japanese boyfriend and my sisters had crushes on David, but there was so much to love about him," she says. "It was the early seventies and I wanted to be a liberated woman—which is what they called feminists back then—and he was supportive of the movement when many men were not. He asked me to marry him, but I had conditions. I would not Americanize my name like a 1940s war bride. Our children would learn to speak Japanese. And I did not want to be a housewife."

"Obviously, he agreed to all of that."

She laughs. "He didn't have a choice."

"Well, he could have married one of your sisters," I say, which cracks her up. "I hope this isn't too forward of a question, but why didn't you give your kids Japanese names?"

"When I was pregnant with Owen, we had so many discussions about names," she says. "Ultimately, we decided that our children would probably be othered, but it didn't have to be because of their names. Forty-four years later, I'm not completely certain that was the right choice."

Yōko looks reflective but then shakes her head. "You do the best you can and hope it turns out okay."

She reaches into the box and takes out a color photo of three children sitting in-line on a wooden toboggan with a curved nose. It's an action shot, caught on their way down a toboggan chute. Their mouths are open wide—caught mid-scream—but their expressions are pure delight.

"Mason, Laurel, and Owen," she says. "A photographer from one of the local papers took it for an article about the toboggan run. I'm sure with a little digital magic, this could be made into a black-and-white photo to match the others."

"Definitely."

I dip into the box and find a photo of Mason as a little boy, wearing a scouting uniform. He's not quite as round as Russell, but his hair is sticking straight up, and his sash is almost completely covered with badges. A laugh escapes me.

"What's funny?" Yōko asks, craning her neck to look at the picture.

I explain.

"Oh yes," she says, laughing. "Even though that movie came out when they were adults, Owen and Laurel called him Russell for the longest time. You probably shouldn't hang that in the taproom, though. Wouldn't want to embarrass him."

"I won't," I say. "I'd like to frame it and put it on his night-stand, though."

"I have a frame that will fit. And I have one more photo for you." She rummages through the box, then brings out the image of an elderly Japanese woman. Her face is deeply lined rinkles and her white hair is pulled up into a bun near the crown of her head. Strapped to her back is a round-faced baby. "This is my grandmother, and this baby is me."

"Oh, this is beautiful. All of the photos are so meaningful, and Mason is going to love them," I say. "Thank you for taking the time to do this with me."

"Thank you for holding my son's heart in such steady hands." Before the moment has the chance to get mushy, Yōko places her palm on my knee and uses me for leverage as she stands. "Before you go, let me get you that ramen recipe."

• • •

I stop to pick up Maisie on the way home, and Avery answers the front door wearing pajamas. Her skin is pale, and she has dark circles under her eyes.

"Maisie isn't here," she says, talking to me through the screen door. "Not long after you left, Leo started complaining that he didn't feel good. He threw up and his temperature was high, and I didn't want Maisie catching it, so Mason came and picked her up."

"Oh no. Why didn't you call me? I would have come back."

"It wasn't dire," Avery says. "And Mason didn't mind."

"Are you okay? You don't look so great."

"I think Leo and I caught the crud together."

"Anything I can do to help?"

"We'll be fine," she says. "Thanks, though. Now, I'm going back to bed before I pass out on the living room floor."

I drive straight home, where I find Mason and Maisie so engrossed in *The Fox and the Hound* that neither even registers my presence. She's snuggled up against his side and he has his arm around her. When Maisie notices me, she scrambles off the couch and flings herself at my legs.

"Mama! I made beer!" The apples of her cheeks are a little pinker than they were when I left, but she doesn't seem sick. She looks happy. "And we went kayaking."

"I let her push the button to start the mash tun," Mason explains, hitting pause on the remote as he gets up from the couch. "After that, I rented a kayak up at the state park and we paddled around the north bay until it was time for a nap."

"That sounds like a lot."

He kisses me. "It was. And it wasn't. We had fun."

"I appreciate you doing it. Thank you," I say, heading toward the kitchen. "By the way, I brought soup base from your mom, and she sent along some *chashu* and *shoyu tamago* for ramen."

Mason follows me. "Can I tell you that hearing you talk about ramen is making me kind of hot?"

"Not right now." I tilt my head toward Maisie. "But maybe around eight thirty you could give me all the details."

His laugh is slightly wicked as he opens the containers I brought from his mom's house. I sit at the island, showing him the photos while he makes dinner. Like his mom, he uses chopsticks while cooking. I don't tell him I ate ramen for lunch, because watching him cook makes *me* kind of hot.

CHAPTER 21

Nepakartojama
Lithuanian
"a never-to-be-repeated perfect situation"

I'm in the sixth cabin, hanging another William Holbrook Beard print—this one with goats marching in a kind of bacchanalian parade—when Mason comes in from picking up Maisie. Except he's alone.

"Hi," I say as he leans down to kiss me. His signature move is touching his fingertips to the back of my neck in the hollow just below my hairline. It sends a sweet little thrill down my spine. Every. Single. Time. "Where's Maisie?"

"Avery and Daniel are keeping her for the night. I figured we should do something for your birthday. Maybe go to Sandusky to grab some dinner and see a movie, maybe spend the night in a hotel with a *pool*."

"I told you we didn't have to do anything special."

"Yeah, but"—he slings his arm around my neck and pulls

me over to kiss my temple—"you only turn twenty-nine for the first time once."

I laugh, shoving him playfully away. "You dork."

Mason locks the cabin door behind us. He takes my hand, and we walk together in the most perfect silence. Sparrows and robins twitter in the trees, and somewhere a cardinal is singing *birdie-birdie-birdie*. I've never known this kind of peace. And I've definitely never known this kind of love.

"Hey, I just realized I left my phone in the office," Mason says as we approach the brewhouse. "Let me grab it real quick, then we'll head to the ferry."

He opens the door for me, and when I step into the tap-room, I'm met with a chorus of "Surprise!" and a building full of people. Avery and Daniel. Vivian and Lucy. Laurel and Mike. Owen and Didie. Mason's parents. The book clubbers. All the people from yoga class—even Walt. *My mom is here.*

Multicolored pennant garlands festoon the airspace above our heads, a birthday cake with brown frosting sits on one table, along with some wrapped gifts, and another table is filled with warming dishes. Overwhelmed, I shuffle back a step and Mason is there, like a wall. He wraps his arms around me from behind, his mouth by my ear. "Happy birthday."

I open my mouth to speak. Instead I burst into tears.

"Hey," he says softly. "It's okay."

"No one has ever thrown a surprise party for me." I give a wet sniffle, and Avery immediately whips a tissue from her purse. "And I've never had so many people in my life who care about me."

"ust here for the cake," Walt deadpans, making every-
and turning me into a blubbering mess of laughter

Mason rubs my back and Vivian brings me a glass of white wine. I blow my snotty nose. "Thank you, all. Your execution was flawless. I had no idea, and . . . where did everyone park?"

Mason laughs. "This was a well-oiled machine."

"So you're saying Avery coordinated it."

He gently swats my backside, then pushes me into the crowd so I can hug my friends. I make brief small talk with everyone, asking Rosemary how her hip is feeling, telling Lucy about an old Chinese checkerboard I scored on eBay, and complimenting Pat's new haircut. Finally I reach my mom.

"I can't believe you came all this way," I say as her arms encircle me.

"Mason booked my flight," she says. "And his parents picked me up from the airport. I spent last night at their house."

"Oh, to be a fly on that wall."

"Yōko and I have some things in common, so we talked a long time," she says. "They think you're good for their son, and it looks like he's good for you, too."

I search the room for Mason and find him holding a glass of beer as he listens intently to something his mother is telling Vivian. Whether by coincidence or the sheer will of my wanting it to happen, he looks at me and grins. He gives me a quick wink before turning back to the conversation.

"Yeah," I say. "He is."

My phone rings in my pocket and my mom says, "Yōko and I spent the afternoon making jaegerschnitzel for the party, so I need to go get it from the house. I'll talk to you more in a little bit."

My stomach growls at the thought of my mom's schnitzel. She makes it every year for my birthday. I wonder if she also ha' a hand in choosing my birthday cake. If so, it's a Black Forest cake layered with whipped cream and cherries, and I can't wait to eat that, too.

I answer the phone, a video call from Anna and Keane.

"Happy birthday, Rachel!" they shout, and Keane launches into an off-key rendition of the birthday song until Anna clamps her hand over his mouth.

"We wish we could be there," she says. "But we're in Bermuda, getting ready to make the transatlantic crossing to Ireland."

"That's so exciting. Are you scared?"

"A little," she says. "We're sailing to Maine first, and from there it will be about a month at sea, which is far beyond the longest I've ever gone without touching land. But we want to get out of the Caribbean before hurricane season. Anyway, enough about us. Were you surprised?"

"Completely. Mason was so stealthy that I had no idea."

"I'm assuming," Keane says, "since he contacted us himself that you've managed to . . . close the deal."

I laugh. "You could say that."

"Well done." He gives me a little two-finger salute.

"We won't keep you from your party," Anna says. "Have fun. Happy birthday. I love you."

I smile because she says it in English instead of German. "I love you too."

I've barely pressed the disconnect button when Avery ⁿⁿⁿ in linking her arm through mine and kissing my cheek. "Happy birthday!"

"This is truly the nicest thing anyone has ever done for me."

"I can't take much credit," she says. "I arranged for a

babysitter for all the kids and chose the party decorations because I wasn't leaving *that* decision to Mason, but he planned everything else and timed the surprise."

I glance at him again and catch him staring at me. He gives me another little grin that not only feels like a private conversation but also makes me want to drag him out of here.

"Don't even think about it," Avery warns, reading my mind. "If you two sneak out and leave me to entertain everyone by myself, I'm breaking up with you."

I smile over at Mason. "We're not going anywhere."

"Then stop with the googly eyes."

"Hey, you're the one who wanted us to get together," I say. "Now you have to take the good, the bad, and the googly."

Avery laughs and leans against the bar. "Your mom and Mrs. Brown are about this close to exchanging friendship bracelets."

"Should I be worried?"

"Mason's mom makes this amazing rice casserole dish called curry doria," she says, and it's so random, I wonder where she's going with this. "She keeps promising she'll give me the recipe, but never does. Today I walked into the kitchen to find her writing it down for your mom."

"She gave me her tonkotsu ramen recipe, so maybe you're not worthy."

"*Rude.*"

I laugh. "Sorry. Can I buy you a sympathy beer?"

"Rachel, it's free. But yes."

I duck behind the bar and pour a couple of glasses of Peach Babe, Mason's new wheat beer made with fresh peaches from Bergman Orchards. It's on a limited summer run because the harvest usually only lasts until September, but he's got the rum stout and a pumpkin ale lined up for fall, and he's already been experimenting with *Glühbier* for Christmas.

The peach scent is delicate, and the taste is slightly juicy.

Avery takes a long drink, then makes a sound that's slightly orgasmic. "God, this is so good."

"I'm going to give you and your beer a little alone time." I nudge her elbow. "Besides, I need to go mingle."

• • •

Walt has dragged me deep into a story about how he's spent the past five years restoring an old Lyman—which is a boat, I think—when my mom and Yōko start setting up a buffet in the warming dishes. Schnitzel, sauerkraut, red cabbage, spätzle, and a small tureen of brown mushroomy jaeger gravy—all my favorites. A lot of people in northern Ohio have German roots, so I'm not surprised when Walt abandons me mid-story, and a buffet line forms almost immediately.

The night unfolds with eating and drinking, punctuated with karaoke tunes whenever someone feels like singing. We slice into the Black Forest birthday cake, but only after I've made a wish and blown out all twenty-nine candles. I don't share, but my wish is to keep this island, these people, forever. Especially Mason.

Later I unwrap a carnelian pendant on a leather cord, which Avery says is one of my birthstones. Vivian and Lucy gift me a vintage globe from the 1950s. Mason's family gives me a generous gift card for Etsy, and Laurel makes me promise I won't use it on stuff for the hotel. The yoga class chipped in on a whole set of yoga equipment, including a mat, grippy socks, a block, and even a set of workout clothes. There's a Led Zeppelin tank top specifically from Walt, who tells me I can stop wearing my ugly rosé shirt. He blushes under his bushy beard when I kiss his cheek.

Mom takes me aside when I've opened all my gifts. She hands me an envelope. Inside is a card, along with a small piece of paper on which my grandparents' names, phone number, and address in Berlin are written.

"You and your sister have always been such brave girls," she says. "And the two of you inspired me to forgive and ask forgiveness, so I called them. I also realized that it wasn't my place to stop you from knowing your family, so if you want to contact them . . ." I hug her so hard, she squeaks a little and comes away wiping her eyes.

"Ich werde dich für immer lieben."

"I'll love you forever too, Mom."

•   •   •

The guests begin trickling away after the presents are unwrapped. At some point, Mom heads for the house to sleep in Maisie's room. Vivian and Lucy stay until they need to catch the late ferry. Until the only people left are Avery, Daniel, Mason, and me, sitting in the Adirondack chairs out back, sipping beer, quietly talking about random stuff and complaining about the mess we're going to have to clean up in the morning.

Daniel keeps nudging Avery's arm and saying, "Babe, we need to go home."

But none of us moves. The crickets chirp in the grass around us, and every now and then a great horned owl will call out *who-who-who who-who,* and the saw-whet will pipe back that single repeated note.

"Mason." Avery waves her glass of beer at him. "I didn't see a gift from you on that table tonight."

"Yeah, I didn't get Rachel one single thing."

I laugh, fingering the orangey-red carnelian stone around my neck. "A surprise party is a huge gift. I'll never forget this."

"Actually," he says. "Your present is . . . out behind the barn."

"You don't have a barn," Avery points out.

"Sex, babe," Daniel says through a yawn. "Maybe there's an actual present too, but he's definitely talking about sex."

She sits upright and grips his forearm dramatically. "We need to go home."

He laughs as he unfolds himself from the chair. "Ya think?"

"Call us for cleanup duty when you're . . . you know . . . tomorrow or whatever," Avery says, kissing my cheek. "Happy birthday, have fun, and don't forget to use bug spray."

As soon as they're gone, Mason takes my hand and pulls me to my feet. He leads me beyond the cabins, into the woods. No path, only a small flashlight to guide us as he weaves between the trees with a confidence that comes from years of experience. Before long, we reach a small clearing, and my breath catches in my chest. Hundreds, maybe thousands, of fairy lights are strung through the branches of the surrounding trees, and on the ground is a *bed*—a mattress fitted with sheets, pillowcases, and a faux fur blanket of deep forest green. Sitting in the middle of the bed is a gift wrapped in brown kraft paper with a twine bow.

"Oh, Mason, this is—"

He interrupts me with a searing kiss that has been all day in the making, his hands on my face and his tongue claiming my mouth. It's the kind of kiss that should be a prelude to tearing off our clothes and having hot, sweaty, gasping sex. But he pulls away abruptly, leaving me breathless.

"I'll be right back," he says. "Open your present."

"Wait. What? Where are you going?"

"Just . . . open your present."

Mason disappears into the dark, leaving me alone in the clearing. I approach the bed, pick up the gift, and tug on the twine bow. It falls away and the paper follows. Inside the box is lingerie—a moss-green lace cami with buttons and a pair of matching high-waisted briefs with a lace panel on the front. The fabric is soft, but substantial. Expensive. Tasteful, yet incredibly sexy. Nothing I would ever dream of buying for myself, but exactly what I would choose if given the option. Exactly what someone would choose for me if they were paying attention. I remove my clothes and put on the lingerie. I have no mirror to see myself, but when Mason emerges from the woods, the hunger in his eyes tells me everything I need to know.

"Where did you go?" I ask.

"Nowhere." His hand covers the lace across my breast and he grazes his lips against the side of my neck. "Just wanted to let you put this on so I could take it off."

August

CHAPTER 22

Saudade
Portuguese
"deep, soul-rending sadness, flavored with longing
 and melancholy"

I would have never guessed that Ohio in August could be as sweltering as Florida, but on a dripping Saturday near the middle of the month, it's too hot to work. Even the construction noises on the second-to-last cabin sound like they're happening in slow motion. Mason locks up the brewhouse. We change into our bathing suits, pack a fast picnic, and take the golf cart to the beach. Leaving Maisie at Avery's house makes me feel slightly guilty, but once the lake water hits my sticky skin, it's easy enough to push the feeling away.

We float on our backs for a long time, then spread out towels on the sand and bake in the sun until we start sweating again. Literal rinse and repeat. We eat salami sandwiches and drink red wine straight from the bottle because we forgot to bring glasses.

When we get tired from the sun and the wine, we head to the house, where we make love and fall asleep in the middle of the afternoon.

I wake to the sound of rain drumming out a melody on the roof. Mason is still asleep as I get out of bed, pull on a tank top and shorts, and go downstairs to make sure the rain isn't coming in through the open windows. I'm standing at the front screen door, listening to thunder rumble across the sky, when the stairs creak and Mason comes up, wrapping his arms around me from behind and kissing the back of my neck. His voice is gravelly from sleep as he says, "Hey, you."

"Hi." I lean my head back against his shoulder. "Thanks for a perfect day."

"I've got plenty more where this one came from."

"Oh yeah?"

"Yep."

He goes quiet, and we stand there watching the rain overflow the eaves and cascade to the ground like a waterfall. Raindrops fall on a set of bamboo wind chimes hanging at the corner of the porch, making it clatter softly.

"Hey, Rachel?" Mason says as lightning crackles in the distance.

"Hmm?"

"I love you."

The first time I said those words to Brian, it should have been a red flag that our relationship was going nowhere. There were moments when he was tender and sweet, and I believed with a Maisie-like devotion that someday he would say it back. He never did. And then I rushed, headlong and foolish, into a relationship with a guy who said I love you too fast, but I was so desperate for it to be true that I swallowed the lie. The voice of experience in my head whispers maybe it's too soon. But the calm in the center of my heart knows that when Mason Brown says those words, he means them.

"I love you too."

"I know it's complicated because Maisie has a father and I . . . have days when I'm not sure I can do that again," he says. "But she's an amazing kid and I love her, too."

"Piper is irreplaceable, and you don't have to be anything to Maisie other than yourself."

When Mason kisses me, I can almost taste the bitter mixed in with the sweet. And that's okay. Sometimes life is like that.

"I'm tempted to take you back upstairs," he says. "But it looks like the rain is starting to let up and one of us needs to go get Maisie."

"Rock-paper-scissors?"

"You're on."

Mason throws rock. I throw scissors.

"Ugh. Fine," I say. "When I leave, order a pizza, and Maisie and I will pick it up on our way home."

"You got it."

• • •

The rain has slowed to a misty drizzle when I turn my car into the driveway with Maisie and a hot pizza in the back. I stop for a second to get out and check the mail. Maisie complains that she needs to use the bathroom, so I unbuckle her from her car seat and let her run to the house by herself. I open the mailbox to a small avalanche of coupon flyers, credit card offers, and legitimate bills. Among them is an envelope addressed to me from a Fort Lauderdale law firm—and it looks official.

I tear it open. Inside is a letter informing me that Brian has established legal paternity and filed a motion for equal time-sharing and parental responsibility of Maisie. A court-ordered mediation date has been set for September 28.

Suddenly everything clicks into focus. Brian's upgraded life goals. His evasive behavior. The well-chosen birthday gift with mermaid wrapping paper. That weird fucking video chat on the Fourth of July. And all of it points to this custody challenge.

For the first time in months, my heart rate skyrockets, and the surge of pain in my chest feels like a heart attack. I inhale huge breaths, but my lungs feel starved of air. My hands tremble so violently, I drop all the mail onto the wet grass. I sink to my knees and spread out, trying to calm myself, but the only thing I can think about is Maisie being taken from me. The letter says *equal,* but I can't wrap my brain around how that would work unless . . . Brian is trying to force me to return to Florida. Making me give up my dreams. This island. This life. Everything I wished for. Fresh panic spirals through me as I think about leaving Mason behind, and the calming techniques I've always used are failing.

Mason finds me sobbing in the grass, my hair and clothes soaked through to the skin. He helps me to my feet. Leaving the car running in the driveway, the driver's door hanging open, the pizza growing cold on the back seat, and the mail scattered on the lawn, he walks me to the house. He doesn't know what set me off and I'm too distraught to tell him. He simply rubs my back in slow circles and speaks to me in a low, calm voice. "Hey, I've got you. I'm here."

By the time we reach the house, my panic has settled into a sense of impending dread. I let him lead me upstairs to the bathroom and wait as he turns on the hot water in the shower. He sends Maisie to fetch my pajamas from the bedroom.

"Listen," he says, touching my chin so I look at him. "Whatever this is, it will be okay."

"No, it won't," I say. "I'm not allowed to have good things. The universe *always* sees to that."

Mason kisses my forehead. "I love you."

After he leaves, I break down in fresh tears, crying as I remove my clothes. I wash my hair and skin, hoping the shower will strip away the feeling that my whole life is about to collapse— again. But when the water starts to go cold, I know I need to face the reality of the situation. I need to go.

Downstairs, the kitchen smells like reheated pizza, and a glance out the window verifies that Mason took care of the mess at the mailbox. Maisie sits at the dining room table, humming a nameless tune as she sculpts a green sphere out of modeling sand. Beside her is a slice of pizza that Mason has cut into manageable bites. Fresh tears spring into my eyes. The attorney letter is lying on the island, folded as neatly as a soggy piece of paper can be, and Mason is waiting for an explanation.

"I didn't read it," he says quietly. "But you're worrying me. Tell me what's happening so I can help you fix it."

I sit down at the island. "Brian is suing for partial custody. In Florida, they call it time-sharing, like she's a fun little condo at Disney World, but it amounts to the same thing. The court-ordered mediation is at the end of September, and I have to go."

"Okay," Mason says. "So we hire a lawyer, book a flight, and—"

"No. I mean, I have to move back to Florida."

His head snaps up like I've said something absurd. "What? Why?"

"The reason I was able to relocate to Ohio was because Brian and I never had a formal custody arrangement," I say. "But now that he's established paternity, he actually has an argument for equal time-sharing and parental responsibility. He's got a job with a steady income. He's going to college. He moved to an apartment in a better neighborhood. Now he can tell a judge that I moved his daughter out of state without his approval."

"Okay, but why does any of this mean you have to move?" Mason asks.

"Because it can't work any other way. Am I supposed to put my child on a plane by herself to Florida every other week? Or do I eat up all my savings driving her back and forth whenever it's Brian's turn?"

Mason shoves a hand up through his hair, telegraphing his frustration. "I don't know, but there has to be something we can do. You need to talk to a lawyer."

"Even if he doesn't intend it, Brian is making it impossible for me to stay in Ohio."

"What about us?" Mason says. "I said I love you *today*. And you're just going to leave?"

"I don't see how I have a choice."

He picks up my phone and thrusts it at me. "Call Brian."

My heart is lodged in my throat as I take the phone. My call goes straight to voicemail, but I don't leave a message. I try again with the same result. On my third attempt, someone picks up.

"Our lawyer has advised us not to speak with you until mediation, Rachel." It's Brian's mother, treating me like I'm an unwanted solicitor instead of the mother of her grandchild. "Please stop calling my son."

"Rosalie, can't we talk—" I begin, but she's gone. "She hung up on me."

Mason sits quietly for a long time, worrying his lower lip between his fingers. Finally he says, "I'll move to Florida with you."

I start to laugh, until I realize he's serious. "What about the hotel?"

"Do you think it matters that much to me?"

"It should," I say. "You've invested so much time and energy and money, and I don't want you to throw away everything we've accomplished. This place is special."

"This place is special because of you."

"I love you," I say. "But—"

"Don't finish that sentence." He cuts me off as he heads toward the door. "I really don't want to know what you're going to say next." He steps into his sneakers. "I'm going to the brewery. Need to clear my head."

I go to the living room and sit on the couch, thinking about how Mason made this room for me. Through the doorway I see Yōkai skittering across the sunroom floor as she bats around a fake fish in a room he made for her. When Maisie and I got here, this house echoed with loneliness, but now it absorbs our happiness. Our love. I don't want to leave. I want to make this house—and Mason Brown—my home. I keep trying to think my way out of this custody problem, but the answer always returns to the same place: I have to go back to Florida. There's no fairy godmother. The cavalry is not coming.

"Mama, look. I made a hops," she says, climbing onto the couch beside me. Her ball of modeling clay is now elongated and covered with a three-year-old's idea of leaves. It's not a bad interpretation of a hop cone, and I laugh that of all the things in the universe my daughter could sculpt with the clay her father gave her, she chose something to do with Mason.

"What are hops for, Maisie?"

"You put them in the beer to make it taste and smell good." She presses the sand sculpture into my hand. "Here. I'm gonna go play with Yōkai."

She runs off, and I stretch out on the couch. My earlier panic has subsided, but my chest hurts as if I've been punched, and I can't tell anymore whether it's anxiety, a broken heart, or both. My eyes sting with tears, so I close them, slowly breathing in and out until they go away.

At Maisie's bedtime, I take her upstairs and give her a bath. Mason hasn't returned from the brewery. I humor Maisie when she wants three bedtime stories and snuggle beside her until she falls asleep, but when I go downstairs, Mason still isn't back. I try to watch TV, but I can't concentrate. I try to read, but the words don't stick. Eventually I go to bed alone.

I wake when I feel the bed shift under Mason's weight. I roll over. "Hi."

Without a word, he kisses me. His mouth is demanding. He slides his hand between my thighs. I wonder where this urgency is coming from, but when I feel the friction of his fingers against my underwear, my brain leaves the rational world behind. Mason takes me over the edge, leaving me gasping as he removes my pajamas completely. There are no tender words between us. No whispering or laughing. But my need for him is incomplete. His eyes are fixed on mine, asking silently for consent, as he takes a condom from the nightstand. I nod. He quickly rolls on the condom and moves over me. Then inside me. He is not gentle, but our appetites are matched, and when my body is shuddering with release, he comes with a ferocious groan.

"Fuck." Mason buries his face against my neck, his breathing ragged. "I love you."

"I love you too."

He eases himself off me, kissing my shoulder. "I didn't hurt you, did I?"

"Not even a little."

We go to the bathroom together, where he cleans himself while I use the toilet. It's not nearly as romantic as pillow talk, but we learned early on that neither of us likes feeling squishy after sex. Back in bed, he spoons up behind me.

"I don't want you to go," he says. "I still think there has to be another way. But I get it. Maisie will always be your priority and if I understand nothing else, I understand that. Just know, my feelings are not going to change. If you ever want to come home, I will be here."

CHAPTER 23

Torschlusspanik
German
"the feeling you experience at a certain point in your life
where you see an imaginary door closing on all your
opportunities, and you wonder what could have been"

Mason helps me pack, and each decision on what should stay
and what should go feels like pieces of my heart are being torn
away. He promises he'll water the plants, as if I'm going on vacation for a couple of weeks. We go around in circles over the
question of whether we could sustain a long-distance relationship, deciding and undeciding that a clean break is best. I want
him for always. Seeing each other a few times a year wouldn't be
a satisfying compromise. It would be torture.

Maisie is inconsolable. I try to soften the blow of leaving by
explaining that her daddy wants to spend more time with her,
but she drills down.

"Daddy can come and get me at my house," she insists. My

heart aches that she considers this place home. "And then he can bring me back tomorrow."

"It doesn't work that way, baby," I say. "Remember when we moved to Ohio and we had to sleep in hotels because it was so far away from Florida? Daddy would have to do that too."

"He could fly on a plane like when we went to see Oma."

"Hey, you'll be able to see Oma again," I offer, hoping that will cheer Maisie up, but she shakes her head with a stubbornness that reminds me of Rosalie Schroeder. Although I want to be angry with Brian and his mother, I can't fault them for wanting Maisie in their lives. I only wish we could have worked it out without having to get the courts involved.

"Oma and Daddy can go on the plane together," Maisie says angrily. "I wanna stay here with Yōkai and Leo and Mason."

"I know. Me too."

"Let's don't go, Mama. Let's don't go."

But I can't make that promise. And when the boxes are packed and loaded into the car, it's time for us to leave. Daniel, Avery, and Leo come to see us off.

Avery grabs me up in a tight hug. "Oh God, Rachel, I wish you didn't have to go."

"I feel the same way, but Brian's family won't be satisfied until Maisie is back in Florida."

"Will you be able to come for a visit?"

"I'd love that," I say, even though I know it's unlikely. Living on the island with Mason spared me rent payments, utility bills, and gas for my car, so I started building up my bank account. Now I'm returning to Fort Lauderdale–sized security deposits and interstate commutes. "But I'm not sure when or how. I have to start all over there."

"I'm going to miss you so much."

"Me too. Give my love and goodbyes to the book club, and please don't let Mason go full Havisham again."

Avery snorts a wet laugh as she wipes her eyes with the back of her hand. "I promise we'll take better care of him."

Maisie and Leo are clutching each other, and I hug Avery once more, then Daniel. Both children wail as I put Maisie into the car. She waves to Leo until their golf cart is out of sight. When the Roses are gone, it's just me and Mason. One last time.

He opens the driver's door for me. "You'd better get going so you don't miss the ferry."

"I'm sorry I have to leave."

"Listen," Mason says, resting his palm lightly on my cheek. "If you pulled into my driveway again—even if I knew it meant having to live this day a second time—I'd still fall in love with you."

"Me too." I kiss him softly, then touch my forehead to his. "Every single time."

•   •   •

The drive to Ohio in April was marked by nervous uncertainty and excitement, but the closer we get to Florida, the closer my anxiety comes to the surface.

The amount of time Maisie and I have spent apart is exceedingly small when compared to the amount of time we've been together. There have been moments when I've wanted a break from motherhood, but they have been rare. I don't indulge in fun daydreams about what I'd do with a week or more away from Maisie. I don't want to share her with Brian. I brought her into this world alone. I've raised her without his help or money.

In the darkest, ugliest part of my heart, I don't think he deserves her. But my dad walked away from me and Anna without looking back, and I could never be the one who deprives Maisie of her father.

Despite trying to stay upbeat for her, my mood sinks, and Maisie picks up on it. She's irritable in the car. We stop way too frequently for potty breaks that turn into temper tantrums over not wanting to get back in her car seat. At night, in hotels in Virginia and northern Florida, she turns clingy. We don't explore the cities for interesting restaurants or play in the pool. If I'm not happy to be back in Fort Lauderdale by the time we reach my mom's condo, I'm sure as hell glad to get out of the car.

"Oma! Oma!" Maisie rushes into her grandma's arms, happy to be smothered by someone who isn't me. "Oma, I missed you."

Mom hugs both of us at once. "How are you holding up?"

"I used to think Peter Rhys-Blackwell was the worst thing that ever happened to me," I say. "But I've just quit the job of my dreams, left my home, and broken up with a man who loves me as much as I love him. I'm not holding up."

She strokes my cheek. "I'm so sorry."

"I know." I blink hard, but the tears come anyway. "Thank you."

"Why don't you go have a nap in my room?" Mom suggests. "Maisie and I have some catching up to do."

My life feels like it's been rewound, my mom taking care of Maisie while I sleep. But I don't want to be awake. I want to stop worrying about what might happen when we go to mediation. I want to stop missing Mason. I send him a text message to let him know we made it to Florida, then kick off my flip-flops, climb into bed, and escape into sleep.

I don't wake up feeling better, but my exhaustion is gone, and that helps. I come out of the bedroom to find Maisie standing on a step stool at the counter, stirring batter in a bowl.

"Mama!" She's visibly brighter than she's been for the past three days. "We're making *pfannkuchen*. That means pancakes for dinner."

"Help her for a second," Mom says. "I'll be right back."

I'm plugging in the griddle when she returns with a file folder in her hand.

"You might get mad at me for this, but I've been keeping a record of Brian's visitations with Maisie," she says, handing me the folder. "Whenever he was late picking her up or forgot her car seat or brought her home early to do something else, I wrote it down. Just in case."

Inside the folder are four years' worth of dates and times.

"You thought I was avoiding Brian because I didn't like him," she says. "And . . . okay, maybe I don't like him very much, but whenever I disappeared, this is what I was doing."

I laugh a little. "Six months ago we probably would have had a fight about this, but these notes could be helpful. Thank you."

"I took the day off work tomorrow. I'll watch Maisie while you meet with the lawyer."

"I'm sorry for disrupting your life."

"*Egal*," she says. "You are my Maisie. There is nothing I wouldn't do for you."

· · ·

When I meet April Thomas at the law offices the following day, she's wearing a yellow power pantsuit that pops against her dark skin, and her natural curls are touched with gray. She's close to my mom's age.

"From what I've gathered by talking with the Schroeder family's attorney, Brian's mother is the driving force behind this," she says, gesturing toward a chair in her office. "Mrs. Schroeder is old-school—personally, I think she's watched too many episodes of *Law & Order*—and believes the only way to make this official is to take it to court. Her attorney can't budge her. But he tells me she's been pushing Brian to be a responsible parent for years, so I get a sense that this is not really about you."

"So Rosalie dragged me back to Florida to teach Brian a lesson? That sucks."

"Well, you weren't under any obligation to return, and if you had called a lawyer immediately, you would have known," April says, and I wince a little inside as I remember how I pushed the idea away when Mason suggested it. "But it kind of works in our favor that you did. You have essentially been a single parent for the entirety of Maisie's life, and you've put her well-being first. Quitting your job and returning to Florida is evidence of that. Despite cleaning up his act, Brian has not demonstrated that he is a competent parent."

"Can't they blame me for separating him from Maisie?"

"They can try, but you were within your right to move when you left," she says. "Prior to that, Brian had nearly four years of opportunity, and what did he do with that time?"

I hand her the folder. "My mom kept records of what he did and didn't do."

She flips through the pages, nodding. "Mediation is your opportunity to work things out without going to trial, where a judge would make a decision for you. We can suggest alternating months. Or even alternating quarters, so you could move back to Ohio."

"I don't know how to be away from Maisie for months at a time."

"Before we go to mediation, I'll put together a few options," she says. "The Schroeders are pushing for equal time-sharing and if they force us to trial, they might get it, but we can try to convince them otherwise."

Back at my mom's condo, I look for apartments online, but every place in my budget is in an unsafe neighborhood. Reviews complain of loud neighbors, theft from cars, and palmetto bugs, which is a fancy Florida name for cockroaches. I consider renting a more expensive apartment in a nicer neighborhood, but until I get a job, I can't afford to burn through my savings.

"Stay here with me," Mom says.

"There's not enough room."

"You and Maisie can have my bed, and I'll take the sleeper sofa. I know it's not a perfect situation, but this complex is safe, and I'll be here to watch Maisie."

I'm tired of crying, but I can't stop the tears from coming. It feels like the past five months never happened. Back to sharing a room with my daughter. Back to relying on my mother for childcare. The only difference is that now her condo is even smaller than our old house. We'll be living on top of each other.

I close all the apartment tabs on the computer, and I can understand how Anna spent so many months overwhelmed by grief. I can't raise my daughter in an unsafe apartment, but I can't stay here, either. I don't know what to do, and I feel paralyzed by sadness. Instead of choosing an apartment, I open a bookmarked job finder website and enter in my search terms. I apply for all the management positions available—even if I'm underqualified—but most of the listings are for housekeepers. Even the Sunway Hotel is looking for a housekeeping supervisor. I apply for that job too.

"Rachel, you've only been here two days," Mom says. "Don't jump at the first apartment or the first job. Take time to rest and heal."

"I don't know how."

"You've never been wired that way, but . . . Anna had it right," she says. "You've experienced a loss—more than one—and you need to grieve. You don't always have to be the strong one. You're allowed to fall apart."

"I don't want to fall apart. I want the universe to bend my way for once."

September

CHAPTER 24

Taarradhin
Arabic
"the act of coming to a happy compromise where everyone wins"

"The toilet is clogged. Again."

The problem with being the overnight manager of the Atlantic Waves Motel in Dania Beach is that there's no actual overnight staff to manage. There is only me, sitting in a tiny office behind a bulletproof window. There's a metal vent for talking, and a shallow scoop for checking people in and out of the motel. Some guests stay for months, others stay a few hours, but nothing is my business unless it needs to be. The Atlantic Waves is the kind of old-school place where Sam and Dean Winchester might hole up while solving ghostly mysteries on *Supernatural*—except our rooms weren't styled to look old and out-of-date. They *are* old and out-of-date.

I've applied for management positions at a few of the luxury and boutique hotels in Miami, but so far I haven't heard from any of them. It could be that I'm a pariah, tainted by my encounter with Peter Rhys-Blackwell. Or it could be that no one in South Florida cares about my role in creating a small brew hotel in Ohio. I've been offered housekeeping jobs from Pompano Beach to Homestead, but I don't want to send Maisie to day care for eight-hour stretches. Maybe someday I'll be able to jump ship. Until then, I hang up the office phone, grab the plunger, and head to room 15.

The one good thing about working at the Atlantic Waves is that there's never a dull moment. Complaints about clogged toilets and malfunctioning cable TV. Complaints about the air-conditioning being too cold or not cold enough. Complaints about noisy neighbors in the next room. Complaints about the traffic on Federal Highway. Complaints about the homeless guy who sits on the edge of the dry fountain in the parking lot. So there's not a lot of time for me to think about Mason.

Except every morning, just before rush hour, as I'm making the twenty-minute drive home, my brain always goes there. I miss him with a longing that makes my chest ache. It feels exactly like panic, but it's really the biggest sadness I've ever felt. I consider calling him daily. At least once a week since I returned to Florida I've said, "Hey, Siri . . . never mind."

I don't know where to put all that leftover love.

I don't know how to go back to the way things used to be.

I don't know how to go forward without him.

If there is such a thing as rock bottom, I'm pretty sure I've hit it.

•   •   •

Although I haven't worn business clothes since I was fired from Aquamarine, I dress my best for mediation, in a black pencil skirt, a white blouse, and a textured gray blazer. I style my hair in a sleek, low bun, and right before I'm ready to leave for the mediator's office in Coral Gables, I slip on a pair of black sling-back pumps. Brian's best suit is ill-fitting garbage, and today I feel petty enough to revel in that knowledge. The universe may not be giving me what I want, but I'll look damn fine not getting it.

I meet April in the parking lot, and we walk to the conference room together.

"How are you feeling?" she asks.

"Too many feelings to pick just one," I say. "But I guess I'm okay. I'm ready."

"I've spoken with the Schroeders' lawyer and they want him to speak on their behalf," she says. "It's not uncommon, but you don't need my permission to speak for yourself. The mediator is not a judge, and she does not make the decisions. She is there to keep the negotiations on track rather than letting them devolve into a battle."

Brian and his parents are already in the courtroom with their lawyer, a balding man named Thomas Mortimer, who is taking notes on a yellow pad. Rosalie busies herself, rummaging through her purse, while her husband gives me an uncertain smile. Brian doesn't make eye contact, but he looks uncomfortable sitting there in his awful suit—not like a man fighting for custody of his child—and I feel bad for him. I wish I could tell him that none of my decisions were meant to hurt him. I wish I could apologize for assuming he didn't care.

April leans toward me, her voice barely above a whisper as she says, "That young man is unhappy. I hate to exploit that, but . . . there's something not right here."

We take our seats across from the Schroeders, with the mediator at the head of the table. She tucks a strand of silvery-gray hair behind her ear. "Welcome, everyone. I'm Amy Sheridan and I'll be your mediator throughout these proceedings. Remember, this is not court. I am not a judge. You will be working out the details of the time-sharing and parental responsibility agreements. I'm here to keep the ship pointing in the right direction."

She looks at Brian, then at me. "I will be asking each of you—or your lawyers, if they are speaking on your behalf—to state your case so I can get full understanding of your situation. Mediation is not a therapy session or a place to air grievances against each other. It is meant to help you find an equitable solution without having a judge make the decisions for you."

Since Brian's attorney filed the motion, he goes first.

"Brian Schroeder has spent the last several months making significant changes to his lifestyle," Mr. Mortimer says. "He took a job with regular hours and steady pay. He's begun a course of study in air traffic control. And he recently moved from an apartment he shared with three other people to his own apartment in a safe neighborhood, more conducive to caring for a child. Brian has established legal paternity and he is asking for equal parental responsibility and time-sharing of Maisie Beck, his daughter with Rachel Beck."

Mrs. Schroeder nods a little, the ghost of a smile on her face, and I know she's proud of her son. I'm proud of Brian too.

"Thank you, Mr. Mortimer," the mediator says. "Ms. Thomas, you may proceed."

"My client, Rachel Beck, is the biological mother of Maisie Beck. She's had sole parental responsibility for the child since birth and Mr. Schroeder did not petition the court for legal paternity until four years after Maisie was born," April says. "Ms. Beck has attempted to contact Brian Schroeder prior to mediation in an attempt to work out a parenting plan without getting the courts involved, but her efforts were rebuffed. In addition, my client sacrificed her career and left her home in Ohio, demonstrating willingness to compromise with Mr. Schroeder. Ms. Beck is seeking primary parental responsibility and majority time-sharing."

The lawyers go back and forth, throwing the arguments we expected. The Schroeder family thinks I had no business taking Maisie out of state without Brian's permission. April points out that Brian had no legal rights at the time I moved to Ohio. She offers my mom's record of Brian's visitations as evidence that he has historically been unreliable, and that he made no attempt to visit Maisie in Ohio. His attorney argues that Brian's efforts to improve should be taken into consideration, but April counters that if this were a trial, a judge would consider Brian's past, not his future.

"Maybe we'll take our chances," Mr. Mortimer says, and my stomach twists into a knot of dread. Mediation already makes me feel like Brian and I are selfish people, instead of parents who want what's best for their child. But dredging through this muck again in a courtroom and having a judge decide the terms of our lives would be worse. Any goodwill Brian and I have left would be ruined.

I steal a glance at Brian, who has moved beyond uncomfortable to miserable. For the first time in months, he looks directly at me. For a long moment, our gazes hold. Then he blinks. And stands up.

"Your Honor, I would like to say something."

Ms. Sheridan clears her throat. "As I mentioned, I'm not a judge."

"Sorry."

The room goes still, except for Rosalie Schroeder, who tugs at his sleeve, trying to get him to sit down. Brian's dad exhales long and slow, like he's been holding it in for months.

"This isn't what I wanted," Brian says. "I was pretty bummed when Rachel took Maisie to Ohio, but I started a new job and school is harder than I thought it would be, and I don't think I can even be a half-time dad right now. This feels like fighting, and I never wanted to fight with Rachel about Maisie."

"What do you want, Brian?" the mediator asks.

"I don't know, ma'am," he says. "I'm not ready for Maisie to live with me. I just . . . want to see her more often than . . . never."

Ms. Sheridan nods. "Okay, so we have a starting point. Let's take a short break—say, ten minutes—and when we come back, we'll hammer out the details."

Brian's mother is softly scolding him as I walk out of the conference room and head for the drinking fountain. I stop in my tracks when I see Mason sitting on a chair in the lobby.

"What are you doing here?"

He gives a little shrug as he stands, and I notice he's wearing a tan suit with a white shirt and gray-and-white-striped tie. I've never seen him dressed like this. It's the least opportune time for me to want to drag him off to a broom closet, but my entire body sings for him.

"Had the urge to hang out in the lobby of a mediation office," he says.

Tears fill my eyes as I laugh. "I don't know whether to be happy or sad."

"You can be both. I am."

I slip my arms around his neck, and when I'm encircled in his embrace, it feels good. It feels right. "Thank you for coming," I murmur, some anxious part of me going quiet at his presence.

"Wild horses couldn't stop me," he says, kissing my nose. "But listen, I know you think it's impossible, but I have an idea that might solve everything."

"What is it?" April says, her heels tapping on the tile floor as she approaches us.

"The summer is the busiest time on the island and it's off-season in Florida," Mason says. "Maisie could spend part of the summer with Brian while we're busy at the hotel, and the rest of the year she can live with us, go to school, and be with her friends. And depending on his schedule, Brian would be welcome to a free cabin anytime he wanted to come visit." He turns to me. "We bring Maisie to Florida every other Christmas to be with your mom and Brian's family, and on the alternate year we celebrate Christmas with mine."

April nods. "That's roughly one of the scenarios I had worked out, but I think we have a better chance of getting Brian to agree now that the dynamics have shifted."

•   •   •

Three hours later we've created a parenting plan. I will retain sole parental responsibility for Maisie, and Brian decided that he wanted to start with two weeks in the summer—not the whole summer—along with every other Christmas. He agreed to fly back and forth with Maisie, so she'll never have to be an un-accompanied minor. It's not what Rosalie wanted for him, but after we returned to the conference room from taking a break, she smiled a little more, nodding and squeezing her son's hand when he spoke up for what *he* wanted.

As we shuffle out into the hall, Brian catches my sleeve. "Hey, Rachel, you got a second?"

I hang back and tell Mason I'll meet him in the lobby. Brian and I slow our pace until we're alone outside the conference room door.

"I, um—I haven't been very nice to you and I'm sorry for that. I just didn't know what to do," he says. "I've also been a pretty crappy dad, so thank you for giving me another chance."

"Maybe when Maisie is older and you're feeling more confident about being a parent, we can revisit our agreement," I say. "But please, just talk to me first, okay?"

"I swear I will *never* get my mom involved again."

I smile. "She loves you and wants you to be a good father."

"I want that too."

"You can do it."

"So, that's the new boyfriend, huh?" Brian asks as we reach the lobby. Mason is chatting with April near the water fountain. He glances at me over her shoulder. His dark eyes shine and the corner of his mouth cocks up in a grin that sends a flutter through me.

"No," I say, smiling back at my love. "He's my home."

November

CHAPTER 25

Ikigai
Japanese
"a reason for being"

I squeeze through the crowded taproom to the makeshift stage, where Mason and Matt stand, ready to announce the winner of the Amber Ale Showdown. Around me, people are sampling beers from breweries across northern Ohio, all gathered at the Limestone for the first annual Owl Fest Brewhaha.

Each year, on the first weekend in November, Kelleys Island hosts Owl Fest, a scientific and educational weekend featuring lectures about bird migration and an evening "owl prowl"—a guided tour through the woods at night, looking for northern saw-whet owls and other night birds. The main draw of Owl Fest is the owl banding. Nets are strung each night in the trees at Scheele Preserve and owl calls are played, luring the migrating owls into the nets, where they are banded and released by scientists. The data gathered from the bands is used to track migration patterns, life spans, and population growth. It's a beloved event, but Mason's kicked it up a notch.

The idea blossomed when his best friend, Matt Long, came to celebrate the grand opening of the hotel last month. Matt booked a cabin, and the two of them spent hours hanging out in the brewhouse, catching up, reminiscing, talking shop, and—eventually—talking smack about their beers. Mason had just finished brewing an amber ale that he planned to launch in conjunction with Owl Fest, and said he thought it was better than the original amber ale that made Fish Brothers famous.

"That's a bold claim," Matt said. "Let's try it and see."

"Better idea," Mason said. "Let's plan a beer event during Owl Fest. We'll invite a bunch of Ohio breweries to showcase their fall and winter offerings, book some bands, and we'll have a blind taste test. We'll charge a cover—all the proceeds going to owl research—and give the public a chance to vote for your beer or mine."

"You do realize that you made both beers," I pointed out.

"Oh, I know," Mason said. "But I bet my new amber is better."

"All right, all right, all right." Matt began nodding, his eyes lighting up. "What are the stakes?"

"Loser matches one hundred percent of the cover donations."

Matt extended his hand. "You're on."

So here we are, and in *my* hand is the sealed envelope with the winner of the showdown. But I don't know which beer is which, so even I don't know who won. On the stage between Matt and Mason is a table with a full beer glass labeled A and a second full beer glass labeled B.

Matt switches on a handheld microphone. "On behalf of Fish Brothers and Limestone Beer Company, we'd like to thank you all for coming out today to drink some beer and support owl research. With your cover donations and matching funds from the losing brewery, we've raised nearly six thousand dollars."

"We don't have a giant check to present," Mason chimes in. "Because this whole event was based on an impromptu bet that my little Kelleys Island beer is better than a world-renowned brand. But Fish Brothers—I mean, the loser—will make sure the money makes it into the right hands tonight."

"Before we announce the winner, I want to tell you a story," Matt says. "About two college roommates who decided to start a brewery . . . to save money . . . on beer."

Laughter ripples through the crowd.

"I know, right?" he says. "It was a *terrible* idea, but I think it turned out okay in the end, don't you? But what some of you may not know is that the brewmaster behind Fish Brothers was Mason Brown. Which means both beers you tasted today were created by him. However, there can only be one winner."

"The envelope please," Mason says, reaching out a hand to help me onstage. It's low enough that I don't really need the help, but any chance to hold his hand is fine with me.

Mason slips his arm around my waist as Matt tears open the flap and pulls out an index card. "And the winner is . . ." He turns the card, revealing a big black letter *B,* and sighs heavily. "This is like back in the day when I took the Pepsi Challenge at the Cuyahoga County Fair and picked Coke. The winner is Limestone."

The crowd cheers and whistles, and the two old friends embrace, slapping each other on the back.

"Well done, man," Matt says. "It's good to have you back."

"It's good to *be* back."

As Mason and I move through the room, people pat his shoulder and offer their congratulations. He says thank you dozens of times, the grin never leaving his face. We go outside, leaving the noise behind, and walk hand in hand to the house, where we sit together on the side steps. Maisie runs over from where she's been playing in the sandbox with Leo, and we shift to make room for her between us. The brewhouse is lit up and buzzing with life. We look at this place that we created together, so different from where we started. Our eyes meet over the top of Maisie's head. And as our lips touch, we smile.

ACKNOWLEDGMENTS

Had 2020 not been such a traumatic year, *The Suite Spot* might have turned out to be a different book, but I found myself needing to tell a story that was warm and gentle. If you've just turned the last page, my first and biggest thanks is to you. I hope you felt as much comfort reading as I did while writing.

Thank you to my editor, Vicki Lame, for her patience, guidance, and encouragement. And to the whole team at St. Martin's Griffin, especially Angelica Chong, Vanessa Aguirre, Meghan Harrington, Marissa Sangiacomo, Kejana Ayala, Brant Janeway, Chrisinda Lynch, Adriana Coada, Kaitlin Severini, Katy Robitzski, and Omar Chapa. And a huge shout-out to Olga Grlic for that gorgeous cover!

I am so grateful for my agent, Kate Schafer Testerman. *The Suite Spot* is our seventh book and we've been together so long that I truly can't imagine doing this without her.

Suzanne Young, Cristin Bishara, and Erin Hahn were there when I needed a writing sprint, an objective opinion, or just an email declaring, "I heart Mason!" There is nothing greater than having the best critique partners.

I owe a special thanks to Elissa R. Sloan for her reading and guidance with Mason and his Japanese American experience. And thank you to Shelly Beach for answering my questions about family law. Any inaccuracies or creative liberties are mine.

Andrea Soule, Gail Yates, Stephanie Pierce, and Ginger Phillips have been my early readers for nearly a decade. I can always count on them to let me know when an idea has legs, for cheerleading along the way, and—particularly Ginger and SJP—for music recommendations for my writing playlists.

A toast to the staff at Coastal Dayz Brewery in Fort Myers for answering my brewing questions and for making very tasty beers. *Prost!* Cheers! *Sláinte!*

Thanks to my family—Caroline, Scott, Mom, and Jack. Sometimes they listen when I'm talking about books, sometimes they don't, but they always love me, and that's the only thing that matters.

Finally, always, Phil. I love you best.

ABOUT THE AUTHOR

Jesi Cason Photography

TRISH DOLLER is a writer, traveler, and dog rescuer but not necessarily in that order. She is the author of *Float Plan*, her women's fiction debut, and *The Suite Spot*. She has also written several YA novels, including the critically acclaimed *Something Like Normal*. When she's not writing, Trish loves sailing, camping, and avoiding housework. She lives in southwest Florida with an opinionated herding dog and an ex-pirate.